I0724587

STRONGER THAN LONGING

KATHERINE MCINTYRE

HOT TREE PUBLISHING

ALSO BY KATHERINE MCINTYRE

Rehoboth Pact

Confined Desires

Opposed Desires

Restrained Desires

Chesapeake Days

Stronger Than Hope

Stronger Than Passion

Stronger Than Longing

Outlaws

Midnight Heist

Twilight Heist

STRONGER THAN LONGING

CHESAPEAKE DAYS

BOOK 3

KATHERINE MCINTYRE

Stronger Than Longing © 2022 by Katherine McIntyre

All rights reserved. No part of this book may be used or reproduced in any written, electronic, recorded, or photocopied format without the express permission from the author or publisher as allowed under the terms and conditions with which it was purchased or as strictly permitted by applicable copyright law. Any unauthorized distribution, circulation or use of this text may be a direct infringement of the author's rights, and those responsible may be liable in law accordingly. Thank you for respecting the work of this author.

Stronger Than Longing is a work of fiction. All names, characters, events and places found therein are either from the author's imagination or used fictitiously. Any similarity to persons alive or dead, actual events, locations, or organizations is entirely coincidental and not intended by the author.

For information, contact the publisher, Hot Tree Publishing.

www.hottreepublishing.com

Editing: Hot Tree Editing

Cover Designer: BookSmith Design

E-book ISBN: 978-1-922679-31-4

Paperback ISBN: 978-1-922679-32-1

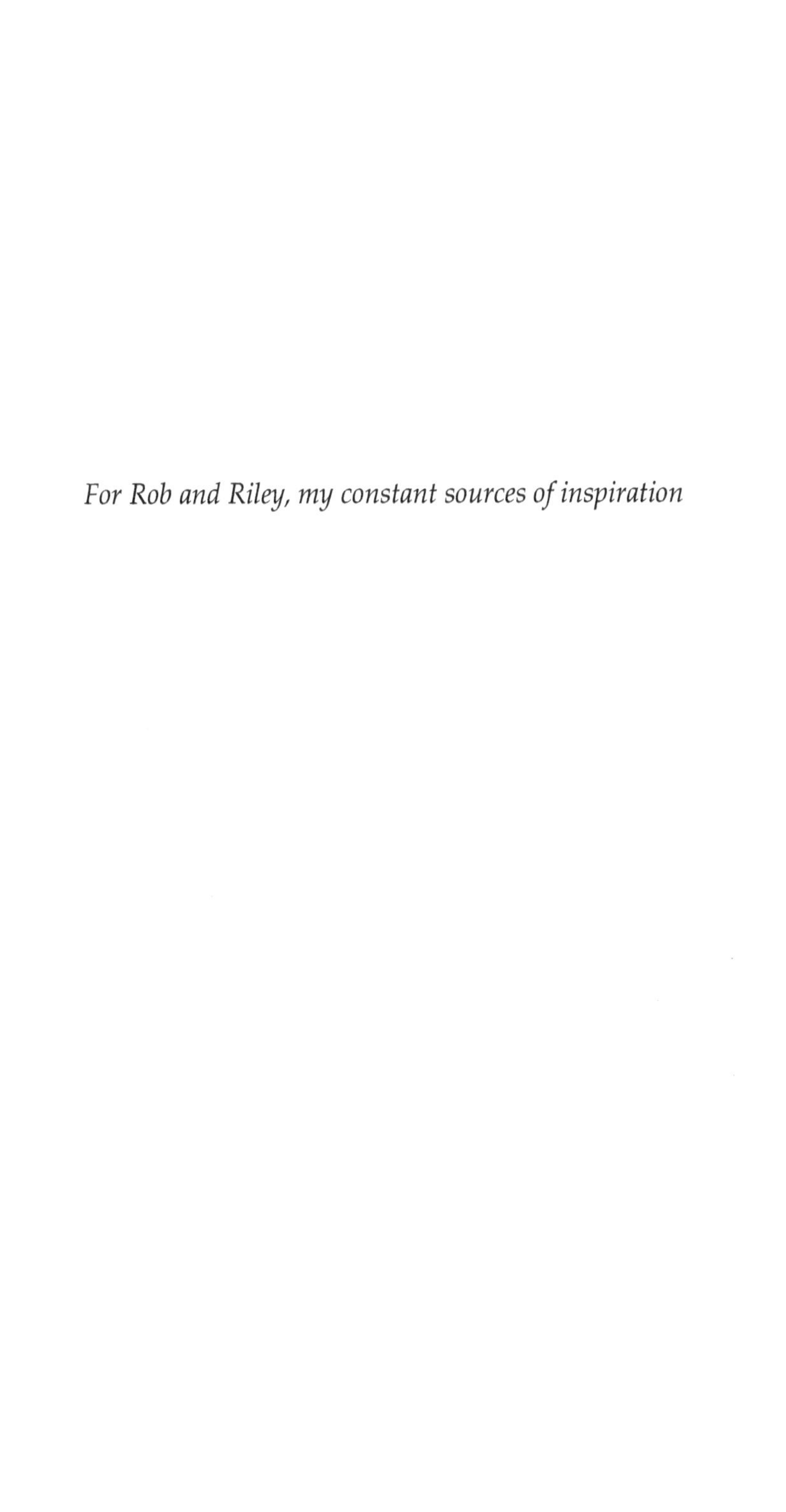

For Rob and Riley, my constant sources of inspiration

CHAPTER 1

Taran had a bad feeling about tonight.

Not because Kevin had chosen Hickory Taproom for dinner instead of one of Taran's brother's establishments in town. Not even because Taran had been getting one-word answers from his boyfriend of eight months all week. No, this ominous premonition hit because it was Friday the Twelfth, and ever since he was a kid, Friday the Thirteenth's cousin caused more heartbreak and devastation than the unlucky day could ever hope to.

Found out his best friend was moving away? Friday the Twelfth.

Caught his first boyfriend cheating on him? Friday the Twelfth.

Dad got into a head-on car collision, killing him instantly? Friday the fucking Twelfth.

There should be a moratorium on the day, honestly.

He looked the menu over, his glazed eyes blurring the black print on cream paper as his nerves tick, tick, ticked. This was just a Friday-night date. No one was going to rob the Hickory Taproom, and Kevin wouldn't show up with his tongue crammed down another guy's throat.

For some reason, neither of those thoughts reassured him.

He glanced up, and Kevin strode in, his blond hair artfully styled and a grim look on his face.

Apparently, the sight of Kevin didn't reassure him either.

Their eyes met, and Kevin headed in his direction, each footstep like the tolling of a bell. The sinking in his chest grew the closer Kevin came. Taran resisted the urge to duck under the table and hide. If he possessed an ounce of self-deception, he might be able to convince himself he was reading too much into the situation. However, Taran had cynicism down to an art form and had learned early on the grim realities life could dole out.

His preppy, pretty, out-of-his-league boyfriend wasn't coming here to talk next steps in their relationship. The resigned way Kevin plunked into the seat opposite him made that clear.

Taran placed the menu down. Suddenly, he wasn't hungry anymore.

"Hey, Kev," Taran said, breaking through the awkward quiet. A prickle crawled up his arms, along with the self-loathing that made frequent appearances.

"Taran," Kevin said, tapping his fingers on the polished surface of the table. He didn't look up to meet Taran's eyes.

Taran sucked in a sharp breath, bracing himself for impact. "Let me guess: you want to talk."

Kevin nodded, reaching over for the container of sugars and running the tips of his fingers across the packets. The waitress had caught sight of another person at the table and was weaving her way over. Taran held back his groan.

"Yeah," Kevin said, his voice heavy.

"Hey, fellas," the waitress called out a few steps before she reached the table.

"We should break up," Kevin blurted.

Taran wanted to die from embarrassment, but they weren't all getting their wishes today. Heat flooded his cheeks as he glanced at the waitress who froze after hearing Kevin. "Do you mind giving us a second?" he forced out, pasting a half smile on his face.

She almost ran to get away from the awkward situation. If only he could join her.

"Look," Kevin continued as if he hadn't just caused that uncomfortableness. "You have to know things haven't been good for a while. Neither of us has been happy."

For at least the past month, Taran had sensed that Kevin had checked out of the relationship, but he hadn't said anything. Relationships were supposed to have their ups and downs, and he'd figured they might be going through a bumpy patch—not a flat-out eviction.

"What happened?" was all Taran could manage.

Kevin shrugged. "Look, you're a great guy," he started, and Taran winced.

The "but" was evident in the statement, and he could already fill in the blanks with a thousand different complaints he'd gotten from exes over the years, not that he'd dated a startling number of guys. Boring, too needy, too geeky, too blunt, and the criticism that still crept in every time he looked into the mirror… not hot enough.

"But I don't think we have a ton in common," Kevin said. "Like, the steampunk stuff you're obsessed with, the conventions you go to—it's a little weird. And I'm sorry, but serial killer documentaries don't scream date night, Taran."

Taran swallowed. Right, so too geeky was the issue this time. "I don't mind keeping my interests to myself," he said. "You don't need to share them with me."

Kevin speared his fingers through his hair. "That's not all, though," he muttered.

Bully for Taran, more agony waited in the bushes to knock him on his ass.

Kevin looked up to meet his eyes at last. "Shouldn't there be more of a zing? I mean, relationships are supposed to have passion, and… yeah. I'm just not feeling this, I guess."

Oh, joy. Another guy who found him boring.

Taran schooled his features into a blank mask. It wasn't that he didn't have feelings—he just didn't see the need in bombarding people with his like they were unwanted dick pics. He called his restraint basic decency, but apparently to everyone else, his reserve was considered boring. Not everyone could have explosive relationships like his brother Nico and his boyfriend Hudson who bickered every two point five seconds. Taran would go insane in a relationship like theirs.

Still, it'd be nice for once if he didn't get labeled the convenient one, the stable one, the sweet one. He longed for the desire he'd seen flare to life in other relationships but never his.

"You understand, right?" Kevin continued, as if Taran wasn't in the middle of processing the frag grenade he dropped.

Taran shrugged helplessly, hoping his shredded self-esteem wasn't bleeding all over the place. He swallowed hard, forcing the words out. "If you're not feeling it, you're not feeling it."

He felt like such a freaking doormat.

"I figured you'd understand," Kevin said. "Look," he started, glancing for the door. Taran's stomach sank. And now he'd be getting ditched tonight too. Kevin splayed his palms on the surface of the table as he made to get up. "I should give you some space to process everything, so I'll take off. Whenever you want to come pick up your stuff that's at my place, give me a ring."

"I'll do that," he muttered, wishing he had some snarky response ready. Yet he was pretty much throwing all his effort into not breaking down into tears at the moment. What was more embarrassing than getting dumped in public? Well, bawling afterward, for one. His throat tightened, and a part of him longed to reach out, to push, to ask for more—yet the words dried on his tongue. Kevin offered a brisk nod as he stood up, and then he stalked out the way he came, those long strides carrying him out like his legs were lit on fire.

Taran's eyes heated with unshed tears, so he glared at the wood grain, as if that might dispel them. Kevin wasn't the love of his life or anything— eight months in and neither of them had exchanged I love yous, so he probably should've seen this coming. Maybe that was where he went wrong? But he didn't see the point in saying the words until he felt them, even if sometimes those feelings took time to develop. His chest ached, though it was less from losing Kevin and more from trying and failing, again.

He was never anyone's top choice, and even when he landed in relationships, he couldn't force the way he was supposed to feel—which always led to the usual comments—boring, not into it, etcetera. He scratched at the surface of the table with his nail. Maybe he really was broken.

Out of the corner of his eye, he noticed the waitress begin to head his way again. He wouldn't be able to stomach food tonight, but he could drink.

"Do you mind if I head to the bar instead?" he said upon her approach.

She nodded, a flare of sympathy in her gaze. "Go for it, sweetie."

Taran pulled himself up from his seat, even though his limbs weighed five thousand pounds. His lips twitched as he forced back the emotion threatening to flood from his eyes again. Friday the Twelfth had struck again, leaving him feeling like he'd been spat out of a washing machine.

He spilled himself into a barstool and rested his elbows on the polished wooden bartop. The older bartender swung over his way for his order.

"Whisky sour," Taran murmured. Tonight was an occasion for hard liquor, because he'd fucking earned it. If he got too wrecked, his roommate Sarah was home and could always come peel him off the floor of this place. Thank fuck he hadn't done something insane like move in with Kevin. He heaved out a dramatic-as-fuck sigh that sounded more like something his brother would do.

In five seconds flat, a whisky sour was settled in front of him, and he tipped the bartender before taking the first sip. It tasted like whisky, lemon, and crushing disappointment. Delicious. His brain felt saturated from all the depressing thoughts soaking up space there, each one weighing him down a little more until it'd be a miracle if he could even pick his head up.

He needed to get drunk tonight. Do something stupid.

Prove once and for all he wasn't as boring as every fucking guy he dated said he was.

Taran took another swig of his drink. And then another.

"Is this seat taken?" a rich, deep, *familiar* voice said beside him.

Taran swung his head to look at the newcomer. The guy was tall and broad-chested, his motorcycle jacket fitting him to perfection, and those jeans didn't leave much room to the imagination with the way they displayed the definition of his muscular thighs. Black ink crept up past his collar and along the side of his neck. The tattoos covered his knuckles as well and were the sort that inspired curiosity. With a wide jaw, windswept deep-mahogany hair brushing his ears, bright too-blue eyes, and thick, stunning lashes, the man was the sort of gorgeous that landed like a punch to the solar plexus.

The sort of gorgeous that had sent Taran walking straight into his locker or tripping over air back in high school. The sort of gorgeous Taran had tried to forget about even though his heart still sped overtime during every moment he spent around the guy who'd been two years ahead of him and was one of his brother's friends.

The guy who'd never given him a second glance, even though Taran had spent far, far too long obsessing and wishing.

Silas King was back in Chesapeake City.

CHAPTER 2

Sink into whatever distraction he could find and shut out all thoughts of the future, even if the diversion only lasted until tomorrow.

His stomach flipped as he pushed those claustrophobic thoughts into the Tomorrow's Problem category. No more dwelling on what was coming, because it'd be crushing in on him fucking soon enough. He pushed against the heavy wooden door for Hickory Taproom and drank in the rich scent of the place—lemon wood cleaner, crisp beer, and seared meat.

He skimmed his gaze over the bar and it landed on an open seat next to a slender guy who was sitting slumped forward. From the slight glimpse Silas had of him, the man had a killer ass, judging by the way he filled out those black jeans, and the silver button-down he wore fit nice and snug in all the right places.

His interest piqued, he headed in that direction. As far as distractions went, finding a hot guy to take to his room for the night wouldn't be a bad one. Granted, his hookup habit had caused this mess in the first place, but that didn't matter right now. Silas slid up to the empty seat at the bar, ready to dive headfirst into this.

As he threw a vague "Is this seat taken" out, he stopped still.

"Little Shah?" came out of his mouth, and he immediately regretted using the nickname. The guy looked nothing like the sweet, shy geek he'd been back in high school, which was something Silas had focused far too much on when he'd swung into town last year. But Nico had been right there and would've killed him if he'd hit on his brother. Nico wasn't here now, and hell, that ass was perfection. With those slender shoulders, deep brown eyes, killer lashes, and pouty lower lip, Taran was a wet dream.

"Think we're ten years too late for that nick-name," Taran responded, his tone deliciously dry.

"You're not wrong," Silas responded, dropping into the seat beside Taran with a creak. His lips curved into a grin as he scanned Taran from head to toe. Those jeans might as well be painted on, and he hadn't been wrong about the way Taran fit snugly into his button-down—the guy was hiding a bit of muscle. "There's nothing little about you anymore." He didn't bother to hide the husky rasp in his voice, because Taran looked fucking delicious.

Taran's eyes widened, and he ducked his head, running his hand along his nape. The sheepish response was adorable, and Silas cursed himself forward and backward for not going after him last year. If he had, he wouldn't be in his current predicament.

The bartender swung over, and Silas placed a quick order. "A beer for me, and whatever his next drink is."

Taran cocked a brow. "Oh, so we're drinking together now, are we?"

Silas didn't bother hiding his smile. "Unless you've got somewhere else to be?" Even though Silas's expression didn't waver, his pulse picked up the pace. A guy like Taran probably had a boyfriend and didn't hook up with high school washouts for a one-night stand.

"You're in luck," Taran muttered, resting his palm on his forehead. "I recently got dumped and could use a drinking partner."

Judging from the slump in his shoulders and the hollow, dejected look in his eyes…. "How recently?" Silas asked, thanking the bartender as he accepted his pint. He took a hearty sip of the rich liquid, though his attention never wavered from Taran.

"Five minutes ago. Kevin showed up to break the

news and then left." Taran scrubbed his palms over his eyes before he tossed back the rest of his drink and ordered another whisky sour. Silas couldn't help but notice the gloss of liquid on that tantalizing lower lip, and he resisted the urge to lean in and lick it off.

Bad. Don't frighten the guy away already.

Taran heaved a sigh. "I mean, it could be worse. No one died, so that's good."

Silas's jaw dropped, and a helpless laugh escaped him. "Do your exes normally wind up dead?"

Taran shot him a droll look. "Why else do you think I neither see nor hear from them again?"

Amusement welled in his chest. "So, I'm guessing you've got quite the kill list."

Taran's eyes crinkled around the edges, and the subtle shift snared Silas's interest. He'd always remembered Taran as having a dry sense of humor, but Nico's loud personality tended to dominate the room, and he'd never spent time with Taran one-on-one like this. He'd been missing out.

"How are you not freaked by the direction of this conversation? My jokes are usually too morbid for most," Taran said, tilting his head to the side. Despite the blasé delivery, the hint of bitterness in his tone suggested Kevin had that specific issue.

The bartender swung by, and Taran wrapped his palms around his drink, the slight hunch in his shoulders a little suspicious and ridiculously cute.

"Likewise," Silas responded, running the tip of his tongue along his teeth. He didn't miss the way Taran's gaze followed it or how those pretty brown eyes flared with interest. Seriously, how had he missed just how hot Nico's little brother was? "Dark humor's my modus operandi, so I guess we're in good company."

"Are you back for a visit?" Taran asked, rubbing his thumb along the side of the glass.

Once Silas had graduated from Chesapeake City High, he'd bolted, not even staying for the summer. He'd hopped from town to town a little bit, but for the most part, stayed around the Philadelphia area.

Silas shook his head, trying to shove down the surge of panic that question brought about. Honestly, all thoughts about what was happening tomorrow made him feel like someone was slowly strangling him. He tipped back more beer, the cooling liquid doing little to soothe his nerves. "Moving back to the area," he forced out, by some miracle keeping his tone level.

Time to dodge this topic. "So, Kevin. Let me guess —frat guy? Bet he loves football games and wears polos."

Taran's jaw dropped. "Did you see him on your way in, or something? Because, yeah, that's a bit too on the nose."

Silas had become a pro at labels over the years

because he didn't have any other option. In this town, he'd always be "Washed-up Loser," which was the one that had stuck with him since childhood, so he leaned into their judgment. However, this guy he'd been able to identify on sight. "The name Kevin says it all. But, yeah, I happened to spot a guy who fit the bill on my way in."

Taran served him another dry look. "Oh? And what does the name Silas say?"

Fuckup, that's what.

Silas plastered on a grin with a confidence he didn't feel. "Hot and a little bit dangerous."

"Sounds more like cocky to me," Taran muttered even as he ran his palm across his nape again. Taran's gaze flickered Silas's way, dragging down his body long enough to indicate.... Oh, yeah. The guy was checking him out. Silas's chest puffed out a little at the perusal. As much as drinking himself into oblivion tonight was an option, as far as distractions went, he could think of much, much better ways to spend time with Taran Shah.

"A little cockiness never hurt anyone," Silas said with a shrug.

Taran snorted. "Don't think that's what you want to be advertising, champ. You'll scare off all the size queens."

A genuine laugh escaped Silas, one that surprised even him. If someone had told him six months ago that he'd be here hitting on Nico Shah's little brother, he would've called them crazy. Taran was too pure, too sweet—too everything Silas wasn't.

However, he hadn't expected Taran to be this snarky wiseass who didn't hesitate to put him in his place all while eyeing Silas up like he was a treat.

"Were you always like this?" Silas asked, unable to help himself. How had he overlooked him in the past? Probably because Taran screamed relationship while Silas was only good for a lay.

Taran arched his brow. "What, world-weary and sarcastic? I'd think you would know by now that sarcasm's hereditary for the Shahs."

Silas hadn't missed the way Taran deflected or the hints of darkness flickering through his eyes. His mental picture of Taran from high school had always been this innocent sweetheart, but some storm clouds had definitely stained the guy's horizon. To be honest, those depths only made Taran more attractive.

Silas arched his brow right back. "I know Nico's sarcastic, but his is about as subtle as a pride parade. You've got this vicious sort of wit, and if I'm honest, that's pretty damn sexy."

Taran blinked, his mouth opening slightly, which put those delicious lips on display. The genuine surprise in his dark brown eyes at the compliment mystified him—seriously, the guy was Grade A gorgeous, and a clever tongue was pure catnip for Silas. This close to Taran, he caught a whiff of the guy's cologne, masculine amber-and-sandalwood notes that traveled straight to Silas's cock.

Taran ran his fingers through his hair, not meeting Silas's eyes. "I'm pretty sure if my wit were actually sexy, I wouldn't be sitting here drinking myself into oblivion after getting dumped."

Silas didn't miss the jagged edges beneath Taran's words, which drew him in even further. This man was clearly hurting, despite the level tone in his voice and the way he tried to pass everything off with nonchalance. Silas knew the game far too well—he was an expert at it. Taran deserved way better than him. He should finish his pint and walk the fuck away.

Except then those deep brown eyes fixed on him, a slight hint of questioning there. Silas's fingers moved before he could stop himself from sliding them under Taran's chin and tilting it up so their gazes locked. The slight skin-to-skin contact sent a jolt right through him like a shot of pure epinephrine.

His tongue slicked his lower lip on instinct, a hunger rising in him unbidden at the close proximity between them. Taran swallowed, the bob of his throat and his blown-out pupils giving him away. Fucking delicious.

"That asshole was an idiot," Silas responded, unable to help the rasp in his voice. "Because the guy who's sitting in front of me? Yeah, he's devastatingly sexy." He could shit on himself all day long, but he couldn't sit here and watch Taran pull the same moves. The guy didn't deserve that hell.

Taran's eyelashes fluttered, long, thick, and far too pretty.

"Bullshit," Taran murmured, his voice low. "Silas fucking King does not find me sexy. I'm the annoying little brother who tries to tag along, right?"

Silas cocked an eyebrow at him. "Hate to break it to you, babe, but I've been known to be a total idiot from time to time, if not always. I was clearly paying attention to all the wrong things back in high school if I missed out on this gorgeousness."

Taran ran his fingers through his hair, looking so adorably sheepish. Their eyes met again, and the sheer intensity there smacked Silas in the face. He should walk away. Taran deserved way better than him, and far better than a single night, which was all Silas could give.

"You're not an idiot," Taran finally said, which was the last thing Silas had expected to hear.

"Please," Silas scoffed, taking a quick swig from his beer. "I almost flunked out a dozen times. I consider it a miracle I even graduated high school."

Taran tipped back the rest of his whisky sour before placing the glass on the bar with a clink. "Hate to break it to you, but idiots don't read Thoreau and Emerson for fun, Silas."

The flush to Silas's cheeks caught him as unaware as Taran's comment had. No one had ever noticed before. In high school, he'd always been the guy someone called if they needed to buy weed or booze, the bad boy with the reputation for sleeping around. At home, he was the disappointment who kept getting into fights and sucked at school. And around town, he was just a danger—menace to society.

No one saw the part of him that dreamed of something bigger, the person who wanted to run off into the woods and chase a higher truth. Who wanted life to be so much more than the confining box he'd been born into.

This was getting too deep too fast. As he met Taran's eyes, witnessing the careful intelligence there, he knew he was screwed. In the span of minutes, his friend's little brother had somehow stripped him bare, and nobody did that.

Silas finished his pint and placed the beer glass on the bar. He should get out of here. Find another bar or go the fuck to sleep rather than chasing after someone as memorable as Taran Shah. It'd destroy the purpose of a one-night stand to distract, distract, distract.

"Look," Silas started, tapping his callused fingers on the surface of the bar.

Before he could say anything more, Taran tossed the rest of his drink back and slammed the glass down next to his. He fixed his gaze on Silas. "Did you mean it?" he asked, his voice barely above a whisper. "That you find me sexy?"

Silas licked his lips.

Yes. In a thousand different ways. Except he should be hightailing it out of here. Leaving before he could do the Silas King trademark and fuck up people's lives. Yet, the slight hint of vulnerability in Taran's voice slayed him. It killed him that this guy couldn't see how gorgeous he really was. That some douchebag had made him feel otherwise, even for a second.

"Hell yes," came out of his mouth instead because self-control was a thing some people had, but not him.

Taran sucked in a soft breath. "Prove it." His voice came out low and fucking incendiary, with the sort of command Silas was helpless to deny.

"I'm staying at the Chesapeake Inn tonight," Silas said. His mind roared a thousand miles a minute, but in this moment, the physical need to touch this man, to kiss him until he couldn't do anything but feel, feel, feel, drowned out everything else. He placed a few bills out on the bar to cover their drinks. "Room six."

Taran's gaze burned into his as the implication settled over both of them. An atomic bomb of lust detonated, the air thickening, the heat rising a thousand degrees between them. Taran Shah was far, far too attractive, and not just physically. The man had an effortless way of making him laugh, and in their short conversation had been the one person to pare back his layers in what felt like a decade.

If they'd only get a single night, he'd make it one to remember.

CHAPTER 3

Taran was pretty sure he was dreaming.

He pulled into a spot right outside of the Chesapeake Inn, his nerves rumbling to the same tempo as the engine. Silas King, the guy he'd entertained five thousand fantasies over in high school, had called him sexy—*devastatingly* sexy. And if the night continued along this trajectory, one of those teenage fantasies would be getting fulfilled.

A light sweat broke out on his palms as he stared at the quaint historic hotel, a dim amber porch light illuminating the entrance. Guaranteed either Mr. Jenkins or his son was working the front desk tonight. Knowing most of the folks in town made clandestine hookups impossible. However, there was no way Taran could pass up this chance. Not after the number of times he'd jerked off as a teenager to the thought of Silas finding him in an empty classroom after school and bending him over a desk to fuck him until he begged to come.

Taran skimmed his fingers over his hair, casting one wayward glance at the mirror to make sure he didn't look like a total mess. The breakup with Kevin felt years away, like it had occurred in a different lifetime, not just earlier in the night. The ache, the confusion, the self-loathing all vanished the second Silas turned his sights on Taran. He'd watched the man flirt for years—smooth, gorgeous, and cocky as hell—and then his targets would all melt into his arms because the man was nuclear-grade hot.

However, no matter how hard Taran wished, he'd never believed the man's attentions would land on him.

Not like anything would happen if he kept sitting out here in his car.

Taran turned off his ignition, opened the door, and stepped out. The late spring breeze swept through the streets, carrying the scents of crisp water and rhododendron. A black Triumph sat out front, and he could guarantee it was Silas's bike. He pinched the collar of his button-down, as if he could somehow summon confidence out of nowhere. He'd been riding to Self-Loathing Station, but the moment he started talking to Silas, he didn't know what sort of bold, assertive stranger possessed his tongue.

He headed to the front door and tugged it open. Taran took a step inside and then stopped.

Silas leaned against the checkout counter, talking to Mr. Jenkins and looking all sorts of gorgeous under the dim lights. So much for any hope of being able to sneak to Silas's room without it being obvious what he'd arrived for. When Silas looked up to meet Taran's gaze, those electric blue eyes seared into him. His dark hair was wind-tossed, thick and glossy, which only made him look more roguish, and his ripped and faded jeans clung to muscular thighs and a biteable ass. Toss in the scruff lining his sharp chin and a knowing smirk, and Taran had been doomed from the start.

"That's my cue, Mr. Jenkins," Silas rapped his knuckles on the counter.

Mr. Jenkins blinked and stared at Taran, the older man unable to hide the sparkle of curiosity in his gaze. Taran sucked in a groan, knowing word would spread through the town by tomorrow that he was one of Silas's dirty hookups. However, after one of those scorching looks from Silas, he couldn't bring himself to care.

"Have a good night, boys," Mr. Jenkins said, a knowing tone in his voice.

Silas snorted and pushed off the counter, already striding toward the corridor leading to the rooms.

Taran rushed after him, tipping his head in a nod as he muttered a "G'night" to Mr. Jenkins, avoiding his eyes. His heart thumped harder and harder as he followed Silas down the hallway. His ass looked like perfection in those jeans, and Taran was so turned on, he could barely breathe. Silas cast a cocky glance back at him, amusement in those cerulean eyes, like the bastard knew he'd follow. He wasn't wrong.

Silas tapped his fingers along the frame of the staircase to the second floor. The dim lighting flickered, casting the stairwell in yellowed hues. Their creaks echoed through the narrow space as they ascended, and the quiet between them amplified the intensity. No one could question what Taran was here for, and part of him wanted to shove that in the faces of every ex who had called him boring.

Granted, he normally wouldn't do a casual hookup with a guy he met at a bar.

The difference here was he'd been longing for a chance with Silas ever since high school when Silas had threatened a guy who'd tripped Taran and called him a queer. Silas had probably just jumped in to look out for Nico's little brother, but having someone stand up for him like that? He'd never forgotten it.

Taran's heartbeat thump, thump, thumped in his ears as they continued down the corridor on the second floor. When Silas's hand rested on the doorknob and his gaze lifted to meet Taran's, the air evacuated the room.

"Still want me to prove it?" Silas asked, an amused smile playing on those clever lips. "Last chance to back out, Tar."

"I'm here, aren't I?" he responded, giving Silas a

look. "Besides, wouldn't want to give you a rap for being quick on the trigger if Mr. Jenkins sees me leaving so fast."

A surprised laugh escaped Silas, one that made those stunning eyes light up. Taran wanted to collect and keep them safe—the rare real responses from Silas, so different from the smirks and cocky smiles he flashed to anyone he felt like.

"We can't disappoint Mr. Jenkins, can we?" Silas murmured as he pushed the door open. He glanced at Taran and crooked a finger. "Come on, gorgeous. I've got some proving to do."

Taran's heart lunged forward before his feet followed.

He hadn't taken two steps inside the hotel room when Silas's hands landed on his shoulders as the man walked him back into the wall. Silas aimed a kick at the door, which shut with a thunk. Silas slammed his arms into the wall on either side of Taran, boxing him in. Taran's heart jackrabbited in his chest, but he barely got the chance to trace the sinuous curve of Silas's mouth or memorize the wicked light in his eyes.

Silas leaned in to press his lips to Taran's, and all thought evaporated from his mind. The scent, all leather, motor oil, and clove, wrapped around him, and the explosive heat between them was a revelation.

Finally.

That scorching mouth caressed his curiously at first, but once a moan slipped from Taran's lips, it was like a switch flipped. Silas took another step closer until his firm chest bumped against Taran's, and he tossed any attempt at civility out the window. He ravaged Taran's mouth with strong, demanding strokes of his tongue that reduced Taran to a puddle. Each time their lips met, the sinful thrill rising inside him traveled straight to his cock. And with the way they pressed against each other, he could feel Silas's hard, sizeable length strain against his jeans. Holy hell.

With Silas's arms surrounding him and his big body pressing him against the wall, Taran surrendered. He melted into their feverish kisses, sank into the broiling heat between them, and dove headfirst into the sensations overtaking him. Taran memorized every second, from the hot puff of Silas's breath when he pulled back until he descended again to the masculine taste of him, all porter and cloves. His heart pounded hard, straining against the confines of his ribs as if at any moment it might escape.

He kissed back with a desperation he'd been holding onto for far too long, drawing on the thousands of times he'd longed for just one extra look in his direction, for Silas to finally *see* him. Silas's teeth nipped at his bottom lip, his lips whispering across Taran's cheek, and those long lashes tickled, brushing across his skin as Silas pressed kisses down his neck.

Taran couldn't help the liquid sunshine that bubbled up inside him in reaction to the singular focus from the man he'd wanted for ages.

Taran let out another moan as he thrust his hips against Silas's. Without realizing it, he'd curled his fist into the fabric of Silas's thin T-shirt, as if he wanted to keep them pinned together.

"Fuck, Taran," Silas purred, his raspy voice vibrating against his neck. "You taste so goddamn sweet." His hand slid down to Taran's belt, and he wrestled with it for a second before the latch snicked open and he tugged the belt from Taran's hips. "I think I need more."

Lust coursed straight through him, strong enough that he struggled to suck in another breath.

Silas tossed Taran's belt to the floor, the wicked smirk on his face pure sin, and then his fingers found the button to Taran's jeans. Before Taran could blink let alone respond, his pants were unbuttoned and the zipper traveling down. He let go of his hold on Silas's shirt to shimmy out of his jeans and boxer briefs, kicking them off to the side. Silas's palms slipped under his button-down, hot against his abs as those callused, clever fingers traced every dip and ridge. The feel of his fingertips tracing fiery lines over Taran's skin held him captive.

"So damn sexy," Silas continued as he traced lazy circles lower, along the jut of his hipbones. "This tight little body makes me want to wreck it," he purred.

Fuuuuuck. Taran flushed at the careful attention, unable to look away from the piercing intensity in Silas's eyes as the man seemed to memorize every detail. In such a short time, Silas made him feel hotter than Kevin ever had.

Silas sank to his knees in front of him, and Taran just about died on the spot. In the dim light of the hotel room, Silas looked like a fallen angel, those lashes like ink, his pretty white skin making the shadows even starker along his sharp nose and sharper chin. The detailed wing tattoo splayed along the right side of his neck turned even more defined in the dim light, and his dark chocolate strands were a wild mess.

Silas wrapped a rough, callused hand around his cock and gave it a tug. Taran's eyes rolled back in his head, and his knees turned to jelly as pure pleasure shuddered through him.

"What's this?" Silas murmured, drawing his tongue up the length of Taran's shaft. The sensation of that hot wetness had him reaching out and weaving his fingers through Silas's hair, his back slumping against the wall. The tip of Silas's tongue dragged all the way down his cock to the root and licked around the piercing right at the base. He circled it a few times before pulling away to look at Taran with pure, unadulterated heat in his eyes. "Never would've pegged you for a cock piercing."

Taran's lips quirked. "If you think that's the only one, you're in for some surprises."

Silas's eyes widened, and his pink tongue slicked his lower lip. "Fuck, that's hot."

Taran opened his mouth, not even sure what would fly out, when Silas licked along the tip of his cock, right along the slit. Any coherent thought vanished right from his brain when Silas followed through by wrapping his mouth around Taran's length and swallowing him down. Taran squeezed Silas's strands tightly as he succumbed to the heady dose of bliss that rolled right through him. His hot mouth was perfection, and when Silas began to bob forward, taking more of him in, Taran was three seconds from exploding.

He tilted his head back for a moment, resting it against the wall as his legs turned to jelly, his mind whirled, and sweat beaded on his brow in the wake of the intense sensations gripping him almost as tightly as the suction of Silas's mouth.

"Holy shiiiit," Taran moaned as Silas took him in deeper. He looked down at the sight of those pink, spit-slick lips wrapped around his cock, those intense blue eyes staring up at him, rapt, and then he noticed Silas had unbuttoned himself, his thick cock hanging out. He gave it a few rough jerks, bringing Taran's sole attention to the deep flush of the head and the veins traveling up its sides. Fuck, the man was mouthwatering beyond anything he could've dreamed up in any of his fantasies.

Taran tested a few short thrusts with his hips, and Silas tried to bob his head in a nod. Taran swallowed, his throat dry in anticipation. If he wasn't careful, he was going to blow his load far earlier than planned.

Silas slipped a finger in his mouth alongside Taran's cock and pulled it out a second later, dripping wet. A short breath escaped Taran's throat—he was a goner. Silas reached between Taran's legs and began to fondle his balls, adding another layer to the sensory overload assaulting him. Silas's fingertips nudged against the guiche piercing farther up, and his bright eyes widened in surprise before he gave it a light tap. Taran tightened his grip, and a loud, lusty moan escaped his lips.

Then that probing finger circled his rim, and Taran just gave himself over—flat-out surrendered. Whatever the man had planned, he would go along for the ride because being with Silas King was beyond anything he could've ever dreamed or hoped for.

Silas teased his hole a few more times until Taran's legs were shaking, and then he gave his cock a long, loud suck before he plunged his finger inside. The intrusion only burned for a brief moment, then Silas crooked his finger, and Taran saw stars. Sweat trickled from his temple and down his cheek, and his breaths came out in shallow rasps.

That was when Silas continued the onslaught with his mouth.

As Silas's mouth owned his cock and his finger thrust inside him, Taran jerked his hips helplessly forward. His balls drew up, and tension coiled inside him, edging him closer and closer to desperation. His brain shut down, and all he could feel was the hot suction of Silas's mouth, the zing of his finger deep inside, and the ache in his balls threatening imminent explosion.

Silas swallowed him at the same point his thick finger pegged his prostate, the bundle of nerves lighting Taran up from the inside out. It was all over. Cum shot out from him as his cock pulsed, yet Silas kept his mouth around him, swallowing him down. Taran's grip tightened on Silas's silken strands for a moment as his release took over. His mind was scoured clean, and he fucking floated, riding on the bliss that short-circuited his senses.

He relaxed his grip as he slowly began to come down, and Silas pulled off with a pop, wiping the back of his hand against his red, lush mouth. If anything, he looked even hotter than before, his cheeks flushed and his shoulders heaving with lust. Silas's cock had grown harder, if that was possible, the thick length tantalizing. Taran sagged against the wall as his eyes locked with Silas's.

"That enough proof for you?" Silas offered, his lips drawing up with a cocky smirk.

"Fuck me," came out of Taran's mouth before he could stop himself. Sure, part of him wanted to drop to his knees and taste Silas's cock, but if this was the only night he would get, he wanted to feel the man buried deep inside him. The idea of Silas driving into him got his flagging cock already interested again, as if he hadn't just come his brains out.

Silas pushed up from the ground, his pupils blown and the shadows deepening the shade of the stubble on his chin and accentuating the arc of his elegant nose. Taran licked his lips, unable to rein in the sheer amount of want he felt at finally getting to be with this man, even if it was only now, even if it was only for tonight.

He didn't hold any delusions that he was special. Silas flirted shamelessly with everyone, and he'd left a string of one-night stands around town before he moved to Philly. From what Nico said, that hadn't changed.

However, as Silas stood in front of him and began unbuttoning Taran's shirt, none of that mattered. He breathed in the heady scent of him, the spicy clove making him insane with lust, and he reached down to shove at the waistband of Silas's jeans. Taran shrugged his shirt off at the same time that Silas shoved his jeans the rest of the way to the ground to kick them off, and a moment later, Silas tugged at the back of his tee, pulling that off too.

Taran soaked in the full sight of him. His fantasies

paled in comparison to the reality standing inches away. Silas's body was a work of art, from the massive deltoids on those broad shoulders to the defined vee leading down to a thick, delicious cock. And black-and-gray ink covered him from the sleeve depicting an intricate haunted house along his arm to the sloping tree that took over his entire back that was visible as he pivoted and strode toward the bed. Taran followed on reflex, noticing that the lines of the tree were all letters, ones he wanted to spend hours exploring so he could learn just a hint more about this beguiling, beautiful man.

Silas cocked an eyebrow at him as he reached the edge of the bed. "You want to get fucked? Then, ass in the air, gorgeous."

Taran climbed onto the bed, his palms and knees digging into the mattress. Normally, he'd feel too self-conscious being splayed out like this. Most of the time, he topped, partially due to preference and partially due to hating the vulnerability that rolled through him when he was exposed like this.

However, he wanted Silas any way he could get him, and he needed to feel his thick length days after it was over, a reminder that this had happened. That the man he'd lusted after for over a decade had finally looked his way—that he'd found him sexy, desirable.

Not boring.

"Fuck, Taran," Silas said, the mattress creaking as

he settled in behind him. His palms coasted along his thighs and up around his ass. "You're hands down the sexiest thing I've ever seen," he murmured, a reverent note of awe in his voice that made Taran's throat squeeze tight. Sure, he probably sweet-talked all of his hookups, but hearing those words from Silas's lips? It fucking meant something—at least, it did to him.

Taran heard the rip of foil, and he glanced back to see Silas kneeling behind him and rolling the condom up his length. A shiver rushed through his whole body, the anticipation waking him right to life again, even after the way that orgasm had ripped him out of his body. When Silas's palms settled around his ass and those fingers hooked around his hips, Taran let out a whimper. Holy hell, he wanted this so badly.

Silas opened the bottle of lube, slicking up two of his fingers and then his cock. A second later, those two fingers were swirling around his rim in teasing strokes until Taran thrust his ass back. Silas's lips quirked, and he slowly slid both fingers inside. After the way he'd been loosened, they glided right in, and Silas took his time making scissoring motions to open him right up.

Taran couldn't help it—he started fucking himself on Silas's fingers, his cock already stiffening again. He hadn't gotten hard this easily in years, but something about this man coaxed his libido into a full frenzy.

"Thought you were going to fuck me," Taran managed to murmur, even though his eyes rolled back in his head when Silas's fingers thumped against his prostate. He hung his head, gazing down on the sheets beneath him.

Silas squeezed Taran's ass cheek as he drilled him with three more intense thrusts. "Just making sure I can slide right in," Silas replied. "You're tight as hell."

"Haven't bottomed in ages." Taran muttered the admission, barely aware of the words coming out of his mouth.

A moment later, he felt those lips press along his lower back, and then Silas sank his teeth into Taran's ass cheek. The slight sting doused him with pleasure, and he resisted the urge to buck forward and rut into the mattress.

"Then I better make it good for you," Silas responded, his husky voice doing unspeakable things to his mind.

"Good would be sticking your cock in my ass," Taran shot back, so turned on he could barely breathe.

Silas's hands shook with his laughter. "Are you always this mouthy?"

"If you wanted my mouth, you should've just asked," Taran responded as he thrust back again, a short breath escaping him as Silas's fingertips slammed into his prostate again.

"I'll save that for next time," Silas murmured, pulling his fingers out. Taran's hole flared with the intrusion gone, and he bit his lower lip to keep another whimper at bay.

At last, the blunt tip of Silas's cock pressed against Taran's rim. He bore down as Silas pushed in inch by inch. Silas had worked him open to the point that the burn was minimal, and before long, he'd settled all the way inside Taran. The fullness felt perfect, and Taran's heart fluttered at the sensation of being filled up like this. It had been a long, long time.

"Damn, gorgeous, you feel so fucking good," Silas purred as he began to move.

One moment he was sliding back, and the next, he glided in again, beginning to work up the pace. Taran clutched the sheets tightly, the sweat of his palms imprinting on the fabric. Strands of his hair stuck to his forehead, and as Silas ramped up his speed, Taran lowered onto his elbows, barely able to focus on the sheets in front of him let alone hold himself upright. Silas's nails dug into his hips, and he began to slam inside Taran, each hit to his prostate sending a warning flare to his system that critical overload was imminent.

The shudders of pleasure wracked through him, traveling from the inside out until his legs were shaking again, as if the man hadn't just wrung him out earlier. Silas's hips snapped against his ass, the rough movements making his head swirl. The scent of sweat, cloves, and leather drugged his senses, and he breathed it in, memorizing the sting of Silas's nails, the slap of their skin together, and how the strong grip made him feel utterly claimed.

"You're so tight—I'm not going to last long," Silas groaned as he thrust in at a punishing pace. Taran would feel this for days, which was exactly what he'd hoped for.

"Do it," Taran responded, not knowing how he still managed to grasp the English language. "Come."

"Nngh," Silas moaned. His hands left Taran's hips, and a second later, that muscular, sweaty chest pressed against his back. Silas's palms pressed overtop Taran's hands, their fingers tangling together, and Silas bore down on him as he fucked him faster. With Silas's big body draped over his, Taran's system fried. The man's weight felt so fucking perfect as he curved over him like he was meant to be there, and Taran's eyes rolled back in his head.

Silas thrust in hard, and a moment later, his whole body shuddered around Taran as the warmth pulsed inside him. The throb of Silas's cock combined with the way his sweaty body framed his did Taran in. His hips bucked forward as his release shot onto the sheets.

Taran's vision swam, probably as a result of coming twice in such a short span of time, and he felt pummeled by exhaustion. Pleasure swarmed him, and he surrendered to those pristine sensations, letting himself float away into oblivion. Eventually, he began to return to his body. Silas was still draped over him, their sweaty skin pressed together, his softening dick buried in Taran's ass and their palms still pressed together, fingers intertwined.

For a one-night stand, this felt far more intimate than he'd anticipated. He swallowed, hard. He wasn't ready for this to end. To return to his reality.

Silas slowly pulled out of him and slammed his back onto the mattress with a bounce. He flung his forearm over his eyes, but a huge grin stole his face. Taran slumped against the bed, not giving a damn that his cum stuck the sheets to his stomach.

"Goddamn, Taran." Silas lifted his forearm to glance over at him. "Where the hell have you been all my life?"

Right here. Taran swallowed the words back. *Right here.*

Taran sucked in a shaky breath, pushing himself up onto his elbows again. Their eyes met, and Silas's gaze devoured him. He wanted to stay here more than anything, but he should get ready to go. Not like Silas King would want a repeat. The first tendrils of regret trickled through his system.

He should've known Silas would ruin him. He'd never had sex that intense in his life.

Silas reached over to clap a hand on his ass, and

he squeezed. "Don't know about you, but I could use a shower." He waggled his eyebrows and tilted his head in the direction of the bathroom.

Taran cocked his head to the side.

Regret could wait until tomorrow. He wanted to enjoy every damn second he got with this man. Taran swung over the side of the bed and sauntered toward the bathroom, even though his legs were shaky as hell. He glanced back to where Silas still lounged on the bed.

"Thought you wanted my mouth?" Taran mentioned with a grin.

Silas all but leapt off the mattress.

CHAPTER 4

Dappled morning light streamed in through the windows, and as Silas rolled his hips, his morning wood brushed against delicious warm skin.

A slender body lay beside him, all taut muscle and skin that glowed sepia in the morning light. The memories of last night came rushing back to him, from the way Taran's body fit perfectly against his to the tight heat of his ass and later the lazy frotting session they'd done in the shower afterward.

Silas wrinkled his nose. He didn't do overnights. Most times after he'd rolled between the sheets with someone, he tugged his pants on and headed out the door to go sleep in his own bed. He glanced at his traitorous arm that lay draped around Taran's side, yet he didn't make any effort to move it. Taran looked fucking beautiful in his sleep, the sheets pooled around his slim waist and his glossy black hair tousled. With his eyes closed, those long lashes were on full display, his lush bottom lip looking biteable. The vulnerability and innocence on his face reminded Silas of the Taran he'd known back in high school.

Nothing like the pierced up, sarcastic, fucking delectable guy he'd screwed into oblivion last night.

He hadn't been lying either—Taran was the hottest thing he'd ever seen, the combination of self-deprecating, snarky, yet a little bit vulnerable was his total kryptonite. And the sex last night.... Fuck. He hadn't experienced a connection like that *ever*.

Except he wasn't destined for anything lasting. Not after today.

Silas ran his palm along Taran's waist, the smooth, silken skin not helping to deflate his morning wood. As much as he should extricate himself from this, as long as Taran remained here, Silas could linger in this bubble before real life intruded. He wanted to stay here for as long as he could.

The motion caused Taran to stir, and the man's lashes fluttered, revealing those deep brown eyes that saw right through him without even trying. He'd always found Taran cute, even back in high school, but he'd been firmly in the too-pure category. And Silas was like a wrecking ball to innocence, which meant he'd always stayed away.

After last night, though, he needed to reevaluate

his assessment. He didn't doubt that Taran was solid in a way he'd never be, that he was moral when Silas tended to bend, but pure? More like filthy in the best sort of way.

Taran glanced over at him, a wry look on his face as he backed that ass up against Silas's hard cock. "Well, that's one way to wake up." He squinted as he looked over at the neon red numbers of the alarm clock. "Shit, it's ten in the morning?"

"Late for a hot date?" Silas asked, even though the idea left a sour note in his chest. He rubbed at the spot, as if he could rid himself of the shitty emotion. This was the problem with hooking up with people he knew. Though, he'd broken his rule before without these results. This was clearly a Taran Shah problem.

Taran cocked a brow at him. "What part of just got dumped did you not understand last night? The only hot date I've got is with the *Hellraiser* movies and a bag of Swedish Fish tonight."

"Right, because breakups put you in the mood for murder," Silas responded, a smile slipping across his lips before he could help himself. Who the fuck was he right now? He didn't do sleepovers, and he definitely didn't do casual morning-after chats like this. Yet, he couldn't seem to pull away from this man's gravitational force.

Taran shifted to his side, elbow crooked as he propped himself up on his palm. "I'm sorry, would you prefer I sob into a tub of ice cream and watch sappy movies that piss me off instead?"

Silas shrugged, sweeping his fingers through his hair as if he might stand a chance at taming his wild bedhead. "I'm just saying, the *Scream* movies are a better choice than *Hellraiser*. Or you could go classic Romero, some *Dawn of the Dead*."

Taran shot him a look. "You handle your breakup routines the way you want, and I'll handle mine my way. I've got a system." Even with Taran's blithe comments, Silas didn't miss the slight sharpened edge to his tone, as if the reality of their bubble ending had crashed down on him too.

"Kevin doesn't deserve a breakup routine," Silas responded, nudging his leg against Taran's. He rested his palm on the sheets between them, even though he itched to reach over and run his hands along Taran's smooth skin again.

Taran made a move instead, tracing his fingertips down Silas's. "I noticed these last night," he murmured, pausing on the letters inked on his knuckles. "Why'd you get 'turn left' there?"

Taran's careful scrutiny made Silas's stomach clench with want. The man's observations peeled back his skin without even trying, like the masks Silas wore that everyone else took at face value wouldn't hold weight with him.

Silas let out a casual laugh, throwing out his normal excuse. "Oh, my dumb ass still can't tell left from right, so I figured I'd give myself the reminder."

Taran just lifted a brow, clearly not buying it. He continued to rub his thumb over the letters, the intimate motion stripping down Silas's defenses as if he hadn't spent years honing them. "We both know that's bullshit, so what's the actual reason?"

Silas's throat dried. Well, damn. How the fuck was this guy even real? They'd barely spoken in high school, so how did Taran Shah see past his crap when even his own friends hadn't?

Silas leaned back in the bed, propping himself up on his elbows. The sheets almost slipped off his hip, and he didn't miss the hungry way Taran's gaze traced the exposed skin. "So, it's kind of stupid, but you know the sci-fi show *Doctor Who*?"

Taran's eyes widened in surprise for a second, only to deepen to wan amusement. "I'm well aware of the show. Remember, I'm the guy who gets dumped for being too boring and liking weird shit."

"That's a load," Silas retorted on instinct. "Kevin must've been too dull to recognize all of this hotness." Silas gestured up and down Taran's body.

Taran pursed his lips, and for a moment his thumb paused midstroke, but then he continued to circle over the letters. "So, *Doctor Who*...."

"There's an episode that's about the Butterfly Effect, one choice leading to an entirely different life," Silas said, staring at the sheets. The reality settled onto him a little more heavily today. "Turn right and go the safe route or turn left and take a risk. And I'd always rather take the risk than wonder what I could've missed out on."

His skin prickled with vulnerability. He'd never told anyone the truth behind the tattoo before, though to be fair, no one had ever called him on his lie either. When he glanced back at Taran, the man was staring at him with a serious expression that was softer, something that reached right in past his ribcage and tugged.

"That's beautiful, Si," Taran murmured. He pulled his hand away and raked his fingers through his obsidian strands that glowed with chocolate notes in the bright morning light. "Risk taking's never been my strong point. Maybe that's where I've been going wrong."

Silas shook his head, nudging his bare leg against Taran's underneath the sheet, all hot skin and the tickle of coarse hair. "Trust me, you don't want to follow my lead. Look up 'hot mess' in the dictionary and my picture will be plastered there. At least I'm hot though," he joked, forcing his grin. Normally, he had no issue keeping folks at a distance—with him, they preferred to stay there. Silas had learned that lesson from an early age.

No one liked to hear about the sad kid whose dad ditched him.

"Making mistakes doesn't mean you are one,"

Taran murmured, those dark eyes piercing through him.

Oh, fuck.

Silas's eyes burned. They'd switched from hot and casual to deeper than he'd gone with any fucking other person on the planet. And the worst part? Silas wanted more. He'd only planned for a quick distraction, but the brief glimpse into Taran Shah had been addictive, and if he were any other person, if he were coming home for any other reason, maybe this was something he could have pursued.

He opened his mouth, wanting to thank him. Wanting to kiss him. Wanting to say or do anything to get this man to stay.

Instead, all that came out was "I'm meeting my daughter today."

The warm coziness threading between them snapped, and Taran's jaw dropped. Before Silas could say anything else, Taran pushed up from the sheets and hopped out of the bed.

"You've got a kid?" he asked, his brows drawing together. Silas didn't miss the note of panic in his voice. "Fuck, are you married?"

Silas's grip on the sheets tightened as Taran threw on his jeans and hastily fumbled with the buttons of his shirt.

"Please don't tell me I'm a home-wrecker," Taran muttered, sliding his shoes on.

Silas opened his mouth to correct him, but his

tongue dried, words not arriving at his lips. Truth be told, he didn't deserve someone like Taran. He hadn't lied when he said he was a hot mess.

Taran patted his pockets, checking for his keys and wallet. "I've got to go." He didn't meet Silas's eyes, and before Silas could manage to make his mouth work, Taran was already rushing out.

The click of the door shutting echoed around the room.

Silas sagged against the headboard, the sweetness of their connection swirling down the drain, like anything good in his life.

Probably better that Taran think he was some monster who'd cheat on his family. Easier than trying to keep the guy at a distance, because who signed on for this? He sure as hell hadn't. Last year's hookup with Maeve at the Chesapeake Days festival had landed him here, back in town to meet his infant daughter, Fiona. He and Maeve weren't getting together—hell no. Apart from a lay, he wasn't thrilled with her company. However, he'd agreed to come be a part of his daughter's life.

Silas King, high school failure and fuckup extraordinaire, was now a father.

CHAPTER 5

TARAN STARED VACANTLY AT HIS PHONE, SLUMPED IN HIS couch. Somehow, his best friend Cole had picked up on the 'what the fuck is my life?' vibe from his earlier text of *How many Swedish Fish can I cram in my mouth at once?*

Sarah had left to go out to the bar tonight, which meant he had the house to himself, and Cole had decided on an impromptu visit.

The Kevin breakup should've stung—y'know, the guy he'd been seeing for months now. That should've been the thing consuming his mind.

Not the scorching night that was his every teenage fantasy brought to life.

Not this morning when the softness in Silas's eyes and the quiet conversation between them made him feel closer to anyone than he had in a long time.

Not Silas fucking 'I have a kid' King.

A knock sounded at the door, and Taran scrubbed his face. As if he stood a chance at clearing his thoughts. Not likely. He forced himself to go answer, even though he'd already regretted inviting Cole over. Considerate bastard had driven the hour and change from Baltimore, so he couldn't turn him away.

Taran swung the door open to Cole standing in the frame, still wearing a lavender button-down and charcoal slacks from work.

"Before you give me your 'I'm fine' bullshit, let's just agree that you aren't," Cole said, pushing his way inside. "I brought takeout from Strawberry Moon Diner, so you can thank me later."

The exact words Taran had planned on saying exited stage left as he closed the door. His best friend was like a gay man's lottery—hot, well-muscled, high-earning lawyer with a charming grin, shaved head, and deep chocolate eyes. If Taran had ever felt an inkling of chemistry with him, they would've been married by now because Cole had been a solid presence in his life ever since they were kids.

"Thanks," Taran muttered, running his fingers through his hair as he followed Cole through the front hallway and into his kitchen. Cole made himself at home, plunking into a seat at the round kitchen table and pulling out the containers from Strawberry Moon. Taran's stomach rumbled at the scent of strawberries and syrup, already knowing what Cole had brought him.

"So, I'm guessing you and Kevin…." Cole started, popping open the container filled with strawberry pancakes as delicious, delicious bait. His best friend leaned back in his seat and nabbed a crispy chicken wrap from his own container.

Taran slumped into the seat beside Cole, grabbing the disposable fork and stabbing into the delicious pancakes piled high with whipped cream. "Kevin dumped my ass last night. Shock of all shocks, I got too geeky and no spark, yet again."

Cole nodded, an amused grin spreading over his lips. "That makes bingo for me. I'd been waiting for another too geeky."

Taran flipped him the middle finger, even though the droll humor lifted him up a little. The last thing he needed was a pity party, and Cole was never the type to deliver. "Happy to help." He shoved a forkful of pancakes into his mouth, the sweetness coating his tongue as he savored the delicious, delicious carbs.

"So, what horror movies are we watching tonight?" Cole asked. Warmth permeated through some of the confusion and irritation that ran rampant through him after his doozy of a twenty-four hours.

"I'm fucking done with guys," Taran muttered. "They're too much drama and not goddamn worth it." Sad part was, Kevin barely even registered as a blip on his emotional radar at the moment. One man took priority, and Taran only had himself to blame on that front.

"Amen," Cole responded, lifting half of his wrap in salute. "Though I'll keep on fucking them."

Taran rolled his eyes as he chewed on more pancakes. Cole's gaze snagged on his neck, and his brows drew together.

"Excuse me, Taran Tabitha Shah—is that a hickey?"

Taran shot him a look. "My middle name isn't Tabitha." His cheeks heated in response to the memory of Silas's mouth on his neck, on his cock. Fuck…. As much as he hated the way it ended, that had been the most unforgettable sex of his life.

"Care to explain how you got dumped last night yet ended up with a fresh hickey?" Cole asked, those dark eyes zeroing in on him.

Taran chewed on his lower lip. "Not really."

"Well, it sure as hell wasn't with Kevin," Cole muttered.

Taran's fingers went to the spot on his neck and he rubbed it lightly. Even though his head tugged him in a thousand different directions right now, all he wanted to do was bask in the memories of last night. "How do you know that?" Taran responded on instinct, forgetting for a moment how perceptive Cole was.

Cole lifted a brow, those full lips pursed in amusement. "Because you and Kevin weren't fire between the sheets, Tar. Kevin was milk toast, and now that you're not together, I'm free to say you can do much, much better than him. Like whoever you happened to pick up after you got dumped."

Taran stabbed into his pancakes a little harder than necessary, staring at the container as if it might hold answers. "Yeah, that's not happening. Let's put on the *Scream* movies and forget about guys completely. Blood, guts, and ruin about sums up my love life anyway."

He tried to ignore the nagging voice in the back of his head that said *Scream* hadn't been his original post-breakup plan, but *someone* had infected his thoughts like malware.

Cole stared at him hard, scrutinizing him. Clearly, he wasn't about to drop the conversation. However, he took the last few bites of his wrap, tossed the empty container into the garbage, and helped himself to a beer. "We can start the movie," Cole said as he left Taran behind to head in the direction of the living room, "but you can bet I'm going to get you to tell me who Mr. Hickey is. The only reason you'd be squirrely like this is if it's someone we both know." Cole glanced back, and when their eyes met, Taran froze.

Cole's lips quirked with a grin.

Fuck. His best friend needed to stop being able to read him so well. Truth be told, they'd both known he'd be spilling his guts within the first five minutes of the movie, but part of him just wanted to keep the Silas thing secret. As if he could preserve the life-changing night for what it had been before the morning splash of ice water.

"I'm meeting my daughter today."

He'd dissected those words a thousand times, and none of the avenues his logic had taken him on meant even a sliver of hope at pursuing anything with Silas. Not that Taran had an issue with kids—hell, he loved kids. But Silas's situation didn't sound like there'd be room for him in it, and he'd just gotten dumped. He couldn't handle more heartbreak.

The familiar sound of the opening of *Scream* came from his living room. Taran took the final bites of his pancakes and tossed the container before following the noise to where Cole waited for him. Probably the interrogation too.

Taran slid onto the open side of his couch and leaned back into one of the throw pillows. Cole had stretched his legs out, feet resting on the coffee table in front of him. His best friend acted like he was staring at the movie on the screen, but really, the fucker was biding his time, making him sweat. Taran grabbed another throw pillow from the floor and clutched it to his chest, resting his chin on the edge.

"So, have I swayed you to the dark side yet?" Cole asked, tipping back his bottle of porter. "Hookups are far easier than relationships."

Taran crooked a brow. "Then explain to me why

I'm more hung up on my hookup than my ex-boyfriend of eight months."

Cole blinked, dropping his feet to the ground as he sat up. "All right. Who the hell did you hook up with, Tar?"

Taran stared at the gray couch cushions beneath them. Maybe if he looked hard enough, they'd swallow him up. "Silas."

Cole spluttered midsip of porter and a second later slammed the bottle to the table. "Silas King? You mean the guy you've had a fucking hard-on for since we were sophomores in high school?"

Taran's cheeks heated, and he burrowed his chin deeper into the throw pillow, pasting his gaze on the early scenes of *Scream*. "I wouldn't put it like that," Taran muttered. "Sue me for finding the guy interesting."

"The word you're looking for is boxer-meltingly hot. The guy was sexy then, and I can imagine he's aged far too well," Cole responded, more excited than he needed to be. He was the only person on the planet who knew about Taran's old crush on Silas. Nico had no idea, because Taran had made a point of keeping it from his brother. With the amount Nico and Silas hung out back in high school, Taran would've been mortified if Silas had found out.

"Yeah," Taran admitted, his voice husky from the memory. "He's aged damn well." As much as the way things ended had been like stepping into the

Chesapeake midwinter, he couldn't bring himself to regret the incendiary sex from last night. He'd had vivid fantasies of how Silas might be in bed, but the reality had outstripped every damn one of them.

"So why aren't you basking in this?" Cole asked. "You got the rebound sex of your life. Who goes from getting dumped to hooking up with the guy they've been crushing on for ages? This is a good thing."

When Cole said it like that, yeah, Taran sounded like a dumbass.

"Unless you happened to miss the rebound memo and expected to ride off into the sunset with a guy who's never been seen with the same guy or girl twice?" And there came Cole's judgment face.

Not like his best friend was wrong. As much as Taran had convinced himself he was down for one wild no-strings-attached night, he should've known he would always want more with Silas King. The man had been a fascination to him for years, and not just because he was sexy as sin with a voice like honey and spice. And maybe the night before had been full of flirtation and sex, but waking up next to him in the morning had felt right in a way waking up next to Kevin never did. And when Silas shed the cocky mask, even for a minute, those feelings had consumed Taran.

"Fuck," Taran muttered. That had been part of the burn, even if he hadn't wanted to admit it. Maybe longing for a guy for a decade and hooking up with him was a terrible idea after all. "Still, I didn't ask to be a fucking home-wrecker."

Cole's eyes widened and he paused the movie. "Silas is married?"

Taran speared his fingers through his hair, scrubbing his face with his palm. "Things were going well this morning. At least, they were until he dropped the bomb that he was meeting his daughter today."

Cole leaned back on the couch, his arms spread across the top. His lips quivered with unbridled amusement. "Was that all he said? Or did he say, gee, I better head home to the wife and kids?"

This was why no one wanted a prosecutor as a best friend. Absolutely ridiculous. Asshole *never* let any of his dramatics slide. His chest tightened as the realization he'd been trying to push off crawled in. Silas hadn't said anything else. Taran had leapt to the conclusion that Silas was married with a kid and then bolted out of the hotel room before the inevitable could happen.

Before Silas could tell him, "Hey, it's been great, but…."

Because out of all the rejections he'd accumulated over the years, that one had the power to break him the most.

Cole stared at him with an annoying smug look. Taran flipped him the middle finger and pressed play on *Scream* again. "I might've drawn my own conclusions," Taran muttered.

Cole shrugged and tipped back his beer for a sip before continuing. "I'm just here for the show, man. You know how to keep shit entertaining. Though I couldn't blame you if the kid thing scared you off. I'd be running for the hills."

Taran rolled his eyes. "You're as bad as Nic used to be. Like if someone breathes commitment in your direction, you'll die from consumption. The kid thing wouldn't freak me out—just if he had a wife or partner and was cheating on them with me. Look, I know what that feels like, and I'm not about to subject someone else to the misery."

Cole reached over and gave him a light punch to the shoulder. "And that's why we love you, Shah."

"Who's 'we?'" Taran muttered, ignoring the warmth that bubbled up inside him. He fucking missed having Cole living up the street from him the way he had when they were kids.

"The royal we, sweetheart," he shot back. "We both know you don't have any other friends."

Taran kicked the side of his leg. He settled into the couch, clutching his throw pillow as he focused in on the shrill screams coming from the movie. Time to wallow for a little bit about how in twenty-four hours his life had taken some extreme twists.

The doorbell rang.

His brows drew together.

"Expecting company?" Cole asked, cocking his head to the side.

"No," Taran said. "But you're going to come to the door with me in case it's a serial killer waiting to murder me. Besides, I need to grab something to drink, and you could probably use a refill."

"Only you would figure out a way to torture yourself while you're down by watching movies that get you on edge," Cole teased even as he pushed up from the couch. "Come on. I'll make sure Ghostface spares you tonight."

Taran headed for the door, his feet dragging with every step. He didn't want to deal with whoever waited outside, most likely Mama or Nico, though the timing was odd. Cole's footsteps creaked from behind, bolstering him. Another knock rapped at the door.

Taran rested his hand on the cool knob for a moment before swinging the door open.

Kevin stood in the doorway, all-American good looks in his salmon-colored polo and khaki chinos. He held a large overflowing box, a few old fantasy books sticking out at the top that Taran recognized. Taran's chest squeezed tight. Not like Kevin had planned on reading them anyway—the guy had never bothered to try to understand his interests. They were better off split. He knew that the moment he saw Silas King and remembered what real attraction felt like.

Their sort of chemistry couldn't be forced, no matter how hard he'd tried.

"Figured I'd bring over your stuff," Kevin said with a shrug and an apologetic wince. "I feel bad for how things went down at the pub last night."

Taran's tongue dried. He sure as hell didn't. No matter how awkward this morning was, last night with Silas had been life-changing.

Kevin's gaze tracked past him to where Cole stood sentinel. "Hey, man," he offered with a casual nod. They'd met a few times, though Cole had always made snide comments when Kevin stepped out of the room. Cole was too busy to bother with subtlety.

"Thanks," Taran said, reaching out to grab the box before Cole could unleash the barbs he had prepared. He placed the box on the ground next to the entrance, fully expecting Kevin to be striding away by the time he straightened up. Instead, Kevin remained awkwardly in the doorframe, scratching his nape.

"You're a good guy, Taran," Kevin said, his tone hesitant.

"So I've heard," Taran muttered, Kevin's words taunting him. Being a "good guy" had become synonymous with taking everyone's shit without complaint, and he'd just about reached the end of his rope. Obligations, favors, and assists piled on him brick after brick until he was about to collapse from the weight of those expectations. He envied Nico and Cole that way, how his brother and best friend just gave a blunt "no" and moved the fuck on.

"Don't lose my number," Kevin said, forcing a grin. "We can still be friends."

Taran could feel Cole's stare behind him, but he didn't acknowledge it. What sort of asshole would he be to say no? The guy hadn't asked for a kidney or anything. "Sure, Kev," he murmured, already wanting to wash the self-loathing off his skin. "I'll see you around."

Kevin jammed his hands into his pockets and turned to the side, looking toward his car by the road. "Have a good night."

Taran brought the door shut with a gentle click, pausing a moment before he turned around.

Cole gave a pointed cough behind him. Taran sucked in a deep breath and let it out slowly as he faced his best friend, Judgy McJudgerson. "What was that?" Cole asked. "Let's be friends?"

Taran shot him a glare. "What am I supposed to say? 'No, go the fuck away'?"

Cole clapped a hand on his shoulder as he steered Taran in the direction of the kitchen again so they could grab drinks. "Yes, that's exactly what douchebags like Kevin deserve. He wants something —either you on the hook, or he's waiting to cash in a favor. I'm telling you."

Taran beat him to the fridge and passed Cole another beer while he nabbed a cider. Once he cracked the top, he took a sip, the refreshing liquid taking the edge off. Not like it could erase the confusion from last night or the extra coating of self-disgust from being such a pushover with his ex. Unlike Mama and Nico, he hated confrontation something fierce. He'd rather sit through a mind-numbingly dull football game than get in a disagreement.

Cole leaned against the kitchen counter, making himself comfortable. "Here's the deal: we can either dive deep into Kevin and Silas, or you can tell me more about the app you've been working on that I'm dying to do the IP contracts for. If you won't put your foot down in your love life, I'll at least settle for you getting ahead professionally."

Taran shook his head, a flutter of vulnerability pricking through the surface. Cole was the best damn person he knew. "All right, all right. We can talk about the Barter app." He'd been working on his baby for the past year, and as much as he wanted to finally launch the thing, it'd be a lot of work. If the app took off, he might need to take the leap and quit his job.

He took another sip of cider, trying to will the cool liquid to suppress the heat that rose at the thought of the fling with Silas.

After last night, he'd taken enough leaps.

CHAPTER 6

Silas strode up the brick walkway toward the door of yet another quaint historical home in Chesapeake City.

This afternoon felt all wrong—the bright, twinkling sunlight, the birds chirping, and the honeyed gardenia breezes sweeping through. Far too cheerful for the end of his freedom. A world away from this morning when he'd woken up next to Taran Shah in all his sultry gorgeousness, and the man cracked him open with a few words. Silas's palms were soaked, and he was pretty sure his temp had turned glacial.

Three weeks ago, he'd gotten the life-changing call, one he should've expected before now in his life after years of flings.

You're a father.

Of course, it wasn't from one of his hookups in Philly. No, this text came from Maeve Johnson, one of the waitresses at Port of Call who he'd taken for a spin in the sheets last year when he'd visited for the Chesapeake Days festival. He'd noticed Taran that night too—adorably hot and looking too fucking cute for words, and like an idiot he'd passed him over. Men like Silas King weren't meant to be dads, but apparently fate loved to fuck with him.

Even if he went down in memory as a total fuckup, there was one thing he refused to be, and that was like his father. He wouldn't abandon his kid.

Still, no amount of time could prepare him for the reality of a three-month-old baby who was *his*.

His phone buzzed, and he glanced down to another text from Mom. Now that he was back in town, she wanted to see him, but little did she know the news he was about to drop. He plunked the phone back into his pocket and reined in his nerves.

Silas tried wiping his palms on his jeans even though they just broke into a fresh sweat after. He lifted his knuckles, sucked in a sharp breath, and knocked. His heart pounded so hard, it was all he could hear, even with the rumble of engines from the street behind him.

The only solace was that it didn't sound like Maeve was angling to get together with him. Their spark had been a shallow flame, quick to burn out after a night, and he couldn't imagine forcing himself into a relationship with someone he didn't know. Not like he knew his daughter, either. At least, not yet.

Footsteps sounded from inside the house, and Silas's whole body locked up. How did people prepare for this? Was there some memo he should've read, some crash course on dealing with surprise fatherhood? Most folks got nine months to get ready, while he got told after the fact.

The door creaked open.

Silas's gaze fell on Maeve, who still looked blonde, snarky, and beautiful even if bags lingered under her eyes and her skin had turned sallow. However, what stole his attention was the small creature bundled in her arms. The baby was wrapped in a pale blue blanket, her eyes shut in slumber and her miniature lips pursed as her whole body trembled with the effort of breathing. She had a thick patch of dark brown hair she'd definitely gotten from him, but apart from that, he wasn't sure if she'd gotten more of her looks from Maeve or him. Hell, he'd barely spared much more than a glance at Maeve the night Fiona was conceived.

Silas swallowed hard. He should feel something here, right? This was his daughter.

His heart hadn't stopped, and he didn't get the overwhelming swarm of warmth or gushiness or protectiveness or whatever the hell you were supposed to feel when you looked at your kid. Clearly, he was more fucked up than he realized.

"Hey, Silas," Maeve said, her tone prim in a way

he hadn't heard the night they'd hooked up. "Glad you could come meet her. This is Fiona."

Silas speared his fingers through his hair, all of his usual cocky charm drying on his tongue. "Didn't realize they made them that small," was all he managed.

Maeve shook her head, annoyed with him if the curl of her lip offered any indication. "Yeah, she's three months old. What did you expect?"

Great. He had eighteen years of co-parenting with Maeve to look forward to, and it was off to an amazing start.

Maeve gave him a pointed look and stepped farther inside the house, so he followed. "Did you want to hold her?" she asked once they shut the door.

The word "no" bubbled to his lips, but that was probably the wrong one. The movies made it look like there'd be some instantaneous bond—as if he'd see his kid and magically feel things, maybe even know how to handle her. Silas stared at the two strangers before him, not sure what the hell he should do next.

"Yeah, sure," he said, even though he very much didn't know the first thing about holding an infant.

Maeve lifted an eyebrow as she passed Fiona over to him. "Make sure to support the head."

Silas placed his callused hands out with tattooed knuckles and covered in scars—not the sort that should be holding something as small and delicate as this. Maeve placed Fiona into his palms, and he couldn't get over how tiny this little creature was. Fuck, she seemed breakable, yet somehow he'd become one of the people responsible for keeping her alive? How was that allowed?

Maeve smoothed a palm over her face. "Why don't the two of you bond? I need to take a shower—it's been way too long." At that, Maeve turned on her heel and trudged up the steps. Stains marred her tank top, and she was barefoot, details he hadn't even noticed when he'd stepped through the door. Before he could say anything or even ask a question, she'd already scaled the staircase halfway.

Silas stared down at the baby in his arms who had barely even stirred at being handed over to him. Fiona let out a shuddering sigh that wracked her whole body as she settled in place, still wrapped like a burrito in a little blue blanket. Panic blared in his mind, but Maeve had disappeared upstairs. Sure, he'd been hoping for a bit more of a preface, an introduction, maybe even to catch up with Maeve and learn what Fiona was like—yet no preparation had been in the cards.

Guys who impregnated their one-night stands didn't get the "how to be a dad" lowdown.

Silas stared at the kid, who was suspiciously quiet. Was she even alive? He leaned down to press his ear to her chest, only to find it rising and falling with her quiet breaths. Weren't babies supposed to scream all the time? Not like he'd ever taken care of an infant in his life. He clutched the bundle tightly, making sure he supported the head as he just stood there in the foyer of Maeve's house. Or was it her parents' house? He'd gotten the barest details from her, and now he was mucking around in the middle of someone else's home, holding a baby girl.

He forced himself to walk with the child, even though she wasn't doing a whole lot besides snoozing peacefully. Silas kept sneaking glances at her, like she was a bomb about to detonate. At any moment, he expected wails, or vomit, or some form of baby-induced horror and he'd have no fucking clue how to react.

Silas's skills ranged from cooking to luring pretty guys and girls to his bed, but none of those talents included a primer on dealing with small humans and their needs. He drifted into the next room, which seemed to be a living room of sorts, with fancy, floral-patterned couches and photographs on the walls of what must be Maeve and her family, as well as Maeve's graduation, a young blond guy's wedding—he could figure out that it was her brother—and a handful of vacations. If he had to take a wild guess, she was living with her parents.

Not like he could blame her. She hadn't signed on to be a single mom. Somehow, he'd figure out a way to be there for this kid, even if he couldn't change a diaper or feed a baby for shit. Silas relaxed his death grip around the bundle as he continued to stride around the room, soaking in the porcelain vases and the bookshelves filled with thick nonfiction tomes. Fiona began to stir in his arms, her little chubby fists poking out to wave around. Her eyes scrunched up, her cheeks turned red, and a second later, the wail erupted.

Silas's heart quickened. What was he supposed to do? Fuck, this kid had lungs. He glanced at the doorway, as if Maeve might appear out of thin air to help him or take Fiona away, but it remained empty. Silas began to sway back and forth.

"Shh, shh, shh," he murmured, repeating the sound over and over again. She started thrashing, those wails persistent and blaring, like a car alarm. His pulse raced, but he tried to seem calm on the surface. At least he'd always been solid at pretending. He just continued to shush and rock, even though the motions didn't seem to do jack shit to help the kid who was becoming an increasingly good imitation of a tomato.

A moment later, a loud fart ripped from the tiny girl, and a stink permeated the air.

Fiona let out a burbling noise, her eyes going wide a moment before her lashes fluttered and they closed again. Silas's jaw dropped. Did the kid literally wake herself up to rip ass? A laugh bubbled up inside him before he could help it, a slow, subtle creep until his shoulders were shaking. All of the fear, the nerves, and the dread spilled out in laughter until he wasn't sure if he was about to teeter into fucking tears. Fiona wrinkled her little nose and fidgeted, so Silas sucked in a lungful of air to try and calm himself.

He clutched the bundle of baby girl tighter to his chest. As he skimmed over her features, he caught those familiar lashes and the same slender lips he had, nothing like Maeve's full ones. Silas waited for the legendary parental protectiveness to wash over him, but nada. Even still, the little fucker was pretty cute.

Whether he felt some bone-deep connection to this child or not, one thing was for sure—he wouldn't walk out on her. The single promise he'd made in life was to not become his father, and he'd uphold it.

Silas found a seat on the couch and plunked onto the cushion, leaning back with Fiona in his arms.

A creak sounded from behind him, and a moment later, Maeve appeared, freshly showered and wearing a fresh pair of pajama pants and white tank top. She pursed her lips and scanned the two of them.

"All right," she murmured, her voice a little softer than it had been before. "We've got a lot to discuss, so let's start figuring some of this out. I know raising a kid together wasn't what either of us planned coming from that night."

Silas nodded, his lips quirking at the sides. "You mean you don't go into all your one-night flings, hoping to impregnate someone?"

Maeve fixed him a glare. "Too fucking soon."

He internally rolled his eyes. Christ, they would've never worked long-term. Silas sucked in a deep breath. "I'm moving back to the area. I want to be a part of Fiona's life."

Maeve swallowed hard, and she stared at the ground. "That's... good to hear. Follow me to the kitchen, and we'll figure out what your involvement looks like. Kiddo needs her next feed."

Silas began to push off from the couch, and Fiona stirred, the chubby fist coming close to decking him in the nose. As if brought to life by the mention of food, Fiona's blue eyes popped open, and a moment later, she opened those tiny lips and squalled. The sound hit him like feedback on a microphone, and Silas winced.

Maeve tilted her head toward the kitchen. "Follow me. Food will solve the problem."

Silas clutched the wailing kid tightly as he strode after Maeve. His heart still lay in tangles, his nerves scraped raw, and he couldn't be more lost if someone dropped him in the middle of the Atlantic, but he was here. He was here, and he was trying.

That would have to be enough.

By the time Silas left Maeve's place, his head was swimming.

They'd gone over the basics—what being in Fiona's life would look like to start, mostly supervised visits until he got comfortable, and then they'd figure out a schedule for which days each of them got her. Stepping into the nursery and seeing all the baby gadgets Maeve utilized with ease had him feeling inept all over again, like he'd shown up to a math final after skipping most of the classes that year. While he visited, Fiona had sucked down a bottle like a beast, and with the same gusto had thrown it all back up again. He'd gone home to change and shower before heading out again.

The rev of the engine beneath him was like reclaiming a part of himself that had gotten tossed adrift the moment he arrived at Maeve's. He turned into the parking lot, the familiar exterior of Port of Call in view. Cozy lights illuminated the gorgeous cream exterior, and the ever-popular deck bar branched out from the side of the building next to the river. It already brimmed with people, even in April. His heart pounded a little harder at the sight of it— not because Nico Shah owned the place but because of who he'd spent last night with.

Nico's little brother. And now here he was, coming to beg Nico for a job.

Not like he could even believe last night had happened. It felt a lifetime away after meeting his daughter had aged him a century.

Silas pulled his bike to a halt and then tugged off his helmet, running his fingers through his hair. Once he shut the bike off, he shoved his hands into the pockets of his leather jacket and braced his shoulders. He had the qualifications to walk into Port of Call and ask for a job—he'd worked in some great restaurants in Philly, and he was competent at what he did. But the approach curdled his stomach as he strode up to the front door, the feeling of permanency settling over him like a collar at the thought of accepting a job in his hometown.

If Nico even had room for him on the roster. Which he definitely wouldn't if he knew Silas had hooked up with his hot-as-fuck little brother. Seriously, Taran came across all pure and sweet, but holy hell was he hiding all his depraved sexiness beneath the surface. Silas had slept with plenty of people over the years and had *never* felt like that before. The electricity between them, the way Taran read him intuitively, how their bodies merged together—Silas had been tempted to offer to bottom, and he'd never done that.

He shook his head and tugged at the handle, stepping into the hopping atmosphere of Port of Call on a Saturday night. People crowded along the mahogany bar on the first floor, most folks watching the Orioles game. Plenty of the tables were filled, and servers bustled around. Before Maeve had the misfortune of hooking up with him, she'd been one of them. She was living at her parents' place as he'd suspected, and she'd quit her job for the time being, at least until Fiona got a little older. After being in the baby's presence for a few hours, he could see why.

Silas bypassed the main floor, heading straight for the steps to the second. His hand skimmed the railing as he traveled past the globe lights along the way and all the nautical swag on the walls, from portholes to a ship's wheel. His tongue dried a little as he reached the second floor and caught sight of Nico working behind the bar.

His friend glanced at him, and his face lit up. "Silas King, what the hell are you doing in town?" His voice boomed, even over the rowdy chatter of the crowds up here.

Silas shook his head, not bothering to hide his smirk. This guy was a goddamn business owner, and a successful one at that. Weird as fuck to see from the guy he knew back in high school. He stalked toward Nico. The man was looking good—happier than ever. Last he'd heard, someone had managed to rope down Nico Shah, which he could barely believe. As much as Silas shouldn't, he couldn't help cataloguing the differences between Nico and Taran. Nico had an edge to him and wielded his charm like a blade—he and Silas were far too alike for either of them to go for each other. But Taran? The pouty lower lip, the big brown eyes that lured you in, and then his dry-as-a-bone humor to cap off such a pretty package? Fucking kryptonite.

Silas plunked himself down onto the barstool closest to Nico, who made a point of sliding an already poured beer in front of him.

"You look like you need it," Nico said, tapping the side of the glass. "Rough day?"

"Man, you've perfected the bartender talk," Silas cracked back. "Let me just unleash all my woes on you as long as you keep the sweet, sweet nectar coming."

"Good to see you too," Nico responded with a grin, tipping his head in a brief nod at a customer down the bar as he reached for a fresh pint glass and pulled the taps, dispensing more lager.

"As much as I wish this was a social visit, I need to talk to you when you've got a second," Silas forced out.

Nico's brows drew together, but he nodded. He swerved down the bar to drop off the beer and returned a moment later. "What's the deal, Si?"

"Remember the server you lost due to her having a kid? I'm here to offer you a full-time sous chef in exchange," Silas responded, his tone deadpan.

Nico stared at him for a moment as the words sank in, and then the jaw drop followed. "Fuck," he hissed. "You're the father of Maeve's kid?"

Silas lifted his palms and waved them in a lack-luster jazz hands. "Bully for me."

"This is why all you bi boys are crazy," Nico shot back, teasing. "At least when I stick my dick in some-one, I don't run the risk of getting them pregnant."

Silas gave him the middle finger. "Clearly, that had been my plan."

Though if he'd stuck his dick in the person he'd been eyeing up like a treat last year, he wouldn't have been in this situation. However, Nico didn't need to hear anything about Silas lusting after his little brother.

Nico pressed his palms to the counter, sinking against it. "Fuck, you're a dad? That makes me feel ancient."

"Y'know, because this is all about you," Silas responded with a shake of his head. Relief soaked through him that Nico wasn't acting weird about the whole thing.

Nico placed a palm to his chest. "Obviously. I mean, you are coming to my bar, asking me for a job, right?"

Silas swallowed the sourness in his throat, because this felt more like slinking home with his tail between his legs than anything. Nico must've noticed since he jumped in again. "By which I mean, the sous chef job is yours if you want it. I don't normally hire friends, but I know the restaurants you worked at in Philly, and I want some of that talent up in my joint.

Besides, if you've got a kid, I'm guessing I don't need to worry about you randomly bolting to a new town."

"Yeah, I'm back for good this time," Silas murmured, taking a sip of beer because Christ, he needed it. He now had the job, and he'd already gotten an apartment in town, so check and check. However, no matter how responsible he was being, he couldn't shake the weight crushing down on his chest, like his time had run out. In Philly, he could be anything he wanted, but here? He'd returned to become the stereotype the town always expected— the fuck-up kid who knocked up a girl and would be stuck in Chesapeake City for the rest of his life.

CHAPTER 7

A week had passed before Cole was proven right in his assumptions.

Taran had been working from home as per usual, clocking hours coding his part of the project for the team when his phone buzzed with a text.

Kevin.

I hate to ask, but Nana's 88th birthday dinner is tonight, and I haven't told the family we broke up yet...

Taran's answer should've been a definitive no. However, Kevin had emphasized at length that he'd only ever ask this once, that Nana wasn't doing well and this might be her last birthday, that she had loved Taran.

Which was how Taran found himself outside of Nico's restaurant one week from when Kevin dumped him, doing a favor for the guy. An awkward, cringey favor that made him feel like garbage. But hey, who needed self-respect when you had bags of Swedish Fish to reassure you afterward?

He ran his fingers through his hair, already wishing he hadn't agreed to this. Chances were, his brother was working, and he'd spot them and have questions. Then this exercise in embarrassment would be a thousand times worse. The second Nico found out he was pretending to still be with his ex, he'd make a scene, and Kevin's nana would probably have a heart attack. Truly, he'd be better off turning around, heading home, and continuing his rewatch of *Doctor Who* he'd started on a total whim that had nothing to do with a certain tattooed, sexy-as-fuck bad boy.

Taran pushed the door open and headed through the entrance he'd traversed five thousand times since his brother first purchased the property. He jammed his hands into his pockets, tempted to head upstairs and visit Nico rather than attempting this appearance. How long was he supposed to stay? Why had he even showed up in the first place?

Cole would have a dozen answers for that question, but he didn't want to hear them.

Taran had only taken a few steps in when he caught sight of Kevin's pale yellow polo and broad-shouldered frame as he stood out amidst a table filled with faces that had become familiar over the past eight months. They'd gone to each other's family holiday traditions without too much hassle, and truth be told, he'd liked Kevin's family. They were welcoming and friendly, and they'd seemed to appreciate him from the start.

Same couldn't be said for the way Mama and Nico viewed Kevin. He should've listened to them a little harder, but he was stubborn on his best day.

Kevin caught sight of him and waved him over, a big smile on his face. For a moment, he could forget that last week had ever happened, that they were still together, going on dates, sleeping over each other's places. Except the unpacked cardboard box in the living room he shared with Sarah said otherwise. She'd already threatened to burn the items in the box if he didn't move it soon.

Taran forced a smile he didn't feel, his stomach sinking with each step forward. This had been a terrible idea. In theory, he thought it wouldn't bother him too much. That he and Kevin hadn't been right together. And they hadn't.

However, he was so, so damn tired of never being right for *anyone*.

The chatter of Port of Call washed over him in the form of low murmurs from the tables and cheerful shouts from the bar. Jer worked the first-floor bar tonight, which meant the chances of his brother being upstairs were increased a thousandfold. Even higher were the chances of Sarah being here, something he hadn't contemplated when he'd agreed to this idiocy.

Maybe he could contract a surprise case of the

laughing death. He probably shouldn't have watched the documentary on Kuru last night, but he never seemed to like sensible things. Which would definitely explain his brain's nonstop fixation on Silas King.

Every day since they'd hooked up, he'd been staring a little harder when he walked around town, as if he might catch a glimpse, even though he shouldn't.

Kevin slid his arms around Taran's shoulders like they'd never broken up a week ago, and Taran's chest squeezed tight at the feeling of solid warmth around him. As much as Kevin might not have been "the one," Taran missed having someone in his bed. He missed the comfort of coming home to share his day with his boyfriend, even if Kevin had only half listened.

"Hey, glad you could make it," Kevin said, a grin on his face that didn't quite meet his eyes.

Taran's stomach soured even more. This had been a mistake. "Yeah," he mumbled, trying to paste on a fake smile as he skimmed his gaze over Kevin's parents, his nana, and a few close aunts and uncles. "Good to see you guys again."

"Kevin was just telling us a little about the project you're doing for work," Kevin's mom said, a sweet woman with an honest smile and tight brown curls that brushed along her shoulders. "He said they're starting to give you more responsibility there."

Taran tried to catch Kevin's eyes, but he refused to look his way, even with the heavy, suppressive weight of his arm around Taran's shoulder. Kevin had always played this game around his family—talk Taran up as the trophy boyfriend to keep them from asking about Kevin's lack of focus when it came to anything work-related. Was that all he'd been dragged out for? Anger ripped through him like a match being struck. Nana wasn't in great health, judging from the lost look in her rheumy eyes, but Kevin didn't seem to be too broken up about it.

Taran had thought maybe he'd be a wall ornament, sit there nodding for a little while and then cut a timely escape, but no, Kevin pulled the same shit he had while they were together, throwing the spotlight on Taran.

"I just wanted to swing by to wish you a happy birthday," he said, locking eyes with Nana. He tried for an apologetic smile which probably came out more like a wince. "I wish I could stay," he murmured, racking his brain for an excuse. "But I promised Mama a visit, and she's been sick with the flu this week."

He met Kevin's eyes, daring him to try and challenge his excuse. Two could play at parental guilt games.

"Glad you could stop by at least," Kevin forced out, even though Taran could hear the edge to his words. Sure, Taran was a model boyfriend to show off to Mom and Dad—steady job, great with the elderly and babies, and responsible to a fault. However, no guy ever wanted him beyond that.

No guy ever wanted *him.*

And the bare blade drove in a little deeper tonight. Before Kevin could offer some more fake affection they'd both try to grin and bear, Taran slipped out from under his arm, tossed his hand up in a half-hearted wave, and made a beeline for the door he'd entered through minutes before.

He stepped out into the brisk April air, his internal reaction to his snap decision shuttling through his veins and leaving him shaky in the aftermath. Taran glanced back toward the door. Part of him wanted to just head to the second floor to see his brother and Sarah, to bask in the chatter and familiar faces tonight rather than the loneliness of his couch at home. However, he'd blown that option out of the water when he delivered that bullshit excuse to Kevin's family.

Why couldn't he just say no?

He should've been heading toward his car, but his hands still trembled, and he didn't want to get on the road like that. Instead, he jammed his hands into his pockets and followed the building to the opposite side of the deck, closer to the employee entrance. Maybe his brother would pop out there and they could catch up. Nico might give him shit, but at least Taran knew his brother cared.

Fucking Kevin Jenkins.

The truth settled in his stomach like acid—he only had himself to blame. No one forced him to come out tonight, to remind himself that he'd been dumped. Again.

He went into each relationship with lofty hopes—memories of how his family had been when Dad was still alive haunting him at every turn. He wanted that for himself. Desperately. Except all of those attempts shattered on the pavement.

Taran ran his palms down his pale blue button-down, wishing he was fucking different. Maybe then someone would want him and not what he could do for them. He stalked over to the closed employee door with the orange pail next to it and found a spot to lean against on the white siding of the restaurant. His eyes ached as liquid threatened to spill from them, but Taran shoved that shit right back. He stared at the starry sky, distant pinpricks of light nestled in a velvet expanse.

A few hesitant clouds threaded through the sky, wheezy little things that threatened to disappear with a puff, just like his confidence. He glanced down at his hands. Still trembling. Damn.

The employee door let out a hearty creak, almost causing him to launch into the air.

The first thread of relief lay within reach as he turned to greet his brother—only, it wasn't Nico.

A helpless laugh slipped from his lips.

Silas King stood before him, looking hotter than fucking ever. His dark hair was tousled, and the white tank top he wore ensured that his ink was on full display. It was glued to his chest with sweat, showcasing those mouthwatering abs. He'd slung his leather jacket over his shoulder, but his striped pants gave him away—Nico had all his chefs wear them.

"You've got to be fucking kidding me," Taran said before he could stop himself.

Silas's eyes widened as he locked and loaded on Taran. He didn't miss the hungry way his gaze devoured him from head to toe or the following wariness that flickered in those blue eyes.

"Not the reception I expected, but I guess I shouldn't be shocked after the way you bolted last week," Silas murmured, the tip of his tongue darting to the side of his mouth in a move that would look self-conscious on anyone else, but on him it was devastatingly sexy.

Taran's shoulders shook, and before he realized it, laughter just ripped from him. Maybe he'd contracted the laughing death after all. Fucking Kuru documentary.

Silas leaned against the wall beside him, watching his complete hysterical breakdown, those blue eyes intense.

Taran sucked in a sharp breath to collect himself and placed a palm on his chest. "One week later, and

I'm in the exact same position I was then—humiliated by my ex and then you show up."

Silas's brows drew together. "I thought he dumped you?"

Taran leaned hard against the side of the building, the cool surface soaking in through the thin fabric of his button-down. He fiddled with the sleeves he'd rolled to his elbows and just stared back up at the sky, unable to face this embarrassment head-on. He should be pissed as hell at Silas for not telling him his situation up front, but in the guy's presence, his lips were loose and his heart tangled in knots.

"He did. And then he asked me to pretend we were still together for his grandmother's birthday dinner." Taran's voice sounded reedy in his own ears, a little incredulous that he'd been such an idiot to agree. When would he fucking learn? "Still not as embarrassing as finding out the guy you slept with has a family."

Well, he hadn't meant to let that slip.

A creak came from behind him, and a shadow shifted. Taran couldn't bring himself to look over at Silas to see whether there was scorn or shame on his face. The man's delicious leather-and-clove scent surrounded him, and his traitorous cock perked up on reflex at the memory of drowning in everything Silas just a week ago.

"I have a daughter," Silas said, his voice low and gravelly. The sound caused Taran to realize Silas had stepped closer to him and was now a mere foot away. Still, Taran didn't have the nerve to lift his gaze as the man continued, "And if that's enough to freak you out, I can't blame you, because the news sure as hell has me spooked. But let's get one thing perfectly clear. I don't cheat. I might have a co-parent relationship with the mother, but that's it."

"Oh." Taran's mouth dried. Every bitter excuse that had rampaged through his mind ever since he left the hotel room dissolved at once.

Silas was single.

Which meant that the real reason for his chickenshit exit rose quickly to the surface, which was actually the expected rejection that had been looming over him in the back of his mind from the moment they hooked up. If Silas delivered it tonight while his skin felt peeled and raw like this, Taran wouldn't recover. Just declare him DOA and toss him in a ditch because he wasn't going to be able to dig himself out of this slump.

Taran slowly lifted his eyes.

"Yeah, oh," Silas said, a slow smirk rising to his lips. Damn but the guy was next-level hot. Whatever protections Taran's mind planned got tossed out once he witnessed the flare of heat in those ocean-blue eyes. His knees trembled a little, but not from any sort of fear. When he sucked in another sharp breath, Silas's gaze seized on the movement, like he was a wolf in the wild stalking down his prey.

"Well, if it isn't clear to you yet, I'm great at coming to terrible conclusions and making bad decisions," Taran mumbled, heat rising to his cheeks.

"Oh, honey, nothing about what we did that night was a bad decision," Silas purred, and holy hell, had it just hit July? Because his temperature soared. What was it about this man that tripped him up every time? He'd been dwelling over his ex again, and there Silas appeared, reminding him of what he should've been feeling the entire time he was with Kevin. The incendiary passion that consumed him like the first page of his favorite book, making a promise to take him to both devastating lows and unimaginable highs.

To etch upon his bones no matter where he and Silas ended up.

Taran licked his lips, unable to help himself with that gorgeous man this damn close.

"No, it wasn't," Taran whispered, knowing the truth deep down, no matter how much he tried to convince himself otherwise.

Silas took another step closer, and Taran felt every inch of his back press against the side of the restaurant, which felt so, so similar to the night they'd spent together. The slight chill of the breeze didn't penetrate past his skin, not with the heat brewing between them. This close, all he could see was the glint in the man's seductive eyes, the scruff along his sharp chin, and the faint scar that ran through his left brow.

The air between them seemed to crackle, but Taran couldn't look away from the curve of Silas's lips mere inches away.

This was a terrible idea. He'd already fallen into Silas's arms last week, and after the reprisal of his shitty feelings of uselessness, he couldn't take another fling. Silas had responsibilities and wasn't in the market for more than that.

Yet when Silas took another step forward, Taran found himself leaning in.

And when Silas's palm wrapped around his nape and those tender lips pressed against his, Taran couldn't help but sink into the kiss.

His mouth caressed Silas's, and a low moan escaped from the back of his throat. The man tasted delicious, masculine with that familiar hint of clove, and Taran lapped it up, sliding his tongue against Silas's with slow strokes. The man settled his other palm against the wall beside Taran, and he tilted his head back, surrendering to the power behind this kiss, to the way the brushing together of their lips made everything else in the known universe just melt away.

Taran settled his hand on Silas's waist as their chests bumped together, and he couldn't help but grind his hard length against the man's thick thigh. The zings that coursed through him in reaction made his knees buckle, but the wall behind kept him upright. Those seeking lips were everything he'd dreamed of, everything he'd memorized from the last time—strong, tender, and mesmerizing. The highs he soared to when kissing this man had him tempted to just drag him to his car and see where the night took them.

The clanging sound of pots and pans banging together came from the other side of the employee door.

Silas pulled back with a start, and the moment between them shattered.

Taran was standing outside of his brother's restaurant, making out with one of his employees. Fuck. Somehow, this guy made him lose his mind even when he was usually more careful. Taran ran his thumb along his lower lip, chasing the phantom sensation of their kiss. He didn't miss the possessive flare in Silas's eyes when he caught the motion.

"I...," Taran started, not sure of what to say. Shouldn't have done that? Shouldn't even be here tonight? Nothing made sense except that when he was around Silas, none of those concerns mattered.

"Look," Silas murmured, carding his fingers through his dark, glossy strands. "I'm off for the night. Do you want to take a drive?"

No. He should say no. Spending more time around Silas was dangerous for his heart, and he'd been too careless with it for years, giving piece after piece to people who didn't deserve it. However, his mouth betrayed him.

"Lead the way," he responded, clearly in a fit of insanity.

"Ever take a ride on a motorcycle?" Silas asked, his lips curving in a smirk so hot it should be illegal. Taran found himself shaking his head, and when Silas spun on his heel, all he could do was follow.

Oh, he was so fucked.

CHAPTER 8

Kissing Taran Shah was a bad idea.

A bad idea that had felt so impossibly good.

After the exhausting week that had sunken into Silas's skin, the sight of Taran outside the employee entrance of Port of Call had jolted him like spark plugs connected to his system. Yet, as much as Silas was tempted to just fall into bed with the guy again and chase the distraction, he hadn't missed the shadow in Taran's eyes or the strain that seemed a little more pervasive than it had the last time they'd seen each other.

He didn't have time for pretty boys with sarcasm for days and hidden piercings and depths. However, the idea of returning alone to his tiny new apartment sat in his gut like a cement block.

Silas stopped in front of his Triumph and grabbed the helmet from the handle of his bike. He turned toward Taran who almost collided with him. The guy looked fucking delicious tonight in his charcoal slacks and pale blue button-down that brought out the rich copper tones of his skin. Taran's round ass was on full display in his snug pants, but Silas could resist the temptation for a little while.

"Pop the helmet on," he said, handing it over to Taran. Silas swung his leg over to settle onto his Triumph, the leather seat familiar when nothing else in his life was. He'd moved into his new apartment, and he'd begun his shifts at Port of Call as well, but he still felt underwater when he spent time with Fiona, as if he might accidentally drop her or feed her the wrong way and then it would be game over, she'd be ruined forever. Why in hell did anyone choose to be a parent?

Taran clicked the helmet into place, and Silas glanced back at him, a smile rolling over his lips. As if the guy could look fucking cuter.

"Hop on behind me and wrap your arms around my waist. I'd promise I won't bite, but we both know that's bullshit." He waited until Taran sank onto the seat behind him before he revved the engine. Taran wrapped his arms around Silas until he found a solid hold, though he clearly tried to keep some space between them. Silas glanced back at him again, drawing in deep the sandalwood scent of his cologne. He cocked a brow. "You're not going to be comfortable like that, and we've been a whole hell of a lot closer."

Taran's lips pursed as he shot him a wry look before scooting up behind him until his chest pressed against Silas's back. The feel of the slender man clinging tightly to him had his cock rising to life. Hell, Silas had no idea what possessed him to not only kiss Taran again but then offer to whisk him away. He'd lived in this small town before and had run into plenty of his hookups in the past without the slightest urge to instigate things a second time, but ever since he'd seen Taran sitting there at Hickory Taproom, the man had been creeping under his skin.

"Ready?" Silas glanced over his shoulder to see those too-pretty eyes staring back at him.

"As much as I'll ever be," Taran responded, even though his arms tightened slightly around Silas's waist. He reveled in the touch, which sent a cascade of sparks traveling through him. Silas pulled out of the spot and started for the road. Heading into town wouldn't do them any good, and they needed to be away from the bar scene right now. If Taran's head was any bit as muddled as his, he'd need to go farther out than Chesapeake City.

Silas zipped over the bridge and onto the highway, a destination in mind. He'd ridden with passengers a few times in the past but not frequently. Most of the time, the trip would be a solid prelude to a good fuck, but this felt different. Even as he soared across the asphalt faster, faster, faster with the inky black stretching ahead of him and a horizon full of unreachable promise up above, Taran's presence at his back was like a mooring amidst a storm.

He hadn't realized it until now, but during their first time together and even here with him now, Silas's mind quieted in a way it rarely did. Too often, he got caught in a spin cycle of self-loathing and poor decisions that continued to plague him long after the fact, and after his most recent one involved an entire life upheaval—yeah, he'd been stuck there. However, as he zoomed along Chesapeake City Road, it was like all those errant thoughts and doubts emptied out and clattered onto the road behind him.

In this moment, all that existed was the pristine moon overhead with its pale, ethereal glow, the brisk wind stinging at his cheeks and whipping through his hair with enough force to remind him he was alive, and the solid weight of Taran behind him, those arms clutching onto him like he meant something. Like he was more than a cautionary tale.

Silas sucked in the sharp air filled with ozone and asphalt, the scents intoxicating as he raced along the road at top speed. Trees loomed on either side, splattering the way ahead with darker shadows, and the lights from his bike cut through the murky blackness with stark clarity. Taran leaned in a little harder, the press of his chest sending a thrill up Silas's spine.

He began to slow as the signs for Lums Pond

State Park came into view right over the border from Maryland into Delaware. His heart puttered in his chest at the same tempo as his motor when he pulled into one of the side entrances into the state park, which would be all sorts of shut down by now. He knew all the back ways to get into this place, though, after years of escaping here to think, a ritual that began when his dad first left. Silas found a spot and pulled into it, parking properly even though the rest of the lot was empty. He shut the engine off.

"We aren't supposed to be here after dark," Taran muttered behind him.

Silas flashed him a smile. "That's what makes it fun."

Taran tugged off the helmet, his ink-stain strands askew as he fixed Silas with a stare. "What would definitely make this night worse is getting arrested."

Silas swung his leg around and turned sideways on the seat, Taran now parked beside him. "Do you trust me?"

Taran arched a brow. "If you think I'm going to say yes just because you're hot, you've got another thing coming."

A genuine smile ripped his face, a surprise after the week of fake flexing he'd done with his muscles. The man continued to knock him off at the knees with his dry sense of humor. "I mean, we could just sit here and hang out on my bike in the parking lot, but if you wanted to take your mind off your ex, the views inside the park are better."

Taran plunged his fingers into his hair. "Fine," he grumbled without much conviction. "But if a serial killer comes after us in the middle of the woods, I'm tripping you and running the other way."

Silas shook his head, his cheeks straining with his smile. "I'll accept being the sacrifice if it gets you to come into the woods with me."

Taran eyed him again. "Way to make it sound creepy."

A laugh escaped Silas as he stood and stepped in front of Taran, offering a hand. "I think we're a little too old to fall into any Hansel and Gretel traps," he responded.

Taran slipped his warm palm against Silas's, and he couldn't deny the zing of electricity that traveled through him at the mere touch. "All right, let's see these illicit views of yours," Taran said, a bit of heat in his eyes as he skimmed his gaze over Silas from head to toe. Silas sucked in a sharp breath, trying to ignore the way his cock stiffened in his pants at the pointed comment. He fought the urge to just hop on the bike with Taran and christen his new apartment.

However, he wasn't in the place to pursue anything more than a single night, which they'd already spent together. With the new job, a new home that needed to be adjusted to having an infant in it, and the brand-new daughter in his life, he was splitting at the seams 24/7. The last thing he wanted to do was drag someone into his clusterfuck of a life. Besides, he didn't even know if he could handle a real relationship, which was what Taran deserved.

Not the mess he was.

Silas pulled Taran up and let go, even though he felt the loss of the warm press of his skin the moment he did. "Come on," he said with a wink. "We've got some trespassing to do."

Silas took the lead as they headed in the direction of the pond, toward one of the little-used trails he'd traveled down too many times to count. Taran kept pace with him, but based on the consistent way Taran's gaze flicked back behind them and to their surroundings, it was less about hiking awareness and more to do with nerves. The trees loomed over them, spidery limbs stretching toward the sky, not yet flush with all their leaves like they would be in the middle of summer. A lonely breeze caressed the uncovered skin of Silas's throat and cheeks, bringing with it the soft scent of loam and the rich tingle of night and shadows.

The quiet between them was companionable, and for once, Silas didn't feel the urge to entertain or to fill the silences, so his mind remained quiet. He caught the glimmer of moonlight across the lake from between some hedges and headed in that direction. Each step closer flooded him with a spectrum of memories—from coming out here to throw rocks into the pond after dad left to escaping after school when he'd caught his supposed girlfriend cheating on him.

You didn't think we were serious, did you?

Yeah, he had. But all too quickly, he saw what expectations people had of the guy whose dad left him, who had almost failed out of school because he couldn't get homework done when he needed to work every day, who started dealing weed on the side just to make sure he and his mom had enough money to pay the electric bill.

They emerged from an opening past the bushes as the trees thinned out and the ground sloped, softening on the way to a wide pond that extended out before them. Moonlight reflected on the surface, silvery and sanguine, the sight flooding his tired soul with new energy. The old docks remained in place, wooden slats that stretched out into the pond at intervals.

Taran sucked in a sharp breath. "Well, damn. Maybe the view is worth it."

Silas took a second to skim his gaze over Taran, who, in his pale button-down and brown loafers, was dressed more for a nice dinner than roaming through the woods, yet he'd followed without complaint. With the lavender moonlight highlighting the man's features, those pretty, wide eyes grew more pronounced, as did his prominent nose and slender jaw. The guy looked so gorgeous, Silas found himself mesmerized.

"I'd say so," Silas responded, his voice coming out husky. Fuck, he needed to stop flirting with him.

Taran arched a thick brow even though a hesitant smile played on his lips. Silas clapped a hand on his shoulder and directed him toward the docks. The moment his boots creaked onto the old, weathered wood, he was at home. Out of everywhere in the area, this was a place he considered his, and he refused to pause and scrutinize too hard why he'd brought Taran along with him tonight.

Silas found a spot at the end of the dock and slumped to the ground like a sack of bones. His shift at Port of Call had been busy as hell but enjoyable. However, the weight of everything that happened during the past few weeks had caught up with him, leaving a perpetual ache in his body he couldn't quite shake.

Taran sat beside him with his knees pulled up and his arms wrapped around them as he stared into the lake ahead. "When did you find out you had a kid?" he asked.

Silas flinched. Not like he'd forgotten about his reality, but hearing those words out loud served as a reminder of why he shouldn't be indulging in this dangerous attraction to Taran.

"If you don't want to talk about it, I've got some fascinating Victorian slang terms I can educate you on. Like a parish pickaxe," Taran continued in his wry tone.

As quick as a snap, the weight in Silas's chest lightened. How the man continued to perform that sorcery, he had no idea, but he was desperate for the respite Taran offered, even just from his companionship.

"Parish pickaxe?" Silas repeated.

"Big nose," Taran responded, his eyes dancing in the gleam of moonlight.

"Maeve told me a month ago," Silas spilled out before he lost the nerve. "I pretty much packed up my entire life in Philly over the past few weeks, found an apartment, and moved here. Your brother's fucking fantastic, so I've got a job, but I still don't have a clue how to deal with an infant."

Taran cast him an amused look. "I don't know… impulsive, reckless, and loud? I'm pretty sure you fit right in with her."

Silas flipped him the middle finger. Fuck, he hadn't smiled this much all week.

Taran leaned his head to the side. "In all honesty, though, you'll learn. Each kid is unique, so even if you'd raised one already, she'll take you on a whole different ride."

"Speaking from experience? Don't tell me you've got secret kids coming out of the woodwork too," Silas responded, kicking his legs back and forth over the side of the dock.

"While you and Nic were getting plastered in high school, I was babysitting," Taran said. "Not like

I'd go to parties even if I had been invited. Not my scene."

His heart twisted at the distance in Taran's voice. How had he overlooked this gorgeous man for so many years? More proof he was a fucking idiot. "You didn't miss much," Silas said. "Just people trying to drown out their problems."

"Did it work?" Taran asked, a hesitance in his voice that stabbed through Silas's heart.

"You deserve better than an asshole like Kevin," Silas murmured.

"That's a sweet sentiment, but I'm better in theory than reality. Everyone thinks they want the sturdy boyfriend, the guy who's going to show up, but after a while, they're all chasing after the glitz of someone more interesting."

Silas cocked a brow. "Trust me, babe, folks think they want glitz until they realize all that shiny's just covering up a mess-load of issues." He ran his fingers through his hair, attempting to ignore the ache in his chest. Somehow, this conversation had gotten real all too fast.

"And what do you want?" Taran asked, the underlying question one they'd never gotten to address on the morning after.

Silas's heart thudded hard, and his mouth grew dry. Truth? He wanted to spend more time around this beguiling, fascinating man, but he also knew himself. He'd made a habit of destroying beautiful things, and Taran Shah deserved far better than him. "I want to survive becoming a father to an infant. Can't handle more than that right now."

Even though he was being honest, those words still shattered the tension in the air.

Taran's head dipped in a nod, but Silas didn't miss the hint of distance in those dark eyes. Fuck, he was an asshole for kissing him earlier and giving him hope.

"I'm done with dating for a while too," Taran said, his voice soft. "I've been going from one relationship to another, yet they all end with the same issues on repeat." He glanced at Silas, locking eyes with him. "I'm not going to lie—a part of me is dying to fall into bed with you again, but that probably isn't a good idea."

"Probably," Silas responded. He swallowed hard. Regret bloomed in his chest even though this was the right choice and what he should be doing.

"Friends?" Taran asked, his lips quirking to the side.

Silas clapped a hand over his chest. "Oof, you just friend-zoned me? Callous, Shah."

Taran knocked his knee against Silas's. "Like you didn't pull the trigger first. Besides, you seem like you could use some friends."

Silas opened his mouth and shut it. His eyes stung, so he glanced away from Taran, not wanting to let show just how right the man was. Even in

Philly, his friends were the folks you could call to grab a beer or hit a party with. No one to talk to when he was drowning with all these new changes. No one who listened or seemed to see through his defenses like Taran did.

"I'd be lucky to have a friend like you, Taran Shah," he responded, his voice coming out hoarse. Taran's gaze fixed on him, steady in a way he'd searched far too long for.

If he wanted more? Well, that was one of the too-many secrets he'd keep to himself.

CHAPTER 9

Taran shoved his feet into shoes as Max whined by the door. Sarah's corgi only loved him when walk time arrived—otherwise the hyper little beast ignored him. At least the sun glittered high up in the sky, and Taran was gunning for an excuse to escape work, even if just for his lunch break. He glared at the screen of his work laptop as if it was mocking him. After the meeting this morning, he wasn't sure if he needed to scream into a paper bag or set something on fire. Either way, he needed to leave.

He slipped his phone into his pocket, a message already on the screen from Cole, which he could check in a second, right after he responded to the one Mama had sent a half hour ago. His keys jangled as he got them out, and a second later, he locked up, Max tugging on the leash as the stubby-legged monster tried to make a mad break for the street. The scents of fresh grass and tulips from the next-door neighbors' yard threaded through the crisp air, but he made sure to veer away from their house so they didn't catch Max taking a shit on their lawn. Even though he and Sarah cleaned up, Ellen and Ted always got bitchy about it.

Taran made it a few paces down the sidewalk before he checked the text.

You should get the demo version of Barter ready.

Taran's heart pounded a little faster. If he launched the app, there was a chance it would fall flat and his life wouldn't change. However, there was also the chance it would take off, and if that happened, not only would he be leaving the secure job he'd worked since graduating college, but he'd be a hell of a lot busier. He didn't know if he was up for the challenge.

He tugged on the cord of his hoodie. With the way this current project was going, the idea of leaving his company sounded real damn good though. The same thing that had happened in high school occurred now, and it exhausted him—in group projects, he'd shouldered all the work while everyone else took credit. Now, they were just called teams instead of groups.

He was pretty sure one of these days he'd go postal. All his sure, sure, sure would push him to the edge and he'd snap, going on a killing spree at his work. Which reminded him of the new slasher movie he wanted to check out. Max let out a yappy bark and scampered ahead, tugging at the leash. He cast a petulant glare at Taran, who rolled his eyes.

"Oh shit," a voice said from farther down the street, followed by the loud caterwaul of a small creature.

Taran glanced up. There at the end of the block was a sight he didn't think he could've imagined if he tried. Silas was walking along the sidewalk, pushing a stroller with a small, squalling infant in the seat. Even with his leather jacket, tattoos, and sexy rockstar hair, something about seeing the guy frazzled over the red-cheeked infant he was strolling around twisted Taran's chest into knots. He'd already thought Silas King was the sexiest thing on earth, but this? Seeing him with a baby? Well, damn.

"Hey, *friend*," Taran called out, emphasizing the word teasingly. Even as he said it, he couldn't ignore the pang in his chest. They'd danced around the conversation the other night, but it had become abundantly clear that Silas was drowning in this new life. Besides, Taran was fresh out of a relationship and should be doing some soul-searching so he didn't end up with another repeat of Kevin, or Brent, or Mike.

Maybe he needed to stop dating preppy dudes.

Maybe he needed to stop dating until he learned to put his foot down.

If that sounded suspiciously like Cole's voice in

his head, it was only because the man had repeated the sentiment so often.

Silas glanced up at him and flashed a smile that dissolved when the baby let out a fresh, lusty wail. He began to push the stroller forward while Taran closed the distance between them with Max in tow.

"My plan had been to take Fiona on a walk," Silas muttered, spearing his fingers through his hair.

Taran caught the exact reason for his use of the past tense—spit-up covered the blanket nestled over her and drenched her little outfit as well. The child was still squalling, clearly looking uncomfortable, though the culprit causing her wails could've been a bunch of different reasons. Silas pushed the stroller back and forth along the sidewalk, staring at the little girl helplessly.

"Maeve needed to run errands this morning, and I'm supposed to be bonding with her," he murmured, a slight pink in his cheeks.

"Just a fair warning, but I think the ship has sailed on a walk," Taran said, eyeing the little girl. Fiona was gorgeous, with a round head, rosy cheeks that were currently the color of a ripe plum tomato, and a thatch of dark hair just like her father's. Taran stepped closer to the stroller, and Silas stopped rolling. The little girl had pipes, that was for sure.

He glanced at Silas whose eyes sent out panicked signals loud and clear. "Do you want me to come with? I could help you troubleshoot what's causing the current meltdown."

Once the words left his lips, Taran wanted to kick himself. What was more offensive than calling someone out on their lack of parenting skills? Great job on that one.

"You'd seriously show me?" Silas asked, meeting his eyes. "Fuck yes. I'd offer to blow you, but been there, done that, right?"

A snort ripped from Taran. "As long as you don't mind Max tagging along, yeah. I've got the rest of my lunch break." His eyes danced. "As far as helping with the kiddo, I mean. Don't think blowjobs are part of the whole friend thing."

"Clearly, you've never heard of bro-jobs," Silas shot back as he wheeled Fiona back the way they'd come from. The little girl continued to caterwaul, though with interspersions of sniffles and brief moments of confused staring until she broke out into cries all over again. "Fuck, I shouldn't be talking about this in front of my infant daughter. That's a parenting fail, right?"

Taran shook his head as he restrained his smile, tugging Max along with him. "The kiddo has no concept of what you're saying right now. If you're speaking in a pleasant tone, you can talk about everything from cumshots to murder sprees and she's not going to have the slightest idea."

Silas's jaw dropped. An incredulous laugh

slipped past his lips. "How the hell did any of your boyfriends find you boring, Shah? I can't remember the last time someone's cracked me up this much." They strode in time with each other as they headed down the sidewalk, Fiona offering her lustful wails as tribute to the angry gods above.

Taran tried to ignore the way his heart swooped at the statement. Safe. Reliable. Trustworthy. He was used to being described like an economy car rather than a person. Yet, Silas bypassed all of that and called him sexy, funny—everything he didn't dare believe he could be. Which was why the man was all too dangerous. Far too easily, Taran could fall for him, and then he'd be collecting the pieces of his heart all over again.

"Clearly, I've been dating some stellar specimens," Taran responded at last, his tone bone dry.

Silas arched his brow. "If Kevin is any indicator, yeah, you could do far better. I'd offer to wingman, but I'm not the king of good decisions."

Taran cocked a brow right back, mirroring him. "Don't know—I gotta say, showing up to be a father to this little girl seems like a damn good decision to me. Even if she has the shriek of a Nazgul."

Silas's cheeks flushed, and he clamped a hand around his nape as he walked a step faster with the stroller. "Didn't realize we'd plucked her out of Middle Earth."

Taran couldn't miss how Silas dodged around the

compliment, but he didn't push. As someone who took compliments abysmally at best—and at worst as active insults—he couldn't blame him. Max barked as he hurried along the sidewalk, tugging at the leash, which Taran pulled back.

Silas slowed in front of a twin Victorian at the end of the block. "This is the stop," he said.

"Where Maeve lives?" Taran asked, following as they headed up the walkway to the front door.

"It's her folks' place, but she's been living here since she had Fiona. They were in Florida for the winter, but they've been swinging up to help her with the baby on occasion and will be returning soon," Silas said, wearing discomfort like a second leather jacket. He unlocked the door, turned the knob, and stepped inside, rolling the stroller into the house. Fiona stopped bawling for a moment to observe her settings, those big blue eyes soaking in what little she could see. After a few seconds of being inside, though, the big-band noise burst from the baby once more. Taran stifled a laugh.

Silas passed him a look. "Is something hilarious about her never-ending screams? How does anyone even think when they cry like this?"

Taran shrugged, unable to help his grin. "Yeah, it gets grating, but it's cute too. Everything's all high drama with babies and toddlers, end-of-the-world type of shit, and it's hard not to find that amusing." He tied Max's leash to the railing so the little guy didn't go off destroying property. Taran sank to a crouch in front of the stroller and began unsnapping her out of it. "Now, let's see what's bugging her." He glanced up at Silas. "It's okay if I hold her?"

Silas made a sweeping gesture. "Be my guest. You'll probably hold her better than I do. I feel like I'm going to break her half the time."

Taran's lips quirked. The mental image of Silas holding an infant wasn't doing anything to tamp down his attraction to the man. If anything, it just made the guy hotter. He sucked in a sharp breath and focused on Screamy McScreamerson in front of him. Once he got her unbuckled, he plucked the baby from the stroller and cradled her in his arms. She was tiny, flexing little fingers, and he couldn't help the warmth in his chest as he brought her close.

He identified the issue at once. Taran glanced at Silas. "Lead the way to the changing table. She shit herself."

Silas shook his head as he hit the steps. "How did I miss that one?"

"I'm not sure," Taran responded, his tone wry. "Because that's some noxious waste in her diaper."

The stairs creaked, and the motion distracted Fiona from her mission to wail herself into hysteria. Taran took the opportunity to rock her back and forth as they ascended. By the time they'd reached the hall-way, she'd started to calm down, those wails growing weaker with every pass. Taran kept her pressed against his chest, enjoying the way the little one shuddered against him as the cries subsided. Once they reached the baby's room, she'd stopped altogether.

Silas stared at him, those gorgeous blues fringed with thick, dark lashes. "How the hell did you get her quiet? Do you have baby sorcery or something?"

Taran brought her over to the changing table, but he didn't set her down yet. The second he did, those wails would begin all over again. "It's just experience, something you're about to get a mess-load of. And because she's yours, you'll start to pick up her cues." He tilted his head toward the changing table. "Now, do you want to change her, do you want me to, or do you want me to walk you through it?"

"Walk me through it," Silas said. "Every time I've shown up to see her so far, Maeve's dumped her on me and left the room, probably desperate for time away from the baby. But she never showed me how to do anything, and I've got zero experience with kids. Don't even have any siblings, so no nieces or nephews scuttling around."

Damn if Taran didn't like that answer. He was used to people throwing problems or responsibilities on him because they could, because he offered to help, but Silas didn't try to take advantage. Taran hadn't forgotten the way Silas had driven him to Lums Pond State Park just because he'd had a bad night and needed the distraction. Guys didn't do that for him. No, they asked him to show up and pretend to still be dating in front of their fucking families.

"All right," Taran said, tilting his head toward the changing table as he settled Fiona on the surface. The shift hadn't helped her attitude at all and was causing her to squall again. "Grab a diaper and the wipes and come stand next to me."

He kept his hand on her belly as she writhed around on the changing pad, the stench wafting their way. Taran wrinkled his nose. Handling a dirty diaper wasn't what he thought he'd be doing on his lunch break, but life had liked throwing him curveballs recently. "You want to make sure you've got a hand on her at all times, because over the next few months, this chick is gonna start rolling at some point, and they like to be unpredictable."

Silas settled beside him, the height difference a stark contrast as he loomed. Taran could feel Silas stare in his direction, and he fought to focus on walking him through the process. The words trailed out of his mouth as he grabbed the dirty diaper, cleaned her up, and disposed of it, even though all he could focus on was the man's proximity.

Once he brought out the fresh one, though, he glanced at Silas. "This is your time to shine," he said. "Wrap her back up."

Silas chewed on his lower lip as he gently laid his palm on Fiona's stomach, the tattooed knuckles such a gorgeous contrast against the baby's soft porcelain skin. Taran watched as Silas struggled to bring the tabs around while Fiona decided to up the challenge by kicking her little legs. Taran's lips quirked with a grin, but he didn't say anything except to tell Silas to bring the tabs in a little closer on the front.

"All right, now snap the onesie into place and you're set," Taran said, placing a hand on Silas's shoulder. His brows furrowed in concentration as he fought with her little legs to snap the flower-printed onesie back together and then tugged the blue pants up.

"All done," he said, beaming as he looked up at Taran.

Taran's throat dried. With Silas's blue eyes sparkling, the earnest brightness emanating from his expression, he wasn't just hot—the man stole his breath away. He offered a weak smile in return. "Great job. Now you're equipped for next time."

"Thanks to you," Silas said, his gaze searing and his voice husky.

Friends. Just friends. As much as Taran reminded himself, his heart hadn't taken the memo and was beating a thousand miles a minute. Clearly, hooking up with the guy had only made those fantasies of his from high school worse because now he knew how scorching the reality really was.

"Right, I should get going," Taran said. "I've got to shove something down my throat before my lunch break ends." He paused, realizing what had come out of his mouth and fixed Silas with an arch look. "And that wasn't an invitation."

Silas's lips curled into a wicked smirk, those gorgeous eyes sparkling with amusement. "Thought we'd established that blowjobs between friends are just courtesy."

Taran eyed him. "A courtesy I reserve for the guy I'm with. Gonna have to just fantasize about my lack of a gag reflex."

Silas blew out a breath and shifted his hips, drawing attention to the slight bulge in his jeans. "Fuck, warn a guy next time." He cradled Fiona in his arm and strode toward the door. "I've got a sub I brought over, so let's split it. It's the least I can do for wasting your lunch break."

A waste wasn't what Taran considered time spent with him. Surprising, yes, but he couldn't get over how much he enjoyed Silas's company, even when doing something domestic like dealing with a squalling baby and changing a diaper. The guy made him comfortable in a way he rarely was around other people, and he didn't know what to make of that.

He should say no and head home. As much as they'd agreed to friendship, he couldn't help but feel like he stepped closer and closer to a riptide with each moment they stole together.

"Sure," came from his mouth instead.

Silas flashed him a sexy-as-fuck grin and clutched Fiona tight to his chest, the little girl's eyes fluttering shut as she started to snore. "Follow me, then. Let's get you fed."

Taran almost whimpered at the seductive purr of those words, but his feet moved on instinct as he followed Silas down the hall. He speared his fingers through his hair.

This guy was a fire, and he couldn't help but thrust his hand into the flame every damn time.

CHAPTER 10

Silas wiped a sweaty arm across his forehead, not sure if the majority of the sweat had come from steam or exertion. He glanced at the clock, taking note of the time. Even if he hadn't been aware of the end of his shift, he'd already started to get a sense of the ebb and flow of orders based on the time of day at Port of Call. Nico was beginning to put him on some of the later shifts, but for the most part, he still worked the earlier ones, especially during the weekends. After two weeks at the job, he'd lost the nervous edge caused by the pressure soaking in everything from the environment and learning the different recipes, and since then he had found it easier to enjoy himself.

"See you later," Silas called out to Gia as he slipped out of his chef's coat. Woman was a firecracker, and he didn't mind being on the line with her any day of the week.

"Fuck, I hope not," Gia called back. "Go home, Silas. Don't you have some wife and kids to fucking worry about?"

He snorted, lifting his middle finger. Not like he'd been able to keep his business quiet for a hot minute with Nico being his boss. "Kid, singular, and I'm a card-carrying member of the hit-it-and-quit-it club."

"More like the hit-it-and-knock-someone-up club," Jer responded, dropping his jacket off by the hooks. He flashed a saucy grin.

Silas rolled his eyes, even though he couldn't help the amusement. This lot of sarcastic fuckers made him feel right at home from the get-go. He shouldn't have expected anything less from Nico's place. He ran a hand through his hair in an attempt to coax the sweaty strands into place but gave up fast. Not like he had far to go—from the back of the house to the front of the house. Maeve wanted to meet with him tonight, probably to discuss more about Fiona's care or some shit. Her parents would be returning soon from wherever the hell they'd been vacationing, which meant an extra two pairs of hands to help out.

His phone buzzed as he grabbed his shit and slipped through the double doors. Silas checked the screen while he sauntered over to the first-floor bar. Taran. A stupid smile curled his lips, one that made him feel like an idiot even before he checked the text. He plunked into the seat to wait for Maeve.

Hey, Mr. Chef. How long are chicken leftovers good for?

Silas pursed his lips, trying to tamp down his grin as he typed a message back. *If you're asking, you should probably throw them out.*

A minute later, Taran shot back another response. *Too late. Make sure to avenge me when the chicken flu takes me out.*

What the fuck is the chicken flu? Silas sent in return. He glanced up as Nina, one of Nico's new bartenders, swung over to place a pint of beer in front of him. He nodded his thanks, barely looking up from the dot, dot, dot on the screen.

Ever since they'd hung out the other week, texts flowed between them constantly. Taran's wit had become the highlight of his day, and he enjoyed how the guy kept him on his toes. He was never sure where their conversations would start, and he sure as hell had no idea where they would go, though they had a tendency to get downright filthy at times. He'd regretted the way shit had gone down at Lums Pond at least twice a day because if he had any balls, he would've kissed the everloving hell out of Taran Shah a second time that night and staked a claim.

He hadn't been lying though—he had one relationship on the agenda right now, and that was with his daughter, who was turning out to be a pretty cool little human when she wasn't screaming her face off at him or shitting up a storm.

Silas brought the pint of lager to his lips and skimmed a glance down the bar. His gaze snagged on a guy in a pale blue polo whose blond locks and blue eyes screamed preppy douchebag. A thinner guy sat on his lap, his lips pressed against the preppy's neck like they were two seconds away from fucking on top of the bar. His eyes narrowed.

He recognized that guy.

Preppy douchebag was the same one he'd seen leaving Hickory Taproom the night he hooked up with Taran. The ex, Kevin. Despite being ballsy enough to ask Taran to pretend to be his boyfriend after fucking dumping him, Kevin clearly had no problem moving on. Silas was relieved Taran wasn't here tonight. The last thing he'd need to see was his ex-boyfriend already getting with a new guy. Silas took an angry swig from his beer, trying to dampen the burn in his chest.

His phone buzzed and he checked it again. *Chicken flu, you know, the mutant virus that fowls up your insides.*

Silas choked on his beer. *Pun jail. Now.*

"Hey." Maeve's voice drew his attention upward.

Silas blinked a few times in surprise. Most of the time when he'd seen Maeve she lived in some form of pajamas or sweatpants, which made perfect sense since she was dealing with the constant feeding and care of a tiny, demanding human. However, she'd seized the chance her parents gave her to get out of the house and ran with it. Her blonde hair was tamed, her blue eyes lined in delicate eyeliner and carefully applied shadow, and her pink lips looked lush. She'd even worn jeans and a low-cut black top that showcased a healthy amount of cleavage.

"You look nice, Maeve," Silas offered. With the stress she'd been under lately, she'd probably needed the chance to doll up.

"Thanks," she murmured with a winsome smirk as she slid into the stool beside him. "You don't look so bad yourself."

Silas might have made a lifetime's worth of dumbass decisions, but there was one thing he'd always been good at—reading people and situations. Those instincts had gotten him out of too many scrapes to count. And based on the flirty way Maeve scanned him, she wasn't here for a chat about Fiona's care. His stomach soured.

Maeve wasn't a bad person, and she seemed to be a good mom, but Silas had zero interest. Their one night together had barely been memorable, and the more they interacted, the clearer it became that nothing beyond the surface existed between them. No common interests, not even remotely similar sense of humor, and unless they were talking about Fiona, he didn't enjoy spending time around her.

"Nah, I'm a mess from work. I'll need to get going

soon to change," Silas said, trying to reroute her as fast as possible. "But you should spend the night out and enjoy yourself. I know you haven't gotten much time away from Fiona."

"My god, it's such a relief to escape the perpetual screams," Maeve muttered. "I swear, all that kid does is cry."

Silas pressed his lips together. Maybe that had been the case when he held her at first, but he'd witnessed Taran's magic with Fiona, and bit by bit, the guy was teaching him some new tricks. Every time he picked up Fiona from Maeve's, Taran had come over on his lunch break and they'd taken her to the park, gone for walks up and down the street, or even just hung out in the house while Maeve escaped. Taran made him laugh in the face of a daunting situation, and he enjoyed his time with the guy more than he'd ever expected.

His gaze lingered on Taran's stupid fucking ex who was still up close and personal with his boy toy. Rage gripped his chest, and he fought the urge to march up to the guy and call him out for the piece of shit he was.

Maeve snapped her fingers in front of his face. "What are you even looking at? We finally get the chance to see each other away from the baby and you're, what, staring down some guy at the bar?"

Silas blinked. Irritation rose even higher in his chest. "I was under the impression we were meeting up to talk about Fiona. If you're looking for a bar night, you're chatting up the wrong tree, sweetheart. I've been working all day, and I'm fucking beat."

Maeve's brows drew together. "What else would we talk about over her? She's eating, sleeping, and vomiting all over my existence. Sue me for needing a break."

Silas's throat tightened. She deserved time away from the baby, but something about the edge to her voice made him careful. He didn't want to lead her on, but he also didn't want to piss her off and ruin their co-parenting relationship before it even began. "You're all dolled up, so you should enjoy your night out, Maeve. I'm sure there'll be guys lining up to sweep you off your feet."

Just not me.

Silas placed a crumpled bill next to his empty pint glass as he rose from his seat. He needed to get out of here before she got any other ideas about this meeting being something it wasn't. "Let me know if you want me to start taking her more. I'm working on making my apartment more baby friendly."

As much as he was adjusting to the squalling munchkin that sometimes got him so frustrated he wanted to scream, he'd been sunk the moment the little girl wrapped her chubby hand around his finger. Even if he still needed to learn a lot about her, those protective instincts had flared to life, the mythical ones he'd been waiting to arrive.

"Yeah, that'd be good," Maeve said, her crimson lips in a pout. "Let me know when we can come over."

He wasn't falling for that shit again.

Silas clapped a hand on her shoulder. "Have a good night, Maeve." He began to head toward the big glass doors. He could feel her stare boring into him, but man, he couldn't deal with this tonight.

His phone buzzed again, and he pulled it out reflexively. When Taran's name lit up the screen, his heart started bouncing harder.

Looks like the flu didn't last. I'm already feeling peckish again.

...

Don't get too eggscited. I have more.

The grin that broke out on Silas's face strained his cheeks. Fuck, this guy just did it for him. And that was the crux of his problem. While right now he was focused on the new relationship in his life, the one with his daughter, if he had time for someone else, it sure as hell wouldn't be Maeve.

No, it would be the guy who cropped up in his thoughts on an hourly basis from the moment they'd first hooked up.

The one who he reached out to any time he needed to talk.

The one who, even for a moment, made him feel lighter than air, like he might be able to climb over this hurdle after all.

The guy who'd probably get snatched up before Silas ever got his shit together, and damn if the thought didn't kill him.

He sucked in a sharp breath and pushed his way into the brisk April air, heading for home.

CHAPTER 11

Friday night was beginning to be a bit of a harbinger at this point.

This time, though, work was the culprit, not Kevin.

Taran stared at his shut down laptop vacantly, like a puppet sans strings. The situation at work had gotten progressively worse throughout the week. Everyone kept piling their problems onto him and expecting him to solve them. Of course, no one gave a damn that Taran needed to do his own work on the project and couldn't be shouldering theirs as well. But, hey, just ask the office pushover. He'd tried to get them to handle the issues by themselves, but between Harry's laziness and Lauren's ineptitude, he kept having to pick up the slack.

The Barter app beckoned him from his laptop. The work situation had inspired him in one way—he'd been tinkering around with it more than ever. The thing had been ready to go into beta-testing for a while now, but every time he considered pulling the trigger, his skin prickled like he was about to break out in hives.

A rap sounded at the door to his home office. Sarah stood in the frame.

"Yo, sulky. I've been recruited by your brother and the rest of the brigade to drag you out to the bar tonight. We're hitting up Hudson's for a change of pace."

"Wouldn't my shitty mood just bring everyone down?" Taran challenged, leaning back in his computer seat.

Sarah shot him a no-nonsense look. The woman intimidated him most days, but he loved her for it. "You say this like we're not well-versed in every variety of your moods. Besides, your shitty mood is like a puppy getting frustrated over not being able to fit all the balls in his mouth. Pun intended."

"So, either you're insinuating I'm helplessly adorable or a total slut?" Taran responded, pushing up from his seat.

"Why not both?" Sarah said. She was clearly all ready to leave in black lace tights, a short black skirt, and a corset-laced shirt that showed off her curves. He and Sarah had perfected the art of being room-mates, not in the cozy hang out together all the time way, but in the casually fling themselves into each other's lives while maintaining a healthy amount of space type. After the roommate fails he'd dealt with in college, he'd been so relieved to move in with someone who was self-sufficient.

Taran tapped his fingers on the table. Part of him wanted to text Silas and see what he was up to tonight, but that wasn't a good idea. Going out and meeting other single guys was. Not indulging in the ocean-sized crush he had on the man who'd rocked his world a few weeks ago, the one firmly in camp friend.

"Yeah, count me in," he said, ignoring the itch of his trigger fingers to type out a text to Silas and invite him along as well. He didn't need to add any more fuel to the fire that had been burning inside him for the guy since he was a teenager. The crinkle of his eyes when his little daughter waved her chubby hands at him, the husky amusement in his voice whenever Taran made a joke, and the intensity in Silas's piercing stare when he thought Taran wasn't looking all added to the heady rush of being around the guy.

Sarah eyed his pajama pants and geek tee attire. "You going like that?"

Taran shot her a look. "Yeah, because nothing says fuck me like a stained shirt and pajama pants."

Sarah shrugged. "Might work better than the business casual you're always buttoned up into. No wonder you attract relationships. After Kevin, you just need a good dicking, not another mess."

Taran snorted, unable to help himself. "Been there, done that. Do I get a badge now?"

Sarah's jaw dropped. "You? Had a one-night stand? And you're not chasing the guy down and trying to marry him?"

Taran lifted his middle finger. "Fuck off and let me get ready." Even as he shut the door in her face, her words still lingered, because he was doing that all over again, right? Getting attached where he shouldn't, chasing after a guy who'd made it clear a relationship was off the table.

Time for a night out to put all thoughts of Silas King out of his mind.

Taran rolled the sleeves up to his elbows, dressed in a navy button-down even if Sarah had hissed her disapproval. They strode in past the gorgeous historical home exterior of the place, the cream walls lit by the rosy, beckoning lights outside. Harbor Pointe had been a spot he didn't visit out of loyalty to Nico until the man had gone and hooked up with the owner, Hudson West. Now with Port of Call and Harbor Pointe as shared businesses between Hudson and Nico, both establishments were fair game.

Sarah took the lead inside, and Taran followed

close behind her, his heart pumping a little faster. He should be getting back out there to date, but he hated this part—the scrutiny, the ghosting, the quick rejections that pared away at him one after another. It was far easier to just not date at all and stay home binging the *Hellraiser* movies instead.

The rich scent of cedar and porter dominated the space inside, a refined atmosphere contrasting with the warmth of Port of Call. Harbor Pointe was more of a white napkin place, the glasses sparkling and on display and the conversation held in amused murmurs rather than shouts and hollers at whatever game played on the TV. While the tables were filled, Taran didn't bother looking for the crew there— they'd be at the bar.

Sure enough, Hudson was working behind the bar tonight, and he leaned forward to press a kiss against Nico's temple, a gesture sweet enough to give Taran a toothache. Taran was happy for his older brother. He seriously was. It just didn't help subdue the intense jealousy that flared at seeing his brother who'd railed long and hard against commitment in the exact sort of forever relationship Taran had been fighting for his entire life.

Whenever the lonesomeness crept in, so did the lingering loss that had rocked through their whole family. Nico had suppressed his grief for years, hurling himself into flings while Taran had done the opposite—struggled long and hard to rebuild what they'd lost.

He sucked in a low, slow breath, trying to ignore the prickle under his skin. Fuck, he wasn't in the mood to meet anyone tonight or start up conversations with strangers. He wanted to feel comfortable. This was why dating sucked.

Taran skimmed the seats beside Nico to see who all had showed up. The usual culprits were there—Nate and Linc. Rachel, Nate's artsy, tattooed employee over at Chesapeake Brew, had arrived too, and Sarah made a beeline for the seat next to her, which left Taran heading to the opposite side... right toward the one guy in the lineup he'd missed.

Because of course Silas would be here tonight.

When Silas glanced to the side and caught his gaze, Taran had to bite back a whimper, because *damn* the man looked good.

His motorcycle jacket hung off the bar chair, and between the ripped jeans and the gray muscle shirt that brought out his too-blue eyes, Taran was driven to distraction. All Silas's luscious ink on display wasn't fair, and he couldn't help but remember tracing those tattoos with his fingers, with his tongue.

Taran steeled himself and plunked into the seat beside Silas. "You do realize sitting next to you is an inconvenience, right?"

Silas cocked a brow. "Why's that? Find me too distracting?"

Damn his husky rasp. The sound mainlined straight to his cock, which gave a hearty twitch. Taran rolled his eyes. "No, it's because it's going to be impossible to meet someone if you're sitting beside me. No one's going to choose me when they could have all of that," he said, making a nebulous gesture at Silas.

"Bull-fucking-shit," Silas exclaimed so loudly that it drew the rest of the group's attention. Taran resisted the urge to duck behind the bar in case he could just turn invisible instead.

Hudson swung by and placed a whisky sour in front of him because Nico's boyfriend was attentive and sweet—nothing like his chaotic brother.

"What's bullshit?" Hudson asked.

"Taran thinking he's not hot enough to pull just about anyone in this bar," Silas said. Taran's cheeks warmed at the vehemence in Silas's voice, the heat there.

"Eww, that's my little brother, King," Nico commented a few seats down.

"He's right though," Nate piped in. "That's total bullshit. You're gorgeous, Tar."

"Right, I'm going to go die now," Taran muttered, pressing fingers to his cheeks, shocked they didn't melt off with the radioactive glow coming from him.

"How about we talk about something else—anything else."

"Okay, explain Kevin to me," Nico said, jumping in. "Why did you even date that douche in the first place? And for eight months?"

Taran shot his brother a look. He'd known Nico and Mama hadn't approved, but neither of them had ever minded being alone all that much. They didn't understand how quickly the loneliness crept in for Taran, how it always had. Growing up a solitary loser left this ache in him that he'd been struggling to fill for so damn long, yet the boyfriends who swung in and out of his life failed to soothe the pain. Most of the time, they just made him feel lonelier and more misunderstood.

The truth he liked to bury was that this pursuit had begun the moment the phone call arrived, the one that shattered the family he'd known. No matter how hard he tried to cement those cracks, some days he just missed his dad more than anything.

Before Taran could shut the conversation down, Silas jumped in.

"On the scale of making mistakes, there's temporary shitty boyfriend and then there's knocking up your one-night stand. I think I win the prize here," he said, a sarcastic note in his voice. Taran glanced at him, gratitude flushing in his chest. Still, he hadn't missed the way Silas tended to put himself down so easily, a habit Taran recognized because he'd stolen the crown for self-deprecating behavior years ago.

Taran stepped in, saying, "Considering your daughter's adorable, I don't think you made a mistake on that front."

"Wait, you've met the mystery baby?" Nico butted in again. "We've been taking bets on if she's real or just an excuse Silas is making for returning to town."

Days like this, Taran wanted to strangle his brother.

"Yeah," Silas jumped in. "We've been hanging out, and when he saw how terrible I was with babies, he took pity on my ass and started showing me how to deal with an infant."

"The two of you? Hanging out?" Nico said, his brows drawing together. His brother started staring at him with an intense look like he was trying to send him mind signals, but Taran understood fuck all about what the hell Nic was attempting to say.

"Is it so unbelievable that I have friends?" Taran shot at him, not sure why Nic's stare bugged him so much. Was his brother operating in overprotective mode, or could he just not believe his friend was spending time with his little brother? Either one came across as insulting.

"Yes," Sarah butted in. Based on her smirk, she understood the minefield she had stepped into and didn't care. "Even more unbelievable that you've had boyfriends, but don't worry, Tar. We'll find you a hot piece of ass tonight."

"That's exactly what you need," Nico said, jabbing a finger in the air. "A hookup."

"Because that worked so well for you, Nic," Linc added in. Rachel snorted, and Silas stared pretty hard at his drink, as if warring with himself over what to say.

"Maybe you shouldn't be the one offering your brother love advice," Hudson mentioned, his tone dry and amused.

"Traitor," Nico shot back, flipping him the middle finger.

Silas glanced up at him with a curious glint in his eyes that Taran couldn't read. He swallowed hard. The man turned him upside down. How was he supposed to be putting himself out there and trying to find someone when the guy he really wanted was sitting right next to him? This close, Taran could smell his leather-and-clove scent, and it was one he wanted to bask in for his entire lifetime. This had been his problem from the start. Despite his attempt to keep his feelings out of the situation, he'd been gone for Silas King for as long as he could remember.

"Excuse me," a low voice said from his opposite side.

Taran glanced to his left to see a slender white guy standing there—fashionable black hair, prominent silver necklaces, and a confident grin.

"Can I buy you a drink?" the guy asked, his voice coming out as smooth as his delivery.

Taran chewed on his lower lip, the word "No" bubbling to the surface. Not because the guy was unattractive. He looked pretty-ish. But he didn't hold a candle to the man by his side. And that was the crux of the problem, wasn't it? Silas had never promised anything beyond one night. All of Taran's wistful hopes were just the same fantasies he'd been indulging in since high school.

"Sure, as long as you don't mind my nosy-ass friends making comments," Taran muttered, shooting a glance behind him. Nic, Hudson, and Silas were all locked and loaded on the interaction. Taran tried hard to ignore the intense look in Silas's eyes.

"A little weird, but they don't intimidate me much," the guy said, slipping into the open seat. Hudson stepped up to him a moment later to take his order.

"They're not intimidating, just annoying," Taran responded, shooting his brother a pointed stare.

"I mean, you should feel a little threatened," Silas muttered.

Taran's heart stuttered at the sullen sound of Silas's words. It'd be far too easy to fall into conversation with him, to argue about who was the best final girl in horror or to piss him off by asking when the touchdown happened during a hockey game, but Silas wanted friendship, nothing more.

And Taran so badly wanted more.

Hudson placed a fresh drink in front of Taran and a beer in front of New Guy.

New Guy lifted the pint. "This is me, quaking in my boots."

Taran's lips quirked. A dry sense of humor, he could handle. However, he wouldn't go down the hookup path again. Silas had been a one and done for him, and clearly, he'd failed at that. "I better drink this fast before you realize I'm a garbage conversationalist unless you want ridiculously detailed knowledge on beekeeping or the 80s wave of horror."

The guy snorted and tipped back another sip of beer. "Do you always throw out a thousand and one reasons to scare newcomers away? If I had feelings, they'd be hurt."

Taran scratched the back of his neck. Fuck, that was exactly what he was doing. It didn't help that he could feel the press of Silas's stare from his right, the intense attention that made his insides melt and his heart soar. The guy he was chatting with was attractive, charming, and focused on him—Taran should be into all of that. However, his stomach churned, and not just with nerves at the idea of pursuing this.

Which was why he needed to. He stuck out a hand. "Let's start fresh, then. I'm Taran. You?"

"Wyatt," he responded, his gaze rolling over Taran from head to toe. Those molten chocolate eyes gleamed with interest, and Taran forced himself to stay present and ignore the guy next to him whose mere presence made him feel the promise of hazy summer nights filled with future nostalgia.

"So, Wyatt, what are you doing in town?" Silas butted in.

Taran shot him a glare, one which Silas batted his eyelashes at, offering an innocent grin.

"Came down from Baltimore for a business meeting scheduled for tomorrow mor ning, so I'm spending the weekend here. I've got a room at the Chesapeake Inn," he said, a sultry note entering his voice as he focused his attention back on Taran.

Taran licked his lips, heat rising through him at the memories of the last time he spent the night at the Chesapeake Inn. He made the mistake of glancing in Silas's direction, and the guy's blue eyes *blazed*.

"They've got some memorable... views there," Silas said, his voice a husky rasp.

Damn. Him. Irritation mingled with the insane lust coursing through Taran's veins right now. The thought of their night together still tangled up his insides—with need, with longing, with a hunger he'd never known before. Taran shot Silas another look before he turned toward Wyatt, who sipped his beer casually even though the flicker in the guy's eyes pegged him as too astute to have missed the weirdness between Taran and Silas.

"So, you're only here this weekend?" Taran asked,

feigning innocence. "Need anyone to show you around town?"

Wyatt's grin widened. "If you're offering, then hell yeah."

Taran pasted a grin on and fixed his attention on Wyatt—available, interested Wyatt, pointedly not looking back at his *friend*.

Yet he couldn't ignore Silas King's intoxicating presence if he tried, nor could he pretend his heart hadn't lunged in his direction a long time before. Even if those fantasies could only end in heartbreak.

CHAPTER 12

After a grueling twelve-hour shift at Port of Call on Saturday night, Silas had been looking forward to Sunday, when he'd be spending time with his daughter again. And also with Taran, who'd agreed to come over and hang out for lunch on a weekend, which wasn't their usual time.

Silas was excited about it, even though Taran had a date with the artsy douchebag Wyatt later that night.

Silas settled in the rocker with Fiona who'd gone down for a nap, since that was most of what she did currently. Taran had explained to him that the need for excessive sleep would start changing in a few months as she started to become more alert and playful. To Silas's own surprise, he found himself looking forward to that. Fiona kept making these little soft cooing sounds as she slept, and her thick eyelashes fluttered whenever a loud car drove by. If someone had told him a few months ago he'd enjoy sitting with a baby on his day off, he would've called them crazy.

However, here he was, basking in the soft warmth the little one offered, surprisingly grounding despite how much she'd shaken up his world.

Maeve had been flirty when she'd left, which made Silas's stomach sour—he didn't know how to handle the situation without stepping on a landmine. It didn't help that the only person he wanted to flirt with right now was Taran Shah, and he'd friend-zoned him so hard that he drove him into another man's willing arms.

Fuck, had he just swallowed an entire vat of acid or what?

And he couldn't help but keep looking at the door and checking his phone, waiting for the telltale buzz or knock to let him know Taran had arrived. The guy was more than punctual—always five to fifteen minutes early, and Silas fucking liked that about him too. There were so many details he'd started collecting about Taran Shah that he could fill a scrap-book with them, yet he didn't have the nerve to ask the man for... what? What could he even offer him?

Silas clutched Fiona a bit more tightly, the answer coiled in his chest even though he didn't want to acknowledge it. He didn't miss the heat when Taran looked at him or the dopey smile that sometimes emerged on his face. If Silas had the balls to ask for more, then maybe Taran wouldn't be going on a date with Wyatt tonight.

A knock sounded on the door. Silas checked his phone with a grin. Fifteen minutes early.

Ever since the night he'd hit on Taran in Hickory Taproom, they'd seen each other frequently and texted nonstop. Everything with Taran felt easy, comfortable in a way that little else ever had in his life. The fact thrilled and terrified him at the same time.

Silas pushed up from the rocker in the half-painted light blue nursery and headed down the steps, managing to walk steadily enough that Fiona remained out like a light.

The smell of the Thai food he'd picked up lingered in the front hallway, which wasn't a far reach from the kitchen. He juggled the bundle of small child, shifting Fiona over to the crook of his arm as he answered the door.

Taran stood in the frame, looking fucking mouth-watering.

He wore a pale yellow dress shirt that strained against his chest, showcasing the delicious abs and tight muscles of his torso, and his chinos were hip hugging and also looked like they had been painted onto him. The heavy gold watch on his wrist was a perfect accent to his sepia skin that soaked in the sun, and he'd tucked sunglasses into his front pocket. Silas hadn't indulged in office fantasies before, but the business-casual look Taran rocked got him hard in seconds.

Taran glanced down at his shirt. "What are you staring at? Is there a stain or something?" His brows furrowed as he checked the fabric.

"Nah, just this really hot guy who showed up on my doorstep," Silas said, unable to help himself when it came to flirting with Taran. He knew he wasn't being fair. He knew the guy deserved better, but hell, he couldn't help himself when the man arrived looking that damn good.

Taran ducked his head in embarrassment as he stepped inside. "Just wanted to not be a total slouch for my date tonight. It's been a while since I've gone on one."

Silas tried to swallow the brick lodged in his throat at the mention of the date. Because of course Taran hadn't dressed up to spend time with him. They were friends. He'd been the one to tell Taran he didn't have the time for anything serious, and the guy was meant for relationships. Taran deserved more than his baggage.

"You look gorgeous," Silas murmured, his voice soft. "He's going to lose his mind."

Taran's eyes flared with intensity for a moment, but he hid it with a quick smile. "Let's hope not. If he goes postal in the middle of the restaurant, that'll be the second-worst date I've been on."

Silas snorted. "Dare I ask what the first one was?" He tilted his head in the direction of the kitchen.

Taran made grabby hands for Fiona first, the gesture driving straight to Silas's heart. Silas passed her over, their arms brushing in the process. He tried to ignore the zing lighting his veins at the simple touch. They'd done a whole lot more, but ever since they'd backed off into friends territory, his libido seemed to run on overdrive around Taran. If the guy even brushed against his cock, Silas would probably come in his goddamn pants.

Taran clutched Fiona close, a goofy smile appearing on his face as he cradled the little girl. Silas swallowed the tightness in his throat as he led the way to the kitchen where he'd left their takeout on the counter. Maeve was getting a haircut and grocery shopping, which meant she wouldn't be back for a while. Currently, Silas came over for daytime visits, giving Maeve a chance to breathe, but sooner rather than later, he'd be doing some overnights with Fiona.

The thought made him feel like he'd waded into deep water, but part of him just wanted to rip the Band-Aid off and learn.

"I picked up food from Thai Café for a change of pace," Silas said. They'd been eating together almost daily now, and that hadn't scared Silas in the slightest. What freaked him out was the idea of using the "b" word and having someone else's expectations on him because Silas failed at those every single time.

"I got us the curry since you said you can handle spice," Silas said, opening up the containers, which was easier than it would have been if Taran wasn't holding the baby. Honestly, he'd started to get used to doing everything one-handed when he was taking care of Fiona, and having another person there with him was more than helpful.

Taran arched his brow. "I grew up on Indian curry—you do realize that, right? Thai curry is the level of spice that can compete with my mother's meals."

"Good," Silas said. "I like a guy who can handle a little heat." Even as he said the words, he realized his tone dripped with flirtation, and based on the stare Taran delivered, the guy had picked up how he'd switched from defense to offense.

"Thought you liked your guys as one-night stands," Taran shot back. Even though his words were light, he'd made his point. "Or friends, in my case."

Silas passed over the takeout container of green curry to Taran, their fingers brushing in the process, and goddamn, the jolt of lust and craving that shot through him almost made his knees buckle. This was his opening. All he needed to do was tell Taran he wanted more. That he wanted to try for something real, even if he couldn't make any promises. He opened his mouth, trying to force those words past his lips.

However, his throat dried. He was in the middle of a storm on a boat that hadn't stopped rocking yet, and if he invited someone else in with him, he'd capsize.

"Oh, you need chopsticks, don't you," Silas muttered, in a total chickenshit move. He dug back in the bag to pluck out the to-go chopsticks and passed them over just in time to see the way Taran's eyes darkened with disappointment. "Where are you guys going tonight?" Silas asked, because apparently he loved to throw salt on his open wounds.

"Well, considering we met at Harbor Pointe, we're heading to the other main bar in town," Taran said, giving him a pointed stare. "I'm not taking a first date to the diner."

"Come on," Silas said, starting on his container of red curry. "That's like a litmus test of how chill your date is though. Do you really want to date a guy who's going to get all bitchy about going to Maverick Diner? You might not have hung around with me and Nic much, but I know you appreciate it as an institution. You were there for most of our zombie contingency plan discussions."

"That's because someone needed to be reasonable," Taran said, an amused grin rising to his lips. "Just because Nic wanted to sleep with half of the football team didn't mean they'd be assets to any sort of zombie survival commune. As if that wouldn't fall through the moment an outbreak happened. Small groups are always the best strategy."

There the man went, filling him with lightness again. "Hey, some of those guys were good lays," Silas defended with a saucy smirk.

Taran shot him an amused look and rocked Fiona back and forth. "Hear that, sweetheart? Your daddy's what some might consider a slut."

Silas flipped his middle finger at Taran, though there was no heat behind the gesture. "Don't be jealous. Anyone can be slutty, even you, Mr. Uptight."

"But only you make it an art form," Taran responded, a full grin on his face. "And we both know I'm not uptight."

Silas fought with his smile and failed. "Oh no, you're definitely tight." Silas regretted those words at once, because fuck, the memory of their night…. His cock hardened in his jeans.

Taran shook his head even though his eyes were dancing. He dipped his chopsticks into his curry, plucking a few pieces as he ate with one hand and held the baby with the other. Taran had her little butt balanced on the counter all while keeping her head tucked into the crook of his arm, a formidable feat.

"Here, hand her over," Silas said, making a gesture for Fiona. "I'm already halfway through my food. You should have yours." That was a bit of a lie because he'd only taken a few bites, but the ship had sailed on his appetite the moment Taran arrived here ready for his date with Wyatt. Fiona's eyes fluttered, as if she knew he was about to pick her up. Chances were, the second he lifted her out of Taran's arms, she'd start crying again. The man was a baby whisperer.

The front door creaked as it opened, drawing Silas's attention up.

"Hey, I'm home," Maeve called, her voice shattering the cozy air between them. Taran froze, discomfort written in the scrunch of his brows. Not like Silas could blame him. She'd never gotten home early on the days they hung out, choosing to squeeze the remaining drops out of her alone time. Except after the weird-as-fuck meetup with her at Port of Call, Silas couldn't be sure of much Maeve was up to anymore.

"We're in the kitchen," Silas called. He met Taran's eyes and shrugged, not sure how to handle this situation. They were hanging out in Maeve's parents' house, after all. And as much as he wished Maeve was walking in on a date between him and Taran, he was the one keeping it from being one.

Maeve stepped into the kitchen and stopped. Her gaze landed square on Taran holding Fiona, and her eyes narrowed. Fuck, was this some faux pas he didn't know about, or was she just pissed he wanted to hang with Taran and not her?

"Taran, what are you doing here?" she asked, her tone unreadable.

Taran untucked Fiona from his chest and passed the munchkin back over to Silas, nearly vibrating with discomfort. Fiona took the cue at once and let out a lusty wail. Silas clutched her to his chest, rocking her back and forth, "Shh, shh, shh" coming from his lips unbidden.

"Silas invited me to hang out, which I thought you knew about. Sorry if I crossed any lines," he apologized, smooth and perfect as always.

Silas immediately felt like shit. He should've told Maeve he'd invited someone into her parents' house and let him hold their daughter. Dammit, he was no good at this parenting thing. Maeve's frown grew as she stared between the two of them, her gaze zeroing in on how close they were standing. If Silas had to place any bets, he didn't think she was upset about that. Fiona let out some loud complaints as she snuggled into his arms, rubbing her nose against his chest.

Maeve glared at him. "Silas, you should be spending time with your daughter, not dragging Nico's brother over to pawn your baby off on him."

Silas's jaw locked. Sure, Taran had started coming over here because he caught Silas mid flail and was a genuinely good person, but Silas wasn't another fucking Kevin. "That's not what this is," he responded, unable to keep the vitriol from his voice even as he maintained his volume control. He made the mistake of looking in Taran's direction, and the uncertainty in his eyes drove a spike through Silas's chest. "Like he said, Maeve, I invited him over to hang out."

"Yeah, okay," she responded, all acerbic sarcasm.

Silas's gut twisted. How had he ever found her attractive?

"I'd better get out of here," Taran said, his voice tight. "I've got a date to head to anyway."

Silas's alarm bells were going off, but Fiona's eyes fluttered open. She let out a lusty squall right as Taran placed his takeout on the counter, offered a brisk nod, and strode toward the door at a pace nearly quick enough to be a run.

"And now she's crying. Good job, Silas," Maeve snapped, bringing a few of the grocery bags she carried over to the countertop.

The front door closed with a click.

"It's fine," he responded, struggling to keep the irritation out of his voice. "I've got her."

Fiona's eyes leaked fat tears as she woke up, and her little arms flailed. Silas clutched her tight to his chest, rocking her back and forth while patting her on the butt, a technique Taran had showed him. All he wanted to do was run after Taran and reassure him that Maeve was wrong. Fuck. But he couldn't rush out, not with Fiona in his arms. His feet planted to the floor even though he wanted to crawl out of his skin at the way their cozy afternoon had ended.

And Taran was going on a date tonight.

Silas's insides iced over.

Guaranteed, he really had just shoved the one person who'd made him feel something for the first time in ages right into another man's arms.

Silas King, Perpetual Fuckup.

CHAPTER 13

Taran tapped his foot along the base of the barstool. His palms were already sweating, and he hadn't even been here five minutes. This was one of those times he regretted his habit of being early.

However, he hadn't wanted to sit with his thoughts anymore.

Maeve's words had splashed over him like ice water. He was doing it again. Letting people take advantage of him like he'd done his entire life. Silas might have denied what she said, but those doubts latched into Taran with powerful hooks once he'd gotten home.

Dad had always said his giving nature was a gift. And he'd believed that too—except time after time, he gave until there was little left, and he just felt hollower in the aftermath.

Taran tipped back the whisky sour that Jer had made him, staring into the tart yellow liquid.

His phone buzzed again for the fifth time in the past few hours. Silas had sent him texts, ones Taran hadn't been ready to look at yet. The last thing he needed was to hear excuses from the guy who couldn't stop hitting on him for five seconds yet froze at the slightest whiff of feelings. Not like he was much better though. He'd never been able to just straight out ask for what he wanted, to make a demand, to take a chance.

Instead, he let people steamroll all over him.

Fucking enough.

He and Wyatt had been texting since they exchanged numbers two nights ago, and the guy seemed chill. Sure, he didn't coax laughs effortlessly the way Silas did, but he was a filmmaker, which Taran found cool as shit, and he wasn't a snobby one at that. Taran needed tonight, if only to put all thoughts of Silas King behind him.

He glanced at his phone. He should check his messages in case any had arrived from Wyatt. When he looked, all he saw was Silas's name.

His fingers itched to check them, but he didn't want to be thinking about another man during his date. Who was now running late. Taran took a swig from his whisky sour, which didn't help the sad state of his stomach in the slightest. He shifted in his seat. Part of him wished he were home right now in his pajama pants, curled up on his couch with a book, not here waiting for a guy he barely knew.

"Date tonight?" Jer asked as he swung by, leaning forward on the counter.

"Yeah," Taran responded. "Sunday-night dates are all the rage."

"They are if you work in the industry," Jer shot back with a grin.

"Not in mine," Taran said, his tone dry. "Though I don't know how it bodes if the guy is ten minutes late already."

Jer shrugged. "Ten minutes isn't bad. Flag me down when he gets here."

Taran typed out a text to Wyatt, letting him know he'd found a spot at the bar, even though he'd sent one telling him he'd arrived. This was one of the five thousand reasons he hated dating. He placed his phone on the counter and wiped his palms again. They immediately bloomed with fresh sweat—joy.

The minutes ticked by slower than ever. Taran passed the time with a whole lot of staring at the door and glancing over his shoulder, as if at any moment, Wyatt would come walking in and the night would reset. Instead, he was left with his own miserable company and the shitty merry-go-round of images from earlier today. Maeve had seemed jealous, which could mean she was still into Silas. He'd sworn up and down they were co-parenting and not interested in each other, but hell, how could Taran compete with the mother of Silas's child?

Not like he was competing. He was on a date with someone else.

Who still hadn't responded to his texts and now neared being twenty minutes late.

The pit in his stomach opened up as he finished his drink. Should he get another one and hope Wyatt showed? Or should he stop drinking after this one and call it quits after a few more minutes? He'd been stood up before, and the lateness, the lack of communication… all of the signs screamed ghosted. Taran swallowed hard, his throat dry, and he didn't have any more liquid to wet it with. He caught a few sympathetic glances from Jer, which only made him feel sicker.

Tonight was supposed to be a distraction from how undesirable he was. How, in the end, no one wanted *him*—just what he could offer.

He stared at the screen of his phone and the unopened messages from Silas.

Before he could talk himself out of it, he clicked on them.

I owe you a huge apology for earlier. What Maeve said couldn't have been more wrong, and I hate that you might have thought for a second she was right.

Taran chewed on his bottom lip, reading on.

Yes, we might've started hanging out during lunches because I was fumbling with Fiona and you offered to help, but honestly, I was just looking for an excuse to spend time with you.

If you don't want to do lunches anymore, I don't care. This was never about me using you. I'm not fucking Kevin or any of those other assholes who hurt you.

I should have told you before, but I just like being around you.

Taran's cheeks heated, and he couldn't rip his gaze away from the messages.

I'll meet you at the diner to argue zombie survival plans or out at the park at night so we can work on the rebellious streak you've got started. Or hell, even just watching shitty horror movies with you, and I don't care what you say, Jason X IS shitty. It's in fucking outer space. But please don't ever think what she said is the truth. You deserve to be treated with the same amazing care you show everyone else, and if I can even show you a fraction of the kindness you've shown me, I'll be damn happy.

Well, shit.

Taran's eyes grew a little glassy as he stared at the text on the screen. He should've known what Maeve said was bullshit. Silas made an effort to never push, to never take advantage of him. Hell, whenever they had lunch, Silas always picked up the tab, a detail he hadn't missed. Maeve's words might've been true for some of his ex-boyfriends, but not for Silas.

He glanced at the door one last time—no sign of his date in sight. Taran typed a text back to Silas.

Looks like I don't have a date after all. Wyatt was a no-show.

If he could be honest with anyone, it was this man. He stared at the screen, watching the dot, dot, dot appear.

Meet me at Elk River Park in fifteen minutes.

Taran tapped his fingers along the surface of the bar for a minute before he pushed his empty glass away from him. The heaviness in his bones grew lighter from the simple message, and instead of the nerves and anxiety buzzing his veins, the thrum steadied to honeyed anticipation. This man made him impulsive in a way he'd never been before, and even though stepping into the unknown of Silas King was terrifying, he craved it.

I'll be there. He shot the message back, tipped his fingers in a goodbye to Jer, and stood up from his bar stool.

He strode out the door and reached his car in a blink. Seconds later, he was peeling out of the Port of Call parking lot and heading down the road in the direction of Elk River Park. All thoughts of Wyatt and the failed date flew out his semi-cracked window, tugged from his mind by the breezes whipping through. The slight chill caused his heart to thump harder, a wild tempo urged by the way he raced across the asphalt.

The truth was, the date with Wyatt had felt wrong from the moment he accepted the guy's number.

Meeting up with Silas? The choice felt right in a way that defied logic, that broke every one of his carefully curated labels and definitions, that thrust him out into this nebulous, hazy future where no boundaries existed. He'd never heard of anything more dangerous.

He soared down the narrow road, letting the thump of the electronica pulse through his speakers and sink into his bones. This man turned him upside down. He'd been collapsing into the mire of failed attempts at dating and feeling like no one would ever want him because they enjoyed him and not for what he could do for them. And then Silas sent those damn texts, making him feel more seen than ever before.

Taran glanced toward the end of the road, the sign for Elk River Park coming into view far too fast. It felt inevitable and too soon all in the same breath.

The main drive was fenced off for the night, but before Taran reached the end of the road, he caught sight of a figure on a bike parked by the side of the road. He slowed and pulled up behind Silas.

Guaranteed, Silas wanted him to go trespassing again, and like before, he wouldn't be able to bring himself to say no.

Not when spending time with this man was all he'd ever wanted.

Taran stepped out of his car, feeling drastically underprepared for a hike through the woods in his chinos, button-down, and loafers. What had he been thinking, driving straight here? He should've swung home to put on something halfway reasonable. Before he could berate himself further, Silas pushed up from the side of his bike and strode in his direction.

The man belonged in this darkness, those elegant features sharpening in the ink-stain shadows until he was so breathtaking Taran couldn't force his gaze away. His dark jeans blended in with the night, and his white tee looked starched from the moonlight. As always, Taran's gaze trailed to the ink crawling up his arms, visible beneath his sleeves that were rolled up to his shoulders, his motorcycle jacket slung over his back and hanging off a crooked finger. His eyes were intense tonight, even more so than usual, like he was one with this great, unfathomable expanse of glittering stars, skeletal tree branches, and whispering breezes.

"Figured you could use an escape," Silas said, cutting through the quiet between them. "Follow me. We can head to the pier."

"You do realize we're right by the water at Chesapeake City," Taran murmured as he stepped in line with Silas who'd already begun to move. Within seconds, they were climbing over the metal bar across the roadway. The chill of the cold metal pressed into Taran's palms, a reminder of the forbidden, but then Silas beckoned with a finger, and he followed anyway.

"Chesapeake City's not far enough away from everything," Silas said, his stride purposeful and his gaze tilting up to the stars above. "Sometimes you need to run off to the woods to find some clarity."

"I appreciate it," Taran said, warmth spreading in his chest with the realization of just how much Silas's actions meant. All it took was a single text about having a bad night, and the man whisked him away to escape it all.

"Well, fuck the asshole who stood you up," Silas spat, a vehemence in his tone that had Taran paying attention.

"Turns out he's not getting fucked, since he'd have to show for that to happen," Taran joked, the response coming out automatically.

"Good," Silas growled, the weight of his words causing Taran's heart to beat faster.

When Silas was flirty, when he was possessive, when he was unwaveringly kind, Taran couldn't help but fall a little harder. He'd been half in love with the man for years, and the fantasies paled in comparison to the reality of getting to know him. And here he was, walking down a paved road with Silas, the trees rearing up beside them on either side. The sky looked like a black canvas smeared with navy and violet, the stars offering a distant glow, everything so immense and heavy he forgot how to breathe.

A shiver ran down Taran's spine.

"Cold?" Silas asked. Before Taran could answer,

Silas draped his jacket around Taran's shoulders. Taran didn't have the heart to tell him the shiver had nothing to do with the chill, not with the scent of the man wrapped around him. He tugged on the still-warm fabric, letting the heat seep into him.

"Where are we heading?" Taran asked, squinting as he tried to make out shapes in the distance. "If you tell me a cabin in the woods, I'm running the other way, screaming."

Silas flicked him on the shoulder, his lopsided grin doing things to Taran's heart. "Not everything is a horror movie."

"In my life, it is," Taran responded. Even though his tone was dry, he couldn't help the scrape in his chest from the words. Truthfully, it'd be easier if he were cursed, or some external reason existed as to why loss followed him around like a specter.

Silas offered a nod. "Well, then you'll just have to trust I'm not leading you to certain doom." His words held a gravity that sank into Taran's bones.

"Easier said than done," Taran said, his voice coming out a little hoarse. He'd given away too many pieces of himself through the years to the point where he wasn't sure what remained. The largest chunk had gotten ripped from him the day Dad died, and it hadn't gotten any easier the older he grew. He tugged at Silas's coat as if it were armor, protection against the blows the world liked to deal.

"We're almost there," Silas murmured, tilting his

head forward.

Taran's breath snagged in his throat at the sight of the Elk River stretched out before them. Piers sprawled to meet the water, which glimmered with silvery promise. The trees in the distance created an even darker backdrop framing the expanse, and Taran almost stopped in his tracks at the stunning sight. He'd never been a step out into nature to clear his mind person, mostly diving into tooling around on a coding project or losing himself in a favorite book or show, but he was beginning to appreciate this avenue more and more.

He'd always been safe, consistent, and predictable, but out here he could feel a wild breathlessness that dared him to do more, to be more.

They slowed as they reached the first pier, and Silas took the lead, his boots creaking over the weathered boards.

"So, why the escape to nature?" Taran asked, unable to help himself.

Silas glanced at him, those blue eyes so hypnotic, Taran couldn't look away. "'I went to the woods because I wished to live deliberately, to front only the essential facts of life, and see if I could not learn what it had to teach, and not, when I came to die, discover that I had not lived.'" His voice was low and full of emotion as he recited the words, a resonance to them that shook every safe, measured piece of Taran's soul.

He pursed his lips, searching his mind for the

source. "Thoreau?" he asked.

"Yeah," Silas said, the hush in his tone brimming with vulnerability.

Taran had known Silas for a long, long time. The man didn't let people in, and yet here he was, cracking the door open.

They stood side by side at the pier, mere inches separating them as the moonlight caressed their skin and the night breezes saturated the thickened air. Taran couldn't look away from Silas, the soft gleam in his eyes, the elegant arch of his nose, and the hesitant purse of his lips. Like this, he seemed raw, as if crafted by clay not granite. Taran understood intrinsically that Silas had shared something rare with him, something that deserved to be treasured, cherished. His heart thumped so hard it was all he could hear, his skin vibrating with the tension stretched between them.

He sucked in a sharp breath, the realization crystallizing inside him. Taran reached across the space between them and pressed his palm to Silas's, weaving their fingers together. Silas glanced up at him, surprise staining his features.

"What are you doing?" he asked, the tentative softness so, so rare.

Taran's heart squeezed tight. He couldn't regret this—no matter how it ended.

"Turning left," Taran murmured. He leaned in, closing the distance, and kissed Silas.

CHAPTER 14

Taran's words rang through him in a sonorous declaration.

Before he could process what was happening, the man's lush lips pressed against his with an intent that had his mind reeling.

He'd been longing to taste Taran again ever since their first night together, but they'd kept their distance, attempting friendship when what existed between them was far more incendiary. Silas enveloped himself in those flames as he sank into the heat of Taran's mouth. He wrapped his palms around Taran's waist, but unlike the first time they'd hooked up, Taran was the one in command. The man's tongue darted into his mouth, the confident strokes causing a whimper to escape him. Something about this man knocked him out at the knees when no one else ever had.

Taran wrapped his fingers around Silas's nape and kissed him harder, as if savoring each brush of their lips like it might be their last. Fuck that. If Taran could put himself out there after all the hurt he'd suffered, Silas could try too. He brought their hips flush together, Taran's thick length brushing against his thigh. Silas drank in the scent of him, all amber and sandalwood, and after all the days they'd spent together, it was embedded under his skin.

Uncontrollable lust raged through his system, pent up from the casual looks, the lingering touches, and the heat he saw sparking in Taran's eyes every time the guy thought Silas wasn't looking. He tasted Taran again and again, savoring the sweet citrus on his tongue and the sultry groans coming from him. Silas reached between them and brushed the pad of his thumb across Taran's nipple, right over the piercing he knew was there. Taran moaned into his mouth, bucking his hips forward. Holy hell, this guy was next-level hot.

Silas pulled back for a breath, the sharp sounds of their exhalations piercing through the night air. "Wait, wait, wait," he murmured. "What is this?"

Taran's Adam's apple bobbed with his swallow. "Whatever you need it to be," Taran said, his voice quiet. "I'm... just tired of pretending I haven't been wanting you ever since we first hooked up. If I'm honest, even before then."

Silas rested his palm against the side of Taran's

face, cupping it. "Yeah, I get that," his voice came out raspy with the truth. "I've been wanting you too."

"Then you have me," Taran responded, the truth shining in those dark, gorgeous eyes.

Silas opened his mouth to speak but hesitated. Taran clearly didn't have any expectations that they'd be throwing a label on their relationship or heading toward anything permanent, but he was in this anyway. The man deserved more. More than him, and more than what he could offer.

Yet Silas was a selfish bastard who longed for him all the same.

"I may not be able to make too many promises," Silas began, sucking in a steadying breath as he brushed his thumb across Taran's plush lower lip swollen from their kisses. "However, I want you. I want this, whatever it is, and from here on out, it's just us, okay?"

"Just us," Taran repeated, his words a hushed promise. Taran's palm rested on his heart, and Silas could feel the thump, thump, thump as if it was trying to leap straight out of his chest.

The past few weeks had been an exercise in restraint, having the man so close yet not touching, not tasting, not kissing him like he'd wanted to. His fault, he knew. However, all the pent-up energy swirled within him, a steady pulse driving him forward.

Silas leaned in to brush his lips against Taran's

neck, a light lick first, followed by a nip that summoned breathy moans from the man. Silas's cock stiffened at the sound, mesmerizing and heady. It had been too long since they'd last come together, and with the way he'd been going out of his mind at those memories, he needed Taran—now. He reached behind to his back pocket, feeling the familiar shape of foil packets.

"Keep moaning like that and I'll fuck you right here on this pier," Silas murmured in his ear.

Taran swore and glanced up at him. "You're serious, aren't you?"

"What do you think?" Silas asked, a grin rising on his lips as he reached down to flick open the button on Taran's chinos before working on the zipper.

"So, you want to add public indecency on our charges on top of trespassing?" Taran hissed, his dismay adorable. "Besides, things never go well for people fucking in the woods. They're always the ones murdered first."

Silas leaned in and captured Taran's mouth, unable to help his grin even as he swept his tongue inside. He loved it when this man got riled up. He slid his hand beneath Taran's shirt and dragged his fingernails down the man's abs before dipping his fingers past the waistband of his boxer briefs. All the hot skin at his perusal, Silas wanted to take the time and savor it, to lick every inch of him, but not now. Not tonight. Silas reached down and wrapped his hand around Taran's firm length. Fuck, his cock felt like silk against his palm, and he gave the man one stroke, then two before brushing his thumb against his slit.

"Fuuuuck," Taran moaned, his hands settling on the waistband of Silas's jeans. "You're not playing fair."

"Where's the fun in that?" Silas responded, drawing the tip of his tongue along the side of Taran's neck before nipping at his earlobe. The man tasted sweet, his skin like velvet. Taran bucked his hips forward again into Silas's grip around his erection. Silas ran his thumb over the pubic piercing at the base of Taran's cock, a silent thrill rolling through him at the feel of the cold metal. This guy was full of so many damn surprises. "You want me to fuck you here on this pier," Silas murmured in his ear. "In fact, I'm sure of it."

He jacked Taran again, rough strokes that got Silas just as worked up. Taran's breaths quickened, and Silas could feel the pound of his pulse as he kissed along his neck, lazy sweeping brushes of his lips against his smooth, hot skin. With his other hand, he reached around behind Taran and slid his fingertip down his crack until he landed on the tight pucker of sensitive skin. Silas began to stroke circles around it, teasing and toying with the hot little hole he was dying to plunge into.

Silas's cock strained in his jeans as he felt the

flutter of the man's hole against his fingertip, and all he could think of was the heat and pressure waiting for him when he sank inside Taran. Fuuuuck. He wasn't going to last long.

"Fine, fine, you win," Taran gasped. "I need you inside me."

"Thought you'd never ask." Silas's grin widened, and he sank his teeth into the side of Taran's neck before he pushed the chinos and the waistband of his boxer-briefs down to the guy's thighs. The slight chill in the air didn't affect him in the slightest, not with the heat detonating between them. Silas pulled away to step behind Taran, his hands resting on the man's bare hips as he drank in the sight of his firm ass. Silas tugged his lower lip between his teeth, needing to be inside that as of yesterday.

How he'd thought he could get this guy out of his system, he didn't know. He'd tried, and the attempt hadn't worked in the slightest. If anything, Silas wanted him more now.

He reached down to unzip himself with a *snick* that echoed through the cool spring air. This place amplified everything, and he couldn't wait to hear Taran's cries on that next-level surround sound of the wild nature around them. Silas dragged his boxers down next, running his hand along his stiff cock, as if he stood a chance of calming it down. Not with Taran's pert ass right in front of him begging to be fucked. He dragged his length along

Taran's crack, rubbing himself against the silken skin.

"Fuck, I could come just like this," Silas murmured, resting his hands on Taran's hips. He leaned in again to press his lips to Taran's neck, the man tilting his neck to grant him immediate access.

"Promises were made," Taran responded even as he thrust his ass against Silas's cock, the friction causing Silas's mind to spin with hazy desire. "If we're going to make ourselves serial-killer bait, I'm at least getting dicked down."

Silas buried his face in Taran's neck, grinding hard against him as he resisted the urge to laugh. "Goddamn, you're mouthy."

"Is that a request?" The sultry drip of words from Taran's lips had Silas close to detonating.

"Not unless you want me to come in two seconds flat," Silas responded, gripping Taran's hips tighter. "I've been fantasizing about your fuckable mouth for far too long, and I won't last."

Taran's lips quirked, but before he could say anything, Silas brought his palm down onto Taran's ass cheek with a loud crack that echoed in the quiet air around them, followed by a moan from Taran. The sensation of his palm against that taut skin drove him insane, and if the way Taran teased his bottom lip between his teeth, pupils blown out with lust, served as an indicator that it had worked for him too. Silas reached back into his pocket and grabbed the lube first, ripping it open as he dribbled some on his fingers. The memory of Taran's tight heat surrounding his cock had carried him through the past few weeks, a slice of pure fucking heaven when things had gotten too tough or bleak.

Except it wasn't just about a place to bury his dick —not when it came to Taran Shah.

The man was total sunshine despite his cynicism and had a way of lighting Silas up from the inside out with every encounter. The tenderness of those memories squeezed his heart tight as he reached down and began to circle the furled muscle with teasing motions that made Taran gasp hard before Silas shoved two fingers inside. Silas let out a low groan at the way Taran's hole clamped around his fingers, the insane heat every bit as tempting as he remembered. The sounds coming from Taran were pornographic and turned him on more than anything else.

Silas's cock throbbed, precum leaking at the tip as the urge to rut against the man rose in urgency. His breaths came out sharp at the sight of his fingers disappearing into Taran's tight hole and how fucking hot that looked.

"Down," Silas murmured. "On the ground." He pulled his fingers out of Taran's ass and dropped to his knees on the planks beneath them, which groaned under his weight. Taran maneuvered in front of him, but Silas didn't wait for him to settle, pressing his palm against Taran's chest and shoving him onto his back. Taran hit the deck with a thump, and Silas slunk over him in a blink, their breaths mingling in the cool night air.

His palms pressed into the weathered boards on either side of Taran, and he stared down, soaking in the perfection of this man. Taran's pouty lower lip glistened, his aquiline nose stark in the sharp shadows and his faint line of scruff delicious. The look in those darkened eyes caused Silas's breath to hitch. He saw not just lust but a yearning there that punched him in the gut.

"I've got you, gorgeous," Silas murmured, tugging Taran's pants farther down his legs and past his knees. Taran knocked his loafers off with two solid thumps. Silas placed his hands on Taran's knees, his skin prickling with awareness at how exposed they were right now, and not just because they were fucking in front of a lake in the middle of a pier. He leaned down between them and brushed his lips over Taran's, tasting the sweet citrus burst of the man's mouth. Silas licked along Taran's lower lip with the tip of his tongue before biting it, and Taran bucked his hips.

"I need it, Si," he murmured, a hesitant pleading in his voice that snapped Silas completely.

Silas pushed Taran's knees up, exposing his beautiful hole, and reached into his pocket. He ripped the foil packet open and slid the condom up his length.

He slicked himself up with lube afterward, his cock throbbing in the process. Need drove him to near insanity. His knees dug into the hard wooden surface beneath him as he settled in front of Taran, cupping that gorgeous ass. The brisk winds skated off the water, a contrast to the inferno brewing between them, and the silvery moon overhead painted Taran in the most stunning light.

Silas lined his cock up, brushing it against the taut, furled skin, and Taran shuddered.

"God, you're fucking beautiful," he purred as he sank the first inch in. He lifted Taran's hips so the man's feet rested against his chest as he waited a moment for him to adjust before driving in deeper, nice and slow. Taran jutted his hips forward, taking more of him in, his eyes so feverish and entrancing that Silas couldn't look away. The pressure consumed him as he pushed in until the tight ring of muscle relaxed, and he sank the rest of the way inside. The breath Silas hadn't realized he'd been holding released. The heat around his cock was mind melting, and the vise of Taran's ass was a perfect fit.

"You going to just park your dick there or are you going to fuck me?" Taran snarked at him, his eyes sparkling with amusement. With his pants around his ankles, knees bent, and ass exposed, Taran looked like a fucking dream. Silas reached between them and palmed Taran's cock before he circled around beneath it to grasp Taran's balls, causing a thready moan to erupt from him. He reached around with his other hand to give Taran's ass a hearty smack, enjoying the breath that shot out of the man on impact.

"You want to get fucked or you want to mouth off?" Silas shot back, even though his lips curled into a grin.

Taran locked gazes with him and thrust his hips up again. The intensity in his stare bowled Silas over, a mixture of clever, challenging, and just plain entrancing. "What do you think?"

Silas's grin widened as he gripped Taran's hips and slid back, enjoying the tight glide. He sank in again, eliciting another groan from Taran, those long lashes fluttering in response. The bliss on that face snapped whatever restraint Silas still clung onto, and he began to fuck him in earnest. Silas gripped hard enough to leave marks, his nails biting into Taran's skin as he lost himself in the back-and-forth glide of his cock into the tight channel. Taran's moans were a melody he couldn't get enough of, and the cool night breezes painting his skin with goosebumps reminded him of where they were, out in the middle of nowhere, surrounded by nothing but sky, water, and stars.

Silas thrust in deep again, pure pleasure rolling through him each time he sank inside Taran, connected to the man in a way he'd longed for ever since their first night together. This man wasn't just a distraction, wasn't just a way to lose himself—being with him felt like taking the first definitive steps on a path when he'd been wandering in circles for far too long. Sweat beaded on his brow and body, several drops rolling down his cheeks and coating his thighs as he moved inside Taran.

Silas couldn't help but memorize the man's responses, how his back bowed every time he plunged all the way in, pegging his prostate. How those sharp, staccato breaths pierced the air, his lashes fluttering as he sank his teeth down on that lush bottom lip. His button-down was rumpled, hiking up his chest, and his socked toes curled each time Silas drove into him, harder and harder as he chased after his release.

His balls began to tighten as pure animalistic reflex took over. Close. He was goddamn close. Silas reached between them and wrapped his hand around Taran's cock, starting to jack him in time with his thrusts. The simple touch had Taran's moans ratcheting louder, and as they collided together with bruising force again and again and again, Silas's vision blurred with sweat, with the consuming need rising higher and higher.

Taran let out a shout, and all of a sudden cum splattered across Silas's knuckles, and some on Taran's shirt. Not like Silas could even focus because the second Taran came, his channel squeezed so tight in fluttering pulses around Silas's cock that it coaxed the orgasm from him. Silas's balls drew tight, and a moment later, his mind was seared into submission as his release flooded out of him and he emptied into the condom. Silas sucked in a sharp breath as the heady sensations bowled him over, pure ecstasy taking over as it coursed through his whole body, making his muscles lax in the wake of the intense orgasm.

Silas slowly returned to earth, his knees aching as they pressed hard into the pier, the night air cooling his sweat-slick skin and his nails still digging into Taran's hips, where they were sure to leave a mark. Their ragged breaths cycled through the silence, amplified by the magnitude of their surroundings. Silas's gaze latched onto Taran's, and he couldn't look away. The quiet vulnerability in those dark eyes and the softness that existed there struck him mute.

What happened between them wasn't a one-night stand or a fling, and they both knew it.

Just us.

The promise he'd made earlier echoed through him, and while it should've been terrifying, he couldn't summon the fear. Not while he was buried inside this man, bared to him in a way he never allowed with anyone else, and all Taran did was accept him completely. Those wild fears, the desperate need to run, the self-loathing that threatened to bury him most days were silenced in Taran's grounding presence, and Silas couldn't pull away.

Silas dipped down and brushed his lips against Taran's in a sweet, satisfying kiss. Despite the cum drying between them, their pants hiked down in the middle of a park, and the way Silas's cock had softened in Taran's ass, he didn't budge, just enjoying the luxurious glide of his lips like they had all the time in the world. Bliss rolled over him, pure and true, and with the stars and moonlit lake as witness, Silas unleashed all the tenderness he'd been holding tightly onto for so many years.

Taran's tongue slipped into his mouth as he deepened the kiss with long, lazy strokes they lost themselves in for minutes, for hours—he couldn't tell. When Silas pulled away, the slow, sated smile on Taran's lips struck him straight in the chest.

Words dried up on Silas's tongue. He didn't want to break the silence that stretched between them in case they'd end once this moment did.

Except that wouldn't happen.

Silas's heart pumped faster as he stared down at Taran's gorgeous features. This was just the beginning, and instead of the terror that normally flooded through him at the thought, tendrils of anticipation crept up inside him, like witnessing the first glimmer of a lake at the end of a long trail.

Taran pursed his lips and glanced to the side. "How long are you planning on keeping your dick in my ass? Because we're prime axe-murderer bait right now, and I'm not loving our odds."

Silas's eyes widened. Before he could help himself, his shoulders shook with laughter. "Never change, beautiful," he murmured with a real grin, nothing like the practiced ones he flashed day in and out.

He slowly slid out from Taran and then rolled the condom down, tying it off at the end. Silas slipped it in his pocket before offering Taran a hand, helping him up off the boards of the pier. They made quick work of tugging up their pants and tucking themselves back in before they faced each other and a hesitant quiet descended.

"So… we're doing this," Taran said, breaking the silence first, a question in his gaze.

Even now, he gave Silas an out.

Silas didn't want one.

He closed the distance between them to place a hot, brief kiss on Taran's lips. "Hell yeah, we're doing this." Heat burned in his chest, a warmth he didn't think he was capable of feeling.

The dip of Taran's head and the giddy grin were fucking adorable. Though Silas couldn't tell in this darkness, he could swear the guy was blushing. "Right. Good. We better head back to our cars before we get caught trespassing though."

"Had enough recklessness for one night?" Silas teased, unable to help himself.

Taran arched his brow. "We just fucked in the middle of a pier, so yeah, I'm tapped out." He tilted his head toward the trail they'd come in on, and before Silas realized it, Taran's palm slipped against his and their fingers threaded together.

This time he was the one to blush.

Fuck, he was so screwed.

CHAPTER 15

Only a few days had passed since the night Taran and Silas fucked in the middle of a park, a phenomenon Taran still wasn't sure had actually happened. The couple of splinters on the backs of his thighs and the crescents of Silas's nails and bruises around his hips were the only proof of that mind-blowing night, one he'd replayed over and over again.

Not like he'd ever believed he would've done something so reckless, but Silas brought out a side of him that broke all his own rules.

Taran shifted in the spot in which he'd camped out at all day while working at Mama's. His work laptop was on his lap at this point, his body contorted in a weird way. However, between Barter, work, and everything else, he hadn't been over nearly as much to visit her, and the guilt had caught up with him.

"Are you sure you can't stay for dinner?" Mama called from the other room. A second later, she entered through the small doorframe. A few wisps of her gray-and-black hair escaped her tidy bun, and perpetual mischief sparkled in her eyes—just like it did in Nico's. "Your brother and Hudson will be coming over," she continued in an effort to sway him.

He lifted a brow. "Haven't you had enough of me yet? I've been here all day, and we had lunch together." Plus, the longer he was under her scrutiny, the more of a chance she'd figure out something was up. He was fairly certain she already had suspicions.

Mama shook her head, leaning against the doorframe. "Never, ever. It's you who's running off on me," she said, placing a hand over her forehead to amp up the mock drama. Taran's lips quirked. He knew she was happy that he'd been by today, but it was clear that some weeks, the loneliness of living in this old house by herself crept in stronger than others.

"You know I love you," Taran reminded her. "I just already made plans."

Mama rapped her knuckles on the doorframe before casting him a fond look. "And I appreciate how you always honor them. Let me go check on the curry."

Taran glanced down to look at the clock on his

work laptop. The time ticked closer and closer, only minutes left until the end of the day, and he couldn't help the anticipation building inside him. He'd be seeing Silas soon.

He and Silas hadn't agreed to any labels—not boyfriends, dating, or whatever, but the promise Silas had made offered enough reassurance. And while they hadn't been able to meet up the past two days due to Silas's long shifts at Port of Call, they'd promised to hang tonight, and Taran felt giddiness welling up in him, like at the start of a movie he'd been waiting years to see or the latest book release from his favorite author. He ran his fingers through his hair, trying to smother the grin rising unbidden to his lips.

His phone buzzed, and he fumbled to check it. *I'll be a few minutes behind. Traffic from Baltimore's brutal right now.*

Cole.

Oh, shit. He'd forgotten about his plans to meet Cole at Maverick Diner tonight. With the way work had been wringing him dry, he'd wanted to at least discuss what the process might be like to get the paperwork for Barter figured out, even though he still hadn't gotten up the nerve to pull the trigger. Though, if he kept skating on the boldness he'd embraced with Silas, maybe he'd find the courage.

Fuck, Silas.

He wanted to see him so damn badly, to make

sure their time the other night hadn't been a fluke, but Cole had already started driving in from the city. He couldn't ditch his best friend. Taran's shoulders sank as he shot off a text to Silas.

Rain check on tonight? I forgot I was meeting Cole for dinner at Maverick.

Taran glanced at the time and clocked out for work, letting out a heavy sigh as he shut his laptop. The fluttering in his chest at the thought of seeing Silas had been crushed under disappointment. Nerves raced through him. What if this rain check led to Silas calling the whole thing off, deciding he was too difficult to deal with? If he could go through a single day without a side order of anxiety, that'd be just peachy, but given his experience thus far, that didn't seem to be a possibility.

Taran got up from the couch to head into the kitchen and bid Mama goodbye. Time to head out.

An hour had passed since Taran arrived at Maverick and met up with Cole, and he couldn't stop checking his phone.

No response.

Which meant he'd pissed Silas off. Guaranteed, the guy regretted fucking him a second time since Silas King had never done repeats in the past. At least not that Taran was aware of. Taran shifted in the vinyl booth, the material cracked and worn. His chicken Caesar wrap stared at him, untouched, because his stomach had been a mess from the moment he realized he'd double-booked himself. He chewed on his lower lip, trying to ignore the way Cole was attempting to laser into him with his stare alone.

"What's so fascinating on your phone?" Cole asked, a faux innocent tone in his voice.

Taran shot his best friend a glare. Cole was definitely fishing, but Taran didn't even know what to call the situation between him and Silas apart from mind-meltingly hot. And Cole would want answers, like the b-word Taran hadn't even broached. Were they friends who fucked? Dating exclusively? Hell, were they even telling anyone they were seeing each other, or were they keeping it quiet?

He needed to talk to Silas, but that might not even happen because the guy was currently giving him radio silence.

"It's the latest Samsung model," Taran responded, tossing back the snark. He'd mastered the avoidance game a long, long time ago. "Got a lot of great features if you're interested."

Cole arched an eyebrow at him. "Fine, don't tell me your secrets. But you dragged me out here to talk about your app, so no putting that off any longer."

Taran poked at his wrap, as if his stomach might

settle enough to eat. Fat chance there. Was he really going to try and launch this thing?

"I can hear your doubts from over here," Cole said, adjusting the cuffs of his pale blue button-down, dressed to kill in charcoal slacks and a blue tie. "But you said you wanted to talk Barter, so we're pushing your anxieties to the side tonight and taking a step forward."

Taran swallowed another sip of water, even though it did little to wet his parched throat. He eyed his phone again, willing a text to appear on the screen, to see it vibrate, any sort of response from Silas. As much as Cole wanted him to pack those insecurities away tonight, they'd already started parading out on main street.

"Okay, okay," Taran said, diving into his messenger bag for some of the folders he'd brought along with all the information he'd collated so far. A sensation of vulnerability prickled along his neck, but this was Cole, who'd been cheerleading this venture from the moment he'd mentioned it. He plopped them onto the tabletop.

Cole took a sip from his coffee, not leaping for the folders. His brows drew together, and his gaze fixed on the front door of the diner. Taran was faced away from it, so he couldn't see what snagged his attention —whoever had arrived, Cole definitely found them fascinating.

"Well, well," Cole said. "If your one-night stand didn't just walk through the door…."

Taran's eyes widened as his heart accelerated.

He turned around to follow Cole's gaze up front to spot Silas King in the flesh.

With his windblown dark hair, leather jacket, and tight jeans, the man looked beyond edible. Entering the diner in his faded Misfits T-shirt made him a blast from the past so similar to the guy Taran had crushed on in high school who'd graced this diner countless times. Silas's gaze landed on him, and those intense blue eyes flared. Taran couldn't help but lick his lips.

"Shit, I'm sorry," Cole said. "I shouldn't have pointed Silas out, should I. You were trying to get over him."

Taran ran his fingers through his hair, a helpless laugh bubbling in his chest. Great job he did on getting over Silas. Instead, he let the guy fuck him in the middle of a pier. His insides fluttered at the memory, a far more intimate one than he'd ever imagined it could be. What was Silas doing here though? Even though Taran faced Cole, he could feel the prickle of Silas's presence as he approached. Not like Cole's curious gaze didn't give him away.

"Hey, beautiful." Silas's voice came out in a purr, and he slid into the booth beside Taran. "Sorry I'm late." Before Taran could register the fact that Silas was here let alone the open affection he'd delivered, Silas slid his arm around Taran's shoulders in a possessive move that had his heart stepping in double time. To Cole's credit, his eyes only widened once before he hid his surprise.

Taran opened his mouth and shut it, not knowing what to say.

Should he tell Cole they were seeing each other? Silas sure as hell was acting like they were. His brain was two seconds from exploding, and with the heavy weight of Silas's arm and his fucking delicious leather-and-clove scent, he didn't know whether he wanted to run away or rub himself all over the man.

Silas's eyes narrowed as he stared at Cole. "Have we met before?"

"Same school," Cole said with an upward nod. "I was in Taran's grade." Even as Cole said the words, his gaze switched back to Taran with an "answers now, bitch" look.

"Uh, I've got to go to the bathroom," Taran said, nudging Silas out of the booth. He just needed a second to adjust to whatever the hell was going on. He didn't look back as he rushed to the men's room on the opposite side of the diner. Taran shut the door closed behind him, the fans whirring and the bright fluorescent lights gleaming down on him. A few splashes of cold water to his face later and he still hadn't figured out what had happened to his night.

The door to the bathroom creaked, and Taran glanced over to see Silas slip inside.

"So...," Silas said, leaning against one of the white sinks. "Cole isn't a date."

Taran's jaw dropped. He thought back to the text he'd sent, but he'd never included a modifier or anything. Oh, lord. Amusement welled up inside him, and he struggled to restrain a grin. "Cole's been my best friend since high school. Definitely not a date. But if this whole flex is a jealousy thing, I've got to say I don't mind in the slightest."

"Right, I probably just should've asked," Silas responded, staring at the paste-white ceiling. "I'm guessing your friend thinks I'm a complete asshole by now, especially because I don't remember him from high school."

Taran shook his head. His heart fluttered at the concern in Silas's tone and the exasperation there. He took the few steps to close the distance between them and brushed his lips against Silas's in a kiss. Silas escalated it seconds later when his hand wrapped around Taran's nape, and he growled against his mouth before sinking his teeth into Taran's lower lip. They were both panting by the time they pulled away.

"Sure you don't want to keep pushing limits by fucking in the bathroom?" Silas asked, his eyes dancing.

Taran shot him a look. "I'm already going to have a hard enough time explaining what this is to Cole without him figuring we snuck off to the bathroom to fuck. I know we're taking this day by day, but the whole possessive move back there is going to leave him with questions."

Silas pursed his lips, running a finger down Taran's chest, slowing it around each button. Based on the hard-on he was barely concealing in those jeans, he was distracted as hell, which had started affecting Taran.

"Seeing each other, I guess?" Silas murmured, attempting to keep his voice light even though Taran could feel the tension.

"I'm pretty sure there's a word for seeing someone exclusively, but I'll let you figure out that one on your own," Taran responded, backing off. As much as he wanted everything defined, he under-stood Silas's need to prioritize Fiona right now, and to be honest, he wasn't keen into leaping headfirst into another relationship. With how deep he was in this with Silas, adding a promise was a recipe for disaster, if his dating history served as any indicator.

If he tried really hard, he could almost believe himself.

"We should avoid telling my brother, since he happens to be your employer," Taran mentioned. Plus, he hadn't missed the weird way Nico had been eyeing them the other night when they'd all been out at Harbor Pointe.

Silas nodded, something unreadable flashing in

his gaze. "Yeah, wouldn't want your brother knowing about me. That'd get messy."

"Clearly, I'm not afraid of a mess." Taran leaned close and ran his palm firmly over the hard length straining Silas's denim, full of intent. And then he turned and headed toward the door. "Coming?" he asked with a smirk.

"Apparently not," Silas muttered, raking his fingers through his wild strands. Taran exited the bathroom, and Silas followed behind him. "You're a fucking tease, you know that?"

"No, really?" Taran glanced behind him, batting his lashes for good measure.

Silas's lips turned up in a grin as he shook his head. "Keep teasing, babe," he murmured. "We'll work on your exhibition kink when I bend you over the table and take you right at the booth."

Taran's cheeks flushed, and he tried to ignore the way his cock woke right to life at the visual. Cole's stare drilled into him as he reached the table, and Taran slipped into the booth quickly so he didn't give his friend an eyeful of his raging hard-on.

Silas plunked into the seat next to him as if he didn't have a care in the world. Even without repeating the possessive overtures from when he'd first arrived, Silas got into his space immediately, reaching past him to steal a fry from his barely touched plate.

Taran smacked his hand. "Order your own food."

"Only if you smack me harder," Silas responded, his lips curling up.

Taran's entire body immolated, and Cole let out a cough.

"So, care to share what's going on here?" his best friend asked.

"We're seeing each other," Silas responded as he snagged another two fries from Taran's plate.

A grin stretched across Cole's face as if Christmas had come early. "Holy shit, you aren't kidding. That was Taran's wet dream through like, what, the entirety of high school?"

Immolation wasn't enough. Now he'd gone supernova out of embarrassment. Taran rested his forearms on the table and pressed his face into them, as if that might hide him from mortification.

"No way. Was I your high school crush?" Silas asked, munching obnoxiously on yet another stolen fry.

Taran flipped him the middle finger, not lifting his head to see the amused faces of Cole and the guy he dated because boyfriend was too scary a word. "Why don't we talk about what we came here to discuss?" His voice came out muffled, but he didn't care.

"You mean the step toward your future that you've been avoiding for a full year now?" Cole said. "While you guys were doing god knows what in the bathroom, I had a chance to look over your paperwork for Barter."

Taran pulled his head up at last since they'd detoured to a less embarrassing topic, even if talking about the Barter app still made him jittery.

Silas's thigh jostled against his. "What's the paperwork for?"

"Just a stupid idea I came up with a few years back," Taran mumbled, picking up half of his Caesar wrap and taking a bite, even though the lettuce had wilted a little by this point after how long he'd let it sit.

Cole crossed his arms over his chest, giving him an arch look. "You mean a brilliant idea for an app that's going to take the hell off. Why don't you stop wasting time tearing yourself down and explain it?"

Taran stared down at the wrap in his hand. "So, not everyone's got the cash to spare for services, but there are a lot of folks with specialized skills. I figured an app where people could exchange similarly valued services would be helpful. Say you need a babysitter for Fiona but you're low on cash that week. You could match up with someone who offers babysitting and is looking for meal services, or whatever other skills you have on offer."

Taran's shoulders tensed as he braced himself for the criticism. Kevin had thought the idea was dumb, and so had Steve, his previous boyfriend. Cole seemed to be the only one who believed in this, and he hadn't brought the app up to Mama or Nico because they'd support him even if this was a bad idea.

"That sounds fucking brilliant," Silas said, nudging him with his thigh. "Why the hell haven't you launched it already?"

Taran peeked over at Silas. The genuine warmth in those blue eyes had his heart beating faster. He swallowed hard, bowled over by the simple way Silas supported him.

"Exactly what I've been telling him," Cole said, jabbing a finger in Taran's direction. "Thank god you're dating someone who isn't tearing you the hell down."

Taran's cheeks flushed. Being around Silas relaxed him like nothing else while at the same time was as thrilling as a cliff dive, but he'd thrown himself headfirst into yet another situation that could explode in his face. However, when a protective arm looped around his shoulders, drawing him in again, his heart soared. Taran couldn't help but lean into Silas's heat, barely believing the guy would pull a public display like this.

"Let me guess: Kevin thought it was a bad idea," Silas muttered, the irritation in his tone sending a silent thrill through Taran. "Man, I could use an app like Barter. Seriously—it's not like I'm swimming in funds right now."

Taran's heart pumped faster. That. That was why he'd been working on the app. All he'd wanted to do was help people, to make their lives a little easier, and Barter might accomplish it. Trickles of excitement filtered through his veins, the intoxicating sort he'd first felt when he started tooling around on the app to begin with. The papers sat in front of him in a folder, all ready to go, and Silas's words were the reminder he'd needed.

He'd never be able to help anyone with it if he never got the nerve to launch.

"All right, Cole," he said, placing his palm on the manila folder between them. "How do we get started on this?"

CHAPTER 16

Silas crouched over the bassinet he'd assembled in his bedroom, popping a fresh set of sheets on the pad. He only had a one-bedroom apartment, so when Fiona crashed over at his place, she'd have to deal with being in the same room as him. He tried to fit the stack of baby clothes his mom had gotten in one of his drawers, which was overflowing at this point. A stack of diapers and wipes sat beside the bassinet, shit he'd ordered in the last week when Maeve had mentioned getting his place baby ready. Her parents were coming home this week, which had her acting odder than ever and setting off all sorts of internal alarms.

She'd be swinging by to check out the setup any minute, but he couldn't even stress too hard over her arrival, not when Taran would be coming over for an actual date in an hour.

Sure, they might already see each other all the time for lunch dates when he went over to take care of Fiona before his shifts, and he'd spent some time with him at Maverick Diner when he'd crashed Taran and Cole's hangout, but that was earlier in the week. And ever since they'd fucked on the pier, he'd gotten so pent up he was a second away from jumping the guy the moment he walked through the door.

An entire night with Taran.

He hadn't gotten that since the first night they spent together, and to his surprise, all the time around each other didn't make him want to run the other way—instead, he craved the guy like a spring night at Lums Pond.

If someone had told him a month ago he'd be seeing someone, let alone wanting to spend every goddamn day with them, he would've called that person crazy. However, he'd also never known anyone who got him like Taran did. Being around him was effortless, easy in a way he hadn't realized was possible.

A knock sounded at the door.

Silas sucked in a breath, surveying the spartan room that morphed into a massive mess over in what he'd dubbed "baby corner." Not like Maeve was CPS or anything. He just needed to show her Fiona had somewhere safe to sleep.

He pushed up from his crouch and strode out of the room and through the main area to the door.

When he swung it open, Maeve stood in the entrance with Fiona resting in her arms, his little girl dressed in a gray onesie and floral pants today. She blinked sleepily up at him in a just-woke-up infant daze he'd begun to recognize.

"Hey," Maeve said, taking a step inside before he had the chance to invite her in. He leaned forward and scooped Fiona out of her arms. As much as Silas had been terrified to even pick her up the first time, he'd started to get the hang of holding her, and he clutched the little warm creature to his chest, those long lashes fluttering. She stared straight up at him with a scrutinizing intensity he couldn't help but grin at.

Fiona looked up at him, and a moment later, her tiny face broke into a smile of her own, those eyes lighting up. The ice around Silas's heart melted like someone had taken a butane torch to it, and warmth flooded through him in an intense sweep. He clutched Fiona even tighter, barely able to believe the MDMA levels of joy bursting through him.

"When did she start smiling?" he asked, giddiness coursing through him.

"What?" Maeve glanced back. She'd already wandered ahead, skating her fingertips along the used couch he'd bought for the living room. "Oh, a few days ago."

He ignored Maeve's blasé tone as he stared into Fiona's eyes, widening his lips in another huge grin.

Her blue eyes sparkled as she mirrored the movement again with pure, unfiltered happiness in her tiny expression. Silas swallowed hard, slammed with more feelings than he was prepared to deal with.

"Well, shit, Fi," Silas breathed out. "Look at you learnin'."

Maeve wandered into his bedroom, probably to check up the setup he had for Fiona. Silas strode through his apartment to show her everything he had in place—which wasn't much if he were being honest, because he was rubbish at this parenting thing. He'd hit up Taran and his mom for suggestions, which caused another cavalcade of excitement from his mother who'd gotten to meet Fiona and wanted so many more visits.

"Let me know if I'm missing anything," Silas said as he stepped into the doorway of his bedroom with Fiona trying to lift her little head up to see what was going on around her. Sometime over the past few weeks, his clutch when he held this munchkin had grown a bit more protective. His attachment to her hadn't been a sudden gut punch but a gradual trickling in until he was flooded with the need to keep Fiona safe and to see that baby happy.

Maeve wasn't picking through the shit he kept beside the bassinet in the heaping, overflowing pile of a few rattles, a stuffed animal, baby blanket, sleep sack, and whatever else had come in. Instead, she leaned over and inspected his bed.

"I thought you had a two bedroom," she said, an edge to her tone that had Silas sucking in a breath. Fucking hell. He knew this wouldn't be the easiest thing, co-parenting with someone who was essentially a stranger, but she was so finicky.

"Nah, I told you, remember?" he said, bringing Fiona over to the bassinet and placing her down on her back to see if she liked it.

"How are we all supposed to fit in one room?" Maeve complained, stalking around the bed and pulling open his drawers. "There's not even any space for another dresser."

Silas's stomach dropped.

The bad feeling that had nagged at him from the moment Maeve arrived now pointed a finger at the blaring problem in her words.

Fucking hell. Maybe he should've been blunt with her from the start. He'd thought they were on the same page when he'd come back to town. Maeve had been his MO in the past—a one-night stand with someone convenient and hot, nothing more.

Nothing like the confusing-as-fuck feelings Taran summoned in him. All of his previous rules, his habits of ditching and keeping people at a distance, collapsed around him. The worst part of it all was that Taran didn't try. He didn't push or ask for more —he just let Silas exist and peered right past every fake smile and pithy comment.

"We're not all fitting in one room," Silas said

slowly, as if he was starting to defuse a bomb. "This is just the setup in my room for when Fiona stays overnight."

Maeve's brows drew together. "But my parents are coming back in a few days."

Silas worked his jaw, fighting to keep his irritation under wraps. Maeve had barely given him an introduction to Fiona, and she'd alternated between hot and cold with him—either flirting or ignoring. Sure, she might've been giving him "fuck me" eyes here or there, but never once had she expressed any intention of moving in with him.

"Which means you'll have help to take care of Fiona," Silas said. "Isn't that a good thing?"

"Not when we could all be living together as a family." Maeve's voice grew icicle sharp now, which mirrored the expression on her face, the pinched-thin lips and the furrow in her brow.

"I'm here for her, not you," Silas said, the words dropping out way harsher than intended. He clutched Fiona a little tighter, as if the baby was a shield. He couldn't bring himself to look up at Maeve. "I want to raise her with you, sure. But as a co-parent. I thought I made that clear from the start. We're not together, Maeve. We're never going to be together."

Fuck, he should've addressed this when he'd first gotten that uneasy feeling. He brushed his fingers across Fiona's dark, soft hair reflexively as he forced himself to look at Maeve. Her blue eyes filled with thunderclouds, and the hurt rolling off her grew strong enough to start her own storm.

"This is because of Taran, isn't it? He's always spending time around you because he clearly has a crush." Maeve crossed her arms over her chest, rage in the downturn of her lips.

"We were never going to get together, Maeve," Silas reiterated, because that hadn't sunk in with her. "I'm sorry if I didn't make that crystal clear. Even if Taran wasn't in the picture, we still wouldn't be a thing. However, you should know…." Silas grappled with saying their situation out loud—mostly because he was terrified that once it became real, he'd fuck it all up. "Taran and I are seeing each other," he forced out.

The tension vibrated off of Maeve, enough to nearly knock him over. "I thought you didn't *do* dating."

Silas swallowed, trying to ignore the prickles of discomfort. He swayed with Fiona in his arms as she reached up and waved her little chubby fists around. "I normally don't."

"Fiona and I need to leave," Maeve gritted out.

Panic flared at the way she phrased that. "Hey," Silas jumped in. "Don't shut me out. We don't have to be a couple to be damned good parents for this little girl. And I've showed you I want to be a part of her life."

"I have to break the news to my parents that I'm not moving out," she snapped, stomping over to him with such erratic movements that he clutched Fiona a little tighter. He didn't want to hand his daughter over to her, not while anger sparked in her eyes. Before he could stop Maeve, she wrenched Fiona out of his arms and turned on her heel. She headed for the door at a brisk pace, and Fiona began crying at once.

Silas started after them, but before he could stop Maeve, she stepped out and slammed the front door in his face.

His heart raced a thousand miles a minute, and he paced around his apartment.

What if she decided she didn't want Silas to be a part of Fiona's life anymore? Didn't he get some sort of say in this? He skimmed his fingers through his hair, trying to ignore the clammy sweat that broke out across his skin. Silas stepped into his kitchen and started to knock through his full sink, scrubbing away at dishes as if that could shake his nerves. He paused to shoot Maeve a text asking when he could take Fiona next.

What if she said never?

His throat turned to sawdust. When he'd found out about Fiona, he had considered the news life-ending type shit—there went nights of hookups, bar hopping, and speeding along the freeway at three in the morning. However, the more time he spent around his daughter, the more he realized life was found in the smaller details. The tender warmth when he held her, the big, curious stare as she soaked in the world through brand-new eyes, and every tiny step along the way—even a simple smile.

His hands were wet with suds, his fingertips pruned by the time a knock sounded at his door.

He wrinkled his nose. Was Maeve back? Silas glanced at the clock above the sink and blinked, realizing an hour had passed while he'd been engrossed in the dishes. He wiped his palms on his threadbare jeans and went to answer the door. Part of him wanted to call off tonight and hole away with his worries, yet his feet seemed to drag him forward regardless. His mind still itched, and his phone remained silent as he reached for the knob and pulled the door open.

Taran stepped inside, carrying two bags of takeout that smelled like garlic and red sauce. "Hey," he said. He'd only gotten a pace inside when he turned to face Silas, his brows drawing together. "What's going on?"

Silas let out a helpless laugh. He didn't know if he'd lost his touch at keeping people out or if this man just knew him better than any damn person in his life. "Oh, you know, just a normal Tuesday, making a complete mess out of my life." He popped his hands into his pockets and rocked back and forth on his heels, panic leaking out of his pores at this point.

Taran walked over to the kitchenette and placed the bags down before he strode back over to him. "Considering your life's not a mess, I'll call bullshit," Taran said, his voice soft. He closed the distance between them and brushed his lips over Silas's. The sweet taste of spiced tea lingered on Taran's tongue, and the heat of his mouth offered the first tendril of relief since Maeve dropped the bomb on him earlier. Silas sank into the kisses, sweeping his tongue into Taran's mouth in lazy strokes as he let those heady sensations coast through him.

His breathing began to even, and his pulse began to calm.

The man was pure fucking magic.

When they pulled away, Taran slipped his fingers through Silas's and tugged him toward the kitchen. "If you want to talk about it, you can, or we can eat the dinner I brought over."

As if on cue, Silas's stomach rumbled. "What did you bring?"

"Picked up takeout from Alessio's," Taran said as he pulled out a few containers from the bags. "Hope you're in the mood for lots and lots of carbs."

His pulse pounded hard as he sank into the seat opposite Taran at his small kitchen table. Even though he still hadn't gotten a response to his text, Taran's presence quieted his nerves at once by the way the man didn't push him, and how he just settled in beside him had his heart lurching.

"Trust me, I'm always ready for carbs," Silas said, grabbing the proffered container and plastic utensils. When he popped it open, the savory, buttery scent of pasta carbonara wafted up at him. Silas snuck a taste, and a moan slipped past his lips at the saltiness of the cheese and pancetta. When he glanced up, Taran was watching him, those dark eyes nearly glowing with lust.

Silas's grin turned feral. "Hungry?"

Taran's tongue slipped out to trace his lush bottom lip. "You could say that." Before Silas could lean forward and close the distance between them, Taran pulled up his takeout container and dug a fork into the lasagna he'd picked up. "Good thing I came prepared." Damn, that smirk was cute as hell.

Silas took a few more bites of his carbonara before the words slipped from his lips. "Maeve thought she and I were getting together."

Taran froze mid bite, and Silas worked his jaw, regretting how he'd dropped it out there. He sucked in a deep breath and continued. "Let me clarify—we're not. However, she showed up today, assuming she was moving in."

Taran's Adam's apple bobbed with his swallow. "Dating her would be convenient," he murmured, his voice growing so quiet that Silas's chest throbbed. "After all, she is Fiona's mother."

"Fuck convenient," Silas growled, not caring if his words came out harsh.

"Isn't that what got you into this in the first place?" Taran replied, his sardonic smile not reaching his eyes.

Silas shook his head and grabbed Taran's hand, holding it tightly. "I'm not interested in Maeve. I want you, Tar."

Taran blinked, as if he couldn't register the answer, and the need to prove it to him drove into Silas.

He summoned his nerves and admitted something he hadn't told a soul before. "I've never had a real relationship before."

Taran's brows drew together. "Never?"

Silas shook his head. He couldn't explain how no one had ever wanted him beyond the façade he put up, how everyone just tolerated the distance he kept them at. As much as he had friends, barely any of them knew the real him. Maybe because if they did, they'd leave, just like his fucking father.

"You're different, okay?" he murmured, even though the vulnerability flayed his skin open, an itch that made him want to scratch. "I'm no one's choice for this, but if the alternative is not having you at all —I want to try."

Taran squeezed his hand, his brow smoothing as the hesitation in the air cleared. "I can handle that."

Silas's phone buzzed, and he reached down on instinct to check. Maeve had texted back.

Watch her tomorrow before your work shift. Next time you're off, she can stay overnight.

Relief prickled through him like a dusting of cinnamon. His shoulders sagged. "She still wants me to take Fiona."

Taran's lips quirked into a grin. "Fiona's lucky to have someone who cares as much as you do."

Silas swallowed hard, emotion welling up in his throat. Taran had this way of making him believe he was valuable—worthy—even if he could never summon those feelings on his own. "You won't be saying that when I fuck up her first time overnight here." He gave Taran's hand another quick squeeze before pulling his away and grabbing his container of takeout. "Why don't we move this over to the couch? I promised we could watch the Caps game, and it's just about to start."

"What sport are they from again?" Taran asked, lifting a brow. "The one where they toss a ball around?"

Silas lifted a middle finger even as amusement bounced through his veins. "You know it's hockey and that they use a puck."

"Do I though?"

Silas' rolled his eyes, grabbing his takeout container in one hand and extending the other to Taran, who quickly accepted. "If you didn't want to watch the game, why did you agree to that for our date?"

Taran's eyes danced. "Because I've got plenty to occupy myself with." The heated way his gaze swept over Silas made his comment crystal clear. "After all, I'm still hungry," he responded, not bothering to even glance at his food.

Silas placed his takeout container on the kitchen table, a smirk rolling over his lips. "Come on, beautiful." He tugged Taran's hand and led him over to the couch, his pulse speeding ahead. "Turns out, I'm starving too."

CHAPTER 17

Taran pulled up to Starlight Drive-In, finding a parking spot with ease. He'd been to this place a thousand and one times, and the showing of the *Evil Dead* trilogy had been enough to drag not just him but Nico and Sarah out as well. At least, those were the original plans he'd made a month ago before he'd started dating Silas.

Which meant Silas was coming tonight, and somehow, they'd have to pretend they weren't fucking. Sarah had already given him the side-eye for insisting on driving up alone. Considering they lived together, that was fair. And then Nico had offered to head up with him as well, and his brother definitely hadn't bought his "I want to leave when I'm ready" excuse for driving up himself, considering Taran almost always carpooled.

Still, things between him and Silas had been beyond good over the past week, and he didn't want to snap the ropes of the tentative bridge they were building. Fuck, on the night he'd slept over, it had been scorching hot when Silas had taken him over the side of the bed, the sort of passionate he didn't think they'd be able to repeat, even if it happened again and again. And then all week he'd continued to see the guy for lunch and spend time with his adorable daughter, when they either came over to Taran's apartment or headed to the park. He couldn't stomach being at Maeve's place with her parents there, knowing she had designs on Silas from the moment he arrived back to town.

Taran squeezed his steering wheel. Silas had reassured him whenever the doubts started creeping in, but he hadn't been able to dispel them completely.

Fuck, Silas had never even been in a real relationship before. What happened the second they had their first fight or life hurdles cropped up? With a kid involved, that was a guarantee. They weren't even telling friends and family about their relationship yet, which didn't inspire confidence. Granted, Cole already knew, and his best friend had lit up his phone for details the moment after they'd left the diner.

Taran sucked in a deep breath, trying to push the errant thoughts from his mind. The evening colors streaked across the sky, a hazy gold with gray-blue puffs of clouds interspersed throughout, casting the whole area in sharper shadows as the sun set. Already, a bunch of cars had pulled into the grass-and-asphalt lot, the white rectangular screen clear from all angles at the edge of the area. Taran's phone buzzed, and he slipped it out on reflex.

Here.

One word and Taran's pulse sped up. He and Silas had agreed to arrive early on the off chance they were able to steal a quick moment to make out before the movie started and everyone else arrived. He couldn't dismiss the illicit thrill that rose in him at the thought of those clever lips on his again, at surrendering to that sensual mouth and Silas's confident, competent hands. His cock stiffened to a semi in his cargos, and he took a second to adjust himself.

He skimmed the rows of cars until his gaze landed on Silas's black Kia. He tugged his keys out, slipped them in his pocket, and exited his Subaru. The air smelled like early summer—all fresh grass, asphalt, and motor oil. The screen and sound systems were already rolling, going through the old trailers handpicked for whatever feature movie they were showing. If it had just been him, Nico, and Sarah here, he would've been shushing them while he paid attention to the trailers too.

However, all he'd been able to think of today was

seeing Silas again. Getting to spend time with him at one of his favorite places in the universe. He wasn't used to that—a guy he dated showing any enthusiasm for his interests. Usually, Taran just shoved them in a corner or entertained them on his own time. He sidled up to the black Kia and leaned close to the window.

Silas rolled it down, a wicked grin on his lips. "What's a handsome piece of ass like you doing in a place like this?"

Taran wrestled with his smile. "Missed you," he murmured, the words slipping out before he could help himself. Shit. The second he started this needy bullshit, Silas was going to head for the hills. His smile fell, and he tried to turn his head to hide the shift. Silas didn't seem to notice, the click echoing when he unlocked his car.

"Come on in," Silas said with a suggestive wink.

Taran took the distraction the invitation offered him and slipped around to the passenger's side, sliding into the seat. Silas glanced over at him, his gaze landing on his shirt. A laugh slipped from his lips.

Taran tugged at the hem of his tee. "Like it?" he grinned back, placing the visual on full display— Boba Fett in a white coat with a pup in his arms and the caption "Boba Vet" below the picture.

"You're a dork," Silas said, leaning in to close the distance between them. "C'mere."

Silas gripped the front of Taran's shirt and brought him nearer. Taran pressed his lips to Silas's in a kiss that turned consuming all too quickly, as if a lifetime had passed since they'd seen each other and not mere hours. The scent of clove-and-leather surrounded him, making him ache, and he lost himself in the heat of Silas's mouth, the powerful strokes of his tongue, and the way this sweet, filthy kiss eviscerated his heart.

When they broke for breath, Taran's cock had already stirred to life, and if the bulge in Silas's jeans served as an indication, he was just as turned on. They hadn't fucked since the night he'd slept over, and his libido ran in overdrive at the idea of being able to fool around. If the thoughts appearing in his brain were any hint, maybe he did have a bit of an exhibitionist kink. Not like he would've ever considered it with any of his past boyfriends.

Taran pulled out his phone to check for messages from Nico or Sarah. All clear. "They're not here yet," he murmured, letting the thought dangle.

Silas's bright blue eyes sparked, those lips curling in a delicious smirk. "Are you suggesting what I think you are, Mr. Shah? How scandalous."

Taran cocked his brow at Silas. "Are we going to be a tease about this or are you going to unzip your pants and get your cock out? We're on a timeline."

Silas licked his lips, heat searing in the look he delivered. "Fuck yeah," came out hoarse. His hands went to his belt as he started to undo it with a jingle and the rasp of leather. "Did I mention it's hot as hell when you get bossy?"

Taran shook his head, unable to help the amusement that rolled through him, even as he watched Silas pull the zipper down and tug out his thick cock. Rock hard with a purplish head and a prominent vein down the side, the thing made his mouth water. He remembered how that hot length felt tapping against his prostate over and over again the other night, but he wasn't about to go that far at the drive-in.

Like this was much smarter.

However, when Silas hiked his jeans down his thighs and he saw the patch of thick pubic hair and heavy balls framing Silas's gorgeous cock, all his worries took second place to the hot lust flowing through him. The sun had mostly set, the shadows long enough that no one would be able to see much beyond their own cars. The movie had begun to play, the familiar opening of *Evil Dead* starting on the big screen, yet the main show was right in front of him.

Silas pushed back the seat and settled in place, giving his cock two strong strokes. He lifted his thick eyebrow. "I believe promises were made?"

Taran pursed his lips. "The only thing I said was to get your cock out."

Silas shrugged, giving him a teasing glance as he

gripped his cock tighter with another stroke. "Then I'll just get the job done myself."

Taran tugged at his arm, pulling it away. He gave one glance up to make sure no one was paying attention to them before he dipped below the dash. The tip of Silas's cock glistened with precum, and he licked it off, savoring the salty taste on his tongue. His cock grew stiff in his jeans as he leaned farther down and drew his tongue in a stripe along the firm length. Silas let out a shuddered breath, causing a grin to rise on Taran's lips. Truth be told, he loved sucking cock. There was a unique power there in being able to reduce a man to a quivering mess.

He teased Silas with slow licks along the length of his cock, inhaling the musky scent of him before he ducked even lower to capture his balls in his mouth, one at a time. He pressed one of his palms against Silas's thigh, and he braced himself with the other on the edge of the seat as he continued to suck Silas's balls, enjoying the sharp exhales and low groans that came from the man's mouth.

Taran pulled off from them and licked his way up Silas's erection. He brushed the tip of his tongue across the slit before swallowing the man whole.

"Fucking hell," Silas moaned, forgetting to be quiet.

Taran lifted his hand from Silas's thigh and thrust two fingers inside Silas's mouth, hooking them there to keep his mouth occupied. He began to bob up and down along Silas's cock, tasting the saltiness from his precum, drawing in the heady scent of him. The man's dick tasted delicious, and the hot length filled his mouth completely, spittle escaping as he focused on making Silas unravel. The man alternated between sucking on his fingers and biting, nipping at them, moaning around them as Taran picked up speed.

Slurping, smacking sounds filled the car as Taran focused on pushing Silas to the edge. He dipped down farther, taking more and more of Silas's cock in with each pass. Silas bucked up with his hips, and his fingers wove into Taran's hair, gripping tightly. He gave Taran's fingers a hard suck as he let out a muffled moan. Taran was tempted to rut against any available surface. His cock had grown so damn hard it throbbed, and the need to stroke it to release amplified with every pass up and down Silas's dick.

Taran lost himself to sensation as Silas's control snapped and he just *took*. His hips pumped up as he thrust into Taran's mouth, the head of his cock hitting the back of his throat. He gagged at first until they found a rhythm, and he focused on breathing through his nose. Taran crooked his fingers a little harder as Silas's moans grew louder, even with them muffled. Silas's thighs tensed, and the saltiness of his imminent orgasm burst in Taran's mouth.

A moment later, Silas's lips clamped around Taran's fingers, and his cock pulsed, his release spurting into Taran's mouth. Taran tried to swallow as much of the hot, sticky cum as he could, but some dribbled down the side of his mouth along with some spit.

Before Taran could pull away and lap the rest up, a sharp knock rapped at the driver's side window.

Taran yanked his fingers out of Silas's mouth, and a second later, the scent of leather surrounded him as Silas tugged his motorcycle jacket over his lap, covering Taran completely. Taran's heart sped a thousand miles a minute.

"Hey, Si," Nico called from right outside the door. "Open up, man."

Fuck. Fuck. Fuck.

Taran's mouth was still wrapped around Silas's softening cock, cum and drool dripping from his lips while his brother stood right the fuck outside. This. This was why people didn't do stupid-as-hell things like give guys blow jobs in the middle of a crowded drive-in.

Taran heard the *shiiick* of the car window rolling down. He slowly removed his mouth from Silas's cock, taking care not to rustle the jacket too much. Nico was the last person he wanted to find him like this—not only because fuck, it was his brother, but also after the way he'd gotten weird about Taran and Silas hanging out, he had the feeling his brother would flip his shit about them fucking around.

"What's up, Nic?" Silas asked, sounding a little breathless.

Taran smirked, even as he slid his tongue out to clean up the mess around his mouth. The leather jacket was a damn sauna, but he didn't dare budge, not with Nico right outside the car door.

"Have you seen Taran at all?" Nico asked. "I checked for him in his car, but he isn't there."

Taran swallowed hard. He should've been more careful. Silas shifted his hips, and Taran couldn't help but snap his fingers at Silas's thigh.

"Nah, haven't seen him yet," Silas said, his voice surprisingly smooth even though seconds ago he'd been moaning around Taran's fingers. Taran had been revving to go, but once he heard his brother's voice, his cock had deflated.

"Hey," Nico said, his voice lowering. Taran's warning bells pealed. "Look, I'm aware you guys have been hanging out more. And that's fine, but I just need to let you know—I'm pretty sure my brother's been crushing on you for ages."

Taran's cheeks heated. As far as mortification levels went, the constant reminder of his crush on Silas embarrassed the hell out of him, especially when he was plastered to his lap, an inch away from his spent cock, and hiding under his jacket. When had this become his life?

"Well, consider me flattered," Silas purred, and Taran jabbed him in the thigh again.

"Yeah, well, flattered or not, you know you can't go there, right?" Nico said, a weird tension in his voice. "Not trying to insult you, man, but you're a card-carrying member of the hit-it-and-quit-it club, and my brother isn't that way. At all. I just don't want to see him hurt."

Taran's chest seared with a mixture of irritation and warmth. Nico loved him and was just watching out for him, but he also didn't have the right to dictate his goddamn relationships. Taran tried to control his breathing, which was becoming increasingly harder to do in this sweat-soaked chamber of hell between Silas's thigh and his leather jacket. He took back every nice thought he ever had about the motorcycle jacket because it overheated worse than a faulty laptop fan.

"I'm pretty sure your brother's smart enough to make his own decisions on the matter," Silas said, in a level, cool voice that most wouldn't blink over. Taran knew better though—he could hear the slightest scrape there, the edge that hinted Nico's comment had pissed him off. Taran's heart fluttered at how Silas hadn't tried to back down or deny. Sure, he wasn't proclaiming their situation to the rooftops, but he never tried to tear Taran down.

"I don't know about that," Nico grumbled, and Taran's urge to wring his brother's neck intensified. "I mean, his last boyfriend was the worst sort of bro-douche."

"What, so you're going to start matchmaking for him? Considering your history, that probably isn't the best idea," Silas said. Taran couldn't help but squeeze his thigh in appreciation. "He's most likely back at his car by now. Why don't I meet you there in a second?"

Taran heard the thumping of knuckles on the car exterior.

"As long as you don't lose your dick into a stranger along the way," Nico called out. "He's parked a few rows back."

An annoyed prickle ripped through Taran at how Nico talked about Silas, but to be honest, Silas had been just as bad as his brother for years. Maybe he was the one being naïve here. This strange spell of seeing each other exclusively—especially considering he was Silas's first? Yeah, it unnerved him a little. But not as much as the rank fucking smell of fetid leather and drying spunk. Jesus fucking hell.

The *shiick* of the window rolling back up sounded, and a moment later, Silas lifted the jacket off him. Taran yanked himself into the passenger seat, making sure to stay down low in case Nico wasn't far enough away yet. He wiped around his mouth with his thumb to clear any remaining residue while Silas tucked himself back in and zipped up.

"Fucking hell, that would've been a hell of a way for Nic to find out," Silas muttered.

"Mark that down on the top ten things I never

want my brother to see," Taran responded, running fingers through his sweat-soaked strands.

"Holy hell, though." Silas turned his focus on him again, his smirk widening and those blue eyes ablaze. "Your mouth is fucking sin."

"Well, that's fitting, because hiding under your jacket is hell, so maybe that was my penance," Taran said, his tone droll.

Silas let a full laugh rip out, the startled kind that Taran had come to adore. "I'd offer to take care of you, but I'm pretty sure that ship has sailed."

"That ship has hurled itself into an iceberg, Titanic style," Taran responded. He glanced around to make sure Nico or Sarah weren't in the peripheral before he leaned in toward Silas and brushed his lips against his. Silas licked into his mouth, turning the kiss feral for a second, but then he let out a reluctant sigh, a puff of air against Taran's lips, and pulled away.

"I'd better get to my car before Nic sends out a search party," Taran muttered as he reached for the car door. Silas flashed him a grin, and Taran made a quick exit. Screams sounded from the big screen as Ash and crew began their cabin in the woods misadventure, but Taran headed for his car, hoping to cut Nico off at the pass.

Even as he quickened his steps, he felt the tug to return to Silas, to spend the rest of the night in his car, watching the movie with him—not as a group, but as a real date.

His heart squeezed tight, the knowledge sitting heavy in his chest that as much as he fantasized, stolen moments might be all he would get.

CHAPTER 18

SILAS FILLED HIS DENTED KETTLE AND SET IT ON THE burner, prepping tea, even though he only had some Tetley shoved in his barren cupboard. He bit back his smile because he could hear his mother's coos from here. He pulled a mug from the cupboard and glanced over at the living area where his mom sat on the floor with Fiona who was kicking to her heart's content on a patchwork blanket. His kiddo was having her first overnight with him, and he was not only petrified she'd somehow suffocate in her sleep but also dreaded the middle-of-the-night wake-ups.

When he'd mentioned to his mom that Fiona was over, she took it upon herself to bring some rotisserie chicken and salad and pay a visit. Her dark waves were streaked with gray and pulled back into a low ponytail, and the soft smile on her face made his heart clench hard. His mother had always been gentle, even after his father's rough edges and the difficulty of raising Silas on her own. The woman was a rarity in a world determined to harden them. And seeing her with Fiona made his chest light up with pure sunlight.

The kettle began to whistle, and Silas pulled it off of the stove to pour his mom a cup of tea. He brought over the steaming liquid, careful to take the long way around so as not to get near Fiona with the cup, which he placed on the coffee table.

"How is this child so damn pretty?" Mom asked, glancing up at him. Her green eyes sparkled.

Fiona must've been tuning into the praise because she chose that moment to give a big gummy smile. Silas couldn't help his own in return as he dropped to a crouch and let her clutch his finger.

"Superior genetics, obviously," Silas responded.

Mom squeezed his shoulder. "You were a beautiful baby too."

Silas's cheeks heated at the compliment. His mother was one of the few people he accepted them from. "Yeah, well, none of that is going to help me with making sure this child keeps breathing through the night."

"I know anything new can be intimidating, but this won't be as bad as you think, sweetheart," Mom said, pulling the steaming cup of tea from the table and taking a brazen sip. Spit-up already covered the sage green blouse she wore because Fiona had decided to imitate a fountain, but his mom hadn't even blinked. Silas had gotten used to the mess far faster than he thought he would too. Fuck, it was hard to stay irritated with the kid when she was handing out smiles like candy and making small burbly noises.

He leaned back and watched Fiona continue to wave her tiny feet in the air. Maeve had all but football tossed her at him when he'd shown to pick Fiona up. Ever since the misunderstanding, she'd been giving him one-word answers. Her parents weren't as cold with him, but they kept their distance. Silas should've felt more twisted up about the situation, but he could barely waste the effort, not when Taran texted him nonstop and they managed to see each other most days.

Fuck, the way that man had worked his way into Silas's bloodstream was like nothing he'd ever experienced.

The warmth that ached in his chest every time Taran walked into a room made him itch with a truth he wasn't ready to acknowledge. Not yet.

Mom leaned over and tapped Fiona's feet. Her tiny toes flexed as she kicked away at the air. "She's something special, Silas," she murmured, her voice filled with a pride that had him swallowing hard. Mom had never been cold—just busy because raising him on her own put her through the wringer. And he had never given her much to be proud of. Bad grades, fights at school, juvie for a hot stint. He'd pretty much broken the poor woman's heart, and all she'd ever tried to do was love him. However, the radiant warmth in her eyes for a situation he'd once thought was his ultimate fuckup—getting a one-night stand knocked up—well, he was coming to fast realize that Fiona had been worth it.

A rap sounded at his door.

Silas's brows drew together as he pushed up from the floor. Maybe Maeve was swinging by to drop something off for Fiona? He padded over on socked feet and opened the door.

Taran stood in the entrance. He'd dressed down today in athletic pants and a gray tee that said "My puns are" followed by a picture of a koala and a cup of tea. His dark hair was combed to the side, and the hesitation in those pretty brown eyes ensnared Silas.

"Hey," he said, lifting up a pair of baby monitors. "Sorry to swing by at random, but I saw you didn't have any of these around. While I know she's going to be staying in the room with you, I thought you might want the ability to duck out of your bedroom while she's sleeping without having to worry about not hearing her."

Silas's chest squeezed tight. Damn the man for being so fucking considerate. A creak sounded behind him, and the realization that his mother was in his apartment crashed in like a speeding car.

"Who's this?" she asked, stepping up beside him with Fiona on her hip.

Taran opened his mouth, panic flaring in his eyes. The poor guy looked like he was two seconds from lobbing the baby monitors into the room and then bolting in the opposite direction. Fiona let out a coo, breaking the quiet, and her face lit up at the sight of Taran.

"He's my boyfriend" slipped out before Silas realized what he'd said.

Well. Apparently, that was where he was at with this relationship.

Taran gaped at him as if he'd just stripped and run naked down the main street of Chesapeake City.

"A boyfriend?" Mom said, her green eyes crinkling with sheer joy. "Please, come in. I've got to meet the first person Silas has ever introduced me to."

Silas stepped back to let Taran in, waiting for the discomfort to set in, the "Fuck, I gotta run" nerves, but for some reason, he felt placid—afternoon sun over a lazy lake vibes. Far, far different from the wide-eyed fritz session going on with Taran. Silas bit back a smile. The guy was so fucking cute.

"What she said, Tar," Silas said, taking the baby monitors from his *boyfriend*'s shaking hands. Guaranteed his self-loathing would kick his ass later tonight, but something about his mother being here and his daughter smiling at the man like she already trusted him just had him blurting out the truth they'd both realized awhile back, the one Taran had allowed him to keep dancing around.

"We're boyfriends now?" Taran mouthed as he walked past him.

Silas flashed him a shit-eating grin. Taran rolled his eyes even though his smile twitched at his lips, threatening to burst free.

Taran walked over to the blanket they had spread out on the floor where Mom was again kneeling to let Fiona keep kicking her way to contentment. His daughter reached up and grabbed Taran's finger, gripping tightly as she offered him a gummy smile.

Taran's expression melted, and damn if that didn't *do* things to Silas's heart.

"Hey there, sweetheart," Taran murmured, reaching down to stroke the soft dark strands off her forehead.

Mom glanced up to meet Silas's eyes, her eyebrows raised. She bobbed her head in an approving nod. Silas's throat squeezed tight. He wasn't shocked Mom would love Taran after spending two seconds around the guy. Who wouldn't? The man was toothache sweet, even though the more Silas had gotten to know him, the more surprises he'd uncovered.

"So, boyfriend of my son's," Mom said, fixing her gaze on Taran. "I'm Beth."

"Taran," he offered as he passed her a grateful

grin.

"How long have the two of you been together?" she asked, glancing between them.

Taran snorted and a second later tried to cover it up with a cough.

Silas plopped on the floor with all of them. "A few weeks now," he said. "We're still pretty new." Taran's eyes widened, and then tremulous delight flickered across those features. Silas met his gaze and nodded. He'd counted from when they'd agreed to do this for real.

Taran had let him set the pace so far, but Silas also needed to start stepping up. The more time he spent around Taran, the less Silas wanted to keep their relationship secret, even if he might never feel like he deserved someone as pure as him.

Fiona had been smiley and happy one moment, but a second later, her small features screwed up and her face turned red as she began to bawl. Taran dove in before Silas even got the chance, scooping her up and starting with the rock and sway he'd perfected. His nose wrinkled.

"Someone needs a change," he said. "I've got it."

Silas shook his head, ready to argue when he saw the way Taran's shoulders were still tensed—if he needed the second to collect himself, he'd give it.

Taran rose and bounced Fiona the whole way over to Silas's bedroom. "Come on, munchkin. Let's get you situated."

The moment Taran disappeared into the room, Mom leaned in toward Silas and batted him on the head. "When were you going to tell me you started seeing someone?"

"When I finally admitted to myself he was my boyfriend," Silas muttered, spearing his fingers through his hair.

Mom smacked his shoulder this time. "I've only met him for a few minutes, and I already know he's not someone you want to give up, Silas. Did you see how sweet he was with your daughter?"

Silas's smile rose unbidden at the memories of just how good Taran was with Fiona. Every time he saw them together, it made his chest warm. He'd never found the trait sexy before, but somehow seeing Taran all competent and in control like that got his motor revving.

Taran wrapped up with the change in record time and popped back out of the room with a fresh and clean Fiona. "Not sure where you want this stink bomb," he said, holding the wrapped diaper in his free hand.

"Shit," Silas said, hopping up to scoop the refuse from his hand and deposit it in his kitchen trash. "I guess that's something else I need to order."

Taran shook his head. "Pro tip: just use plastic grocery bags. I'm sure you've got a few around here somewhere, and it'll keep the mess from stacking up."

"Where did the two of you meet?" Mom asked, her green eyes dancing with eagerness.

"We were at the same high school," Taran said, turning on his polite charm. "Silas was in the same grade as my brother Nico."

"Where were you hiding all that time?" Mom took a sip from her tea.

"Oh, I was there," Taran murmured. An almost indecipherable note emerged in his soft tone, one that took Silas a moment to identify. The sharpness of the yearning stole his breath away. Silas hated himself a little more as he stood witness to the powerful feelings Taran had harbored all these years that he'd been blind to. How had he not seen Taran for the clever, wry, and devastatingly gorgeous man he could be?

"I was just looking in all the wrong places," Silas admitted, the confession heavy on his tongue.

Taran swallowed hard, those brown eyes filled with hesitant emotions. Silas wanted to close the distance between them and claim his luscious mouth, to show the man that he'd meant what he said the one way he knew how, but that would get way beyond PG fast, and he wasn't about to go there with his mother over.

"Are you working at the Chesapeake Days festival this weekend?" Mom asked, pushing herself up from the ground. "I'm going to get myself some more tea."

"Friday and Sunday," Silas said, tapping his fingers on the floor. He reached out for Fiona, and Taran passed her over, the current between them so easy he wondered how he'd existed without a comfort like this. While his mom busied herself in the kitchen, he leaned in, his voice low. "Sorry for surprising you like that."

Taran ducked his head, a shy grin on his lips. "Don't ever apologize for a surprise like that."

Silas's heart thudded a little harder. Fiona sank her little claws into his skin, scratching away as she nuzzled against him. "Let's keep rolling out the surprises then. I was planning on taking Fiona to the festival on Saturday…. Do you want to come with us?"

Taran blinked in surprise. "Like a public date?"

Silas's throat dried a little with nerves. He wasn't anyone's idea of a catch—his life was a fucking mess, and he should push Taran in the other direction to let him find someone better. Yet, he couldn't seem to pull away from him, no matter how hard he tried. "Yeah," he said. "If you want."

Taran nodded furiously. "I want."

The pristine joy in Taran's dark porter eyes reflected back at him. He had put it there. Silas King, fuckup of Chesapeake City. Just being around this man made him feel stronger in ways he'd never anticipated.

Strong enough to take a chance on them.

CHAPTER 19

The Chesapeake Days festival always brought a level of frenetic energy to the town every year of the sort Taran tried to avoid. However, when his brother's and Hudson's became the headlining restaurants for the festival with their Chesapeake Eats collaboration, Taran summoned himself out the door and into the fray each year, even if he wanted to hide away in a dark cave afterward. With the festival being a few blocks away, he'd have to fight hard to avoid it anyway.

This time, Taran didn't need any push to get out the door.

Taran tugged the bottom of his pale blue polo, wondering if he should've just gone with a T-shirt and jeans. But before he could go back and change, a knock sounded at the door.

"Who's here this early?" Sarah asked from the kitchen.

"I've got it," Taran announced, already heading toward the door. Silas's mom and Cole might know about them dating, but he hadn't broken the news to his brother yet, and Sarah had a big mouth. He sped to the entrance of their place, checking his pocket for wallet and keys as he went. Taran swung the door open, and Silas and Fiona were waiting for him on the other side. At the sight of them, a thousand butterflies burst inside him.

Ever since the other night at Silas's place, this devastating sort of hope was building in his chest, unasked for and certainly uninvited. The kind accompanied by a timer and a bomb because he'd never been able to hold onto anything this good for long.

"Ready to go, beautiful?" Silas asked. Silas leaned in and placed a brief kiss on his lips, only interrupted by Fiona reaching out to grip his shirt tightly and yank.

Taran resisted the urge to swoon, though his knees were bad bets at the moment. He detangled Fiona's chubby fingers and took a second to admire the small blue hat and summery blue-and-white polka-dotted outfit she had on. Silas looked delicious as always in a weathered pair of ripped jeans and a black tank top that showed off his muscular frame and the tattoos Taran had spent plenty of time tracing with his tongue. Except this time, Fiona was situated in a baby carrier where she rested on his chest, and somehow that made the man even hotter.

"Bye, Sarah," he called out to his roommate. "I'm heading to the festival."

"Tell Nic I said hi," Sarah shouted back.

Silas's lips crooked into a smirk as he shook his head. "Your roommate relationship is weird as shit."

Taran stepped under the sunshine, the beams seeping into his skin. "So says the man with no roommates. We both dig our space—it's worked for us for five years now."

Fiona let out an excited burble as they headed down the sidewalk, and she reached out to tug on his sleeve. Taran's heart squeezed tight. He'd been half in love with Silas King from high school on, so it was no surprise his daughter had burrowed her way into his heart in record time.

Already, he could hear the shouts and laughs from a few streets over, and cars lined the streets on either side, everyone heading to the closed main street where the businesses in town had set up stands to show off their wares. The food was always next level, and this year for Chesapeake Eats, Hudson and Nico had worked together on an entirely new menu, this one a product of their joint venture—Compass Enterprises.

The sky overhead was the sort of blue that hurt, a perfection rarely reached, but with Silas and Fiona at his side, for once it felt within his grasp. A comfortable quiet settled between them, one Taran basked in. With too many people, he needed to verbally vomit all over the place to put them at ease—either that or total silence, but being around Silas felt more comfortable than he could've ever imagined.

Silas might've been center stage in all his high school fantasies, but nothing about those sex-crazed, horny imaginings of his youth came close to the amazing reality. Because, while their sex was next level scorching, he'd never anticipated the depth of emotion in all their interactions. Silas had always seemed like he coasted through life without a care, but Taran had sensed the man was a loaded grenade waiting for the pin to be pulled.

As they rounded the corner onto the main street, the wall of noise slammed into him. People crowded the streets—midday on a Saturday brought out everyone en masse, and at this point, the boat parade would've already begun.

"What did you want to do at the festival?" Taran asked. The question that stuck to the roof of his mouth was what they'd do when they stopped at the Chesapeake Eats booth, because he'd get skinned alive if he didn't swing by.

"Grab food? Wander around?" Silas shrugged, the motion lifting Fiona in her little carrier in the process. "The last time I came home for this festival, I was nursing a wicked migraine and had apparently just knocked up Fiona's mother, so clearly, I wasn't in the mood to participate."

"Well, I'm thinking it's pretty easy to avoid that route this time," Taran responded. "Food would be good. We could head to Pell Gardens and find a spot under the trees a little ways from the water line, since that's where everyone will be crowding."

"And coffee," Silas punctuated with his finger, pointing to the awning for Chesapeake Brew's stand. "Definitely coffee."

Taran grinned even though his nerves pulsed at the idea of running into anyone he knew. Silas had declared them boyfriends—it was all he'd ever hoped for, but now he was the one filled with nerves. When they'd been in limbo, he'd been able to attempt to lie to himself that he wasn't getting attached, but the second Silas went and proudly announced their relationship to his mother, Taran's ship had sunk. All those hesitant hopes he'd been barely pinning back came flooding in, and then anxiety decided to give him helpful reminders, like how well his relationships always went or just how quickly the people he cared for could get taken away.

He reached over and ran his fingertips across Fiona's soft strands. She lifted her chubby fists up, and a second later, she gripped his finger tightly again. Taran tried to yank it back, but she fought him with an amused look in her eyes. "When does she need to get back for her next bottle?"

"We've got a few hours before meltdown commences," Silas said, tugging at the strap of the diaper bag on his shoulder.

"Damn, babies are the perfect excuse to escape crowds," Taran replied with a grin.

Silas shot him a look. "Is this you going along with something you're not a fan of again? Thought I made my point clear that you can always say no."

Taran shook his head. "No. I mean, yeah, I don't love festivals and crowds, but I'd be heading here anyway to pay Nic a visit. And going with you and Fiona is worth it." He hated how his voice grew hushed at the end there since he was incapable of keeping the emotion out of those words.

They stepped into the line for Chesapeake Brew, which teemed with people. He spotted Nate and Rachel manning the line with bright smiles from Nate and snarky ones from Rachel. In the back of the tent, Linc and his son Beckett bustled around, restocking cups and carrying bags of coffee over to line the front tables. Nate worked through the crowd so quickly that Taran didn't even have time to think of how to approach them before they were stepping up to place their order.

"Hey, guys," Nate said, his big blue eyes sparkling with excitement. If anyone in the universe had golden retriever energy, it was this man. "Good to see you. Swinging by for coffee or just to say hi?"

"Definitely coffee," Silas said as he fidgeted with

Fiona's hat. "Large for me, and—" He paused to glance at Taran. "You want chai, right?"

Taran's heart just about leapt out of his chest at that. He'd never realized how astute this man could be and how much Silas soaked in details about him. That sort of consideration was something he'd never experienced in a relationship before. Taran nodded.

"Right, and a large chai tea for him," Silas said.

Nate glanced curiously between them, a grin playing on his face as he pulled out two cups. Taran's gaze zeroed in on his finger. More specifically the gold band around it.

"Wait… you're engaged?" he asked.

Nate bobbed his head, just about exploding with rainbows and kittens. He glanced at Linc who shot him a smirk from feet away where he was working on stocking more cups. "Just yesterday."

"Well, fuck," Silas swore, then clapped a hand over his mouth as he caught sight of Beckett there. "I mean far out? Shit."

Taran snorted. "What he means to say is congratulations."

Silas pursed his lips and shot him a grateful look. "Yeah, that."

"Dad, when do we get to go see the boats?" Beck asked, tugging on Nate's sleeve.

Nate beamed down at him and rifled his hair. "Once we get these guys their coffee, I think it's safe to go on break. Rach, you should have backup here in a few. Leo's coming in to help out today."

"Shoo," Rachel said as she placed the cup of coffee and the cup of tea in front of Taran and Silas. The punky employee then waved Nate off. "I can manage fine without you."

"Thanks," Nate said, looking just as eager as Beckett to escape.

Linc snuck next to them as they were fixing up their drinks. "Don't think I missed the whole cozy vibe going on here. Does Nic know?"

"That we're dating?" Silas said, the bluntness a mixture of reassuring and nerve-wracking. "Not yet, but we'll tell him soon."

Damn, this was every secret hope Taran'd been holding onto when he'd run into Silas over the years. He found it hard to shake the surreal feeling that he might wake up out of a dream at any moment.

"You better," Linc said with an entertained grin. "You know how protective he gets."

"Like an enraged honey badger," Taran responded. "We're well aware."

He and Silas exchanged a glance, amusement flickering in their gazes. The last time Nic brought his protective side out had been awkward as hell, considering Taran's mouth had been stuffed with Silas's cock. Taran coughed into his hand to try and re-center his attention, otherwise he'd get an inconvenient hard-on in the middle of this conversation.

He clapped a hand on Linc's shoulder. "Congrats to you and Nate though. You guys are meant for each other."

If his well-wishes came with a side of yearning so strong he might as well just carve his heart out? That was for him to keep to himself.

"We'd better get going," Silas said as Fiona began to do her shimmy shake that meant a fuss was on the way. "Good seeing you guys."

"Want me to take a turn with Fiona?" Taran asked. Not like Silas couldn't handle her, but Fiona always quieted down faster around him, something he didn't dare mention out loud. To be fair, he'd always had luck with charming babies and old folks —just never hot guys he was super into. Until now. Goddamn.

Silas nodded. They found a spot to put their drinks down, and a second later he unstrapped Fiona from his chest, and Taran popped the harness over his shoulders and slipped the little girl into place. Silas rolled his shoulders and then stretched his arms up overhead, flexing those sexy-as-hell muscles. Taran settled Fiona in her new vantage point, the shift enough to calm her down. He gave her his finger to latch onto, and in that moment, he was careening for the two of them harder than he could handle.

This quiet peace, the shared partnership with a little one—this was everything he'd dreamed of in private and rarely shared, because dreams in his hands quickly turned to dust. Or sulky horror movie marathons.

"I guess we better go tell my brother," Taran said, wrinkling his nose. His stomach flip-flopped at the prospect. "If Linc and Nate know, word is going to spread like wildfire."

"Don't sound too excited," Silas responded, a slight shadow in his eyes that snagged Taran's attention.

Taran elbowed him in the side. "It has everything to do with my brother being dramatic. I'm honored to be your boyfriend." That statement paled in comparison to the giddiness that erupted inside him every time he said the word. He swallowed down all his joy so he wasn't grinning like an idiot as they walked along. "And don't worry about it on the boss front. As much as my brother might get pissy about us dating, I'd never let him jeopardize your job."

Silas cast him one of those sultry looks he'd perfected a long time ago—pure cocky confidence. "Who said I'm worried?"

Taran let that look roll through him, mingling with the adrenaline coursing through his veins. Lately, all he'd been doing was taking leaps, and he wasn't sure if he could keep up the pace. Yet, after spending so long paralyzed, he wanted to ride this wave as long as he could.

He patted Fiona's stomach as they walked along,

and she waved her fists around, babbling to herself while they headed in the direction of Chesapeake Eats. The big banner stood out at the end of the street, and the surrounding massive crowds showed off just how successful his brother's venture had become. His brother who had told Silas to steer clear of him. As much as he had promised Silas it would be okay, he had no clue how Nic would react when they let him know.

Truth be told, Taran was still reeling from how fast Silas went from no relationships ever to telling everyone he saw that they were boyfriends.

Part of him was waiting to trip and fall into a chasm.

"Are you sure you want to go to Chesapeake Eats?" Taran asked. "I mean, you just worked there all of yesterday. We could go to Eliza's instead." Hopefully, Silas wouldn't see the freaking-the-hell-out energy he was broadcasting. As if Fiona sensed it, she grabbed his finger again, squeezing tightly.

Silas reached over and pinched Taran's nape in a possessive move that made him shiver. "Definitely want to go to Chesapeake Eats, especially with the way you're terrified of telling your brother," he teased. "Come on, beautiful."

Taran's heart pounded as hard as the midday sunshine, and those words bolstered him like nothing else. He nodded, and they took their place in the busy line. Already, he caught sight of Nico and

Hudson manning the bar and grill setups, along with several other employees. He skimmed the crowds around him, all heat and chatter and the rich scents of sunscreen, grilled meat, and fried dough.

Silas stiffened beside him. Taran glanced in the direction he was looking, and his gaze landed feet away.

Kevin approached with a slender, model-gorgeous guy in tow. Taran's stomach dropped at the sight of his ex. He didn't miss Kevin in the slightest, but the last he'd seen of him had been a few weeks ago when he'd begged him to show up at his family's dinner at Port of Call. Had he already been hooking up with this guy? Shame flushed through him in a fierce torrent.

"Hey, Taran," Kevin said as they took their place in line behind him. They were moving closer and closer to the front, but he couldn't get there fast enough.

"Kevin," he said, forcing a smile. He didn't miss the way Silas's jaw clenched and how his deep blue eyes flared.

"Come on, now," Kevin said, the cajoling tone in his voice scraping at Taran's nerves. "Don't be all standoffish like that. I thought we agreed to be friends."

Taran swallowed hard. He hated, hated, hated being a pushover sometimes. If he wasn't such a chickenshit, he would've just told Kevin to fuck off.

"Who's this, babe?" the boy toy asked.

"My ex-boyfriend," Kevin replied, wrapping his arm around his boy toy's shoulders.

"Him?" the guy asked, his voice filled with disbelief.

Oh, screw him. Taran tensed, ready to snipe back.

Kevin leaned in and lowered his voice. "There was a reason we broke up."

Taran's jaw dropped as those words slammed him right in the chest.

In one moment, Silas was by his side.

In the next, Silas's fist hurtled toward Kevin's jaw.

A crack echoed through the area, the gunshot sound shattering the chatter around them.

"Fuck you," Silas spat. Kevin staggered back, clutching his jaw. "That man is the best damn person you'll ever meet, and you were a fucking idiot to give him up. Can't say I'm not grateful though, because now that he's mine, you can bet I'm not letting him go."

Taran blinked, his eyes burning as gratitude rushed through him. No one had ever stuck up for him like that before. No one.

"What the hell?" Kevin hunched over, and his boyfriend fluttered around him making soothing noises. "I should call the cops on you."

"What's going on?" Nico's voice cut through. His brother had stepped away from the bar, and most of the crowd waiting in line turned to look in their direction.

"The asshole made a shitty comment about my boyfriend, so I let him know how I felt about it," Silas responded, ripping the Band-Aid off then and there. Taran's chest swelled, too many feelings overwhelming him at once.

He stepped up beside Silas and leaned in to press a kiss to his cheek. "Thank you."

Nico's jaw dropped for a moment, but a second later, he shook his head, a grin rolling over his lips. "Nothing to see here, folks," he called out, lifting his hands up. "This guy just tripped and fell." He shot a glare at Kevin. "You were a dick when you were dating my brother, and it looks like that hasn't changed. Get the hell out."

Silas shook his fist out. "Fuck, I'm probably not setting the best example for my daughter, am I?"

Taran snorted. "I don't know. I think I'd pay money to see you punch out assholes at the PTA meetings in your future."

Kevin muttered something under his breath, but he quickly exited the scene, his new bimbo boyfriend in tow. Taran's heart still raced a thousand miles a minute as he turned to face his brother.

"So...." He squeezed Fiona's little socked feet for courage. "We were coming over here to tell you."

Nico's broad grin surprised him. He'd been expecting a frown, a warning, or some big dramatic statement after the hesitance he'd seen from his brother regarding the two of them. "I've never, in all the time I've known Silas, heard him call someone his boyfriend or girlfriend. What sort of magic did you pull, Tar?"

Silas leaned in and squeezed his shoulder. "Guess I just never met anyone worth taking the risk for until him. You know how it is."

Nico met his eyes, his expression softening as he glanced at Hudson. "Yeah, I get it."

Silas's phone began to ring. He checked the screen and mouthed, "Got to take this" before stepping away for a moment.

Taran nodded but then realized it was just him and Nico here in the middle of the line, no more buffers. "So, no shaking your fist in warning?"

Nico glanced over at Silas, his dark eyes crinkling with his smile. "If you guys were just fucking around, yeah, I'd have warnings aplenty. Not just because I know you've already gotten attached to him, but guaranteed, you're gone for this little girl too," he said, leaning in to brush a finger against Fiona's cheek. "But I'm serious when I say that in all the time I've known the guy, he's never seriously dated. So, if anyone's going to stand a chance at breaking through his issues—it'll be you."

The words should've been reassuring, but they hadn't discussed those issues. Taran wanted to be the one who deviated from the pattern so, so badly, but he understood more than anyone how hard those emotional habits were to break. For fuck's sake, he'd made a big stink about no more boyfriends and that had lasted for all of five minutes.

He could feel Silas approach again, but when he turned in his direction, his chest sank.

Something was wrong.

Silas's expression was drawn tight, his gaze thunderous, and he brimmed with tension.

"What happened?" Taran asked, the tide of anxiety nipping up to his toes, fast threatening to overtake him.

"That was Maeve's parents," Silas said, his voice hoarse, quiet. Despite the buzz of sound around them, the flurry of activity, Taran's gaze zeroed in on the man before him as he awaited the next words out of his mouth. He had a feeling deep in his gut that they were about to change everything.

"She's gone."

CHAPTER 20

Silas's fingers shook as he strapped Fiona into her car seat.

Taran had offered to come with him, but Silas couldn't bring him to Maeve's parents' place—not when he needed to figure out what the hell they were talking about.

Not dead. She wasn't dead.

That was all he'd gotten from Mrs. Johnson before she'd told him to come over and then hung up.

The coziness he'd been wrapped up in today—the bright sunlight, the way his heart swelled while he was strolling around with Fiona and Taran, and the fucking vindication he'd felt at decking Kevin—all of it shattered with a single phone call.

Fiona began to cry, her eyes screwing up and her face flushing.

Silas swallowed hard. "Me too, sweetheart, me

too," he murmured. He hopped into the driver's seat of his Kia and took off down the street, heading up the crowded road to park closer to Maeve's parents' place. The short drive didn't offer enough time for Silas to collect his thoughts or even begin to process what was going on. His brain had just sort of numbed over, one loop playing on repeat again and again and again.

The taste of grape bubblegum soured his tongue the way it did every time his mind reverted to that day.

Knees skinned from playing in the park, skin lightly burned, and he'd run into the house to tell his folks about the caterpillar he found at the park.

Six fucking years old.

Mom slumped on the couch, head in her hands, shoulders shaking. She wouldn't respond.

He'd checked every room of the house—no Dad.

He'd even gone outside, but Dad's truck wasn't in the driveway anymore. Little did Silas know it at the time, but Dad's truck wouldn't ever be parked in the driveway again.

Silas's car puttered to a stop in front of the house where he found street parking. The bubble of bliss from earlier had shattered, and now he was just left with this empty, aching wondering, a dread that rose by the minute with no end in sight. Fiona had grown quiet, and chances were, she was probably taking a nap, which would soon be rudely awakened when he plucked her out of her comfortable spot. He chewed on his lower lip, clutching the steering wheel as he stared vacantly out the window.

He sucked in a sharp breath and pulled the key from the ignition. Time to face this.

Silas checked the backseat where Fiona had passed out. Fuck, she wasn't going to like this either. He tried as gently as possible to extricate her, but the moment he plucked her from her cozy car seat cocoon, she began the initial tremble that led to the first wail. Silas hugged her close to his body, swaying her back and forth as he walked up to Maeve's parents' house. His heart was thundering so loud that for once he could barely hear Fiona's cries, which had already begun to simmer down by the time he reached the door.

Silas lifted his knuckles and knocked.

A shuffle sounded, followed by hushed voices, and the door swung open.

He'd met Maeve's parents a few times before. Both of them looked like your typical upper-middle-class country-club types—starched polos and pressed blouses and pasted-on smiles—but today the façade was gone. Deep lines etched their faces, the grave expressions telling him everything he needed to know. He clutched Fiona a little tighter, as if he could shield her from this blow.

"She said she was running out to the grocery store," Maeve's mom said, a tremble in her voice as she handed over a piece of paper. Silas stood there, not even entering the house as he skimmed the note.

I can't do this anymore. Don't come looking for me—I'll be fine on my own. Whether Fiona goes to you guys or to Silas, I don't care. I'm just not meant to be a mother.

Love, Maeve

His hands trembled as he read those lines again and again and again. Fiona nuzzled into his chest, and the simple motion shattered his heart.

"She left," Silas said, the words sounding like they came from a stranger.

The reality still hadn't crystallized in his mind, a pervasive numbness trickling through his veins.

Fiona just kept rubbing her face in his chest, blissfully unaware.

Unaware that the woman who gave birth to her had just abandoned her.

Unaware that her whole future was now in limbo.

Unaware that she'd been left behind.

"We don't know where she went," Maeve's father said, his voice hoarse. "We looked around her room, but she didn't leave any clues."

The thump, thump, thump in Silas's ears grew louder and louder. He'd just taken Fiona for her first overnight, and it had been *hard*. He'd been watching her in chunks, segments—never the whole time. Never all at once.

Yet, if Maeve was gone…

He was all she had.

"We will do whatever we can to help," Maeve's mother said. "If you need anything—some extra funds, babysitting—we'll try and help you get settled. We'd… still like to see our granddaughter."

Silas nodded, his mind sailing full speed toward Antarctica. He'd already been thrown for a loop in finding out he was a father—but all of a sudden, he'd be raising her 24/7. He'd gone from skating along with the bare minimum of responsibility, floating from one apartment to the next, one hookup to another, one restaurant to a new one. And now he was the full-time parent of a three-month-old.

Unprepared didn't begin to describe it.

Where was she supposed to go when he needed to work? Maeve had never even given him the name of her pediatrician, let alone most of the other things he should know. The night he'd done the overnight, waking up a few times throughout to feed Fiona—that wouldn't just be an occasional thing. It'd be his new reality. His fingertips numbed, but still he clutched his baby tightly.

He glanced down at her and realized with a start that her next bottle would be coming up soon. Fuck. He needed to get her home and take care of her. While he'd fed her plenty over here in the past, Maeve had always been around before her parents returned. He felt like an intruder in this place, especially while they were trying to digest the fact their own daughter had disappeared.

"Look, I've got to go home and feed Fiona," he said, feeling so damn distant.

"I know you don't have childcare at the moment, and you still have a job to go to," Maeve's mother said. "We can watch her when you work while you figure out what you want to do."

"Thanks," he murmured even though he could barely process what they were saying. "I'll bring her over tomorrow when I'm due in."

He trudged out of the house, not looking back to soak in the shattered faces of Maeve's parents. Her departure had been a frag grenade for all three of them, and he didn't have the capacity to pick up their pieces. The only thing he could focus on was the fact that he needed to get Fiona fed. If he tried to think beyond that about anything else, that this wasn't just an overnight visit tonight, he would teeter close to a full shutdown. He strapped Fiona into her car seat and took off back in the direction of his apartment.

Silas only had a few minutes' drive—everything was nearby in this town—but part of him just wanted to hit the open road and sail down the highway at top speed. The feeling of a noose around his neck had dissipated as he'd gotten to know his daughter, but it descended big-time now. How had his mother done it? How had she raised him by herself? He pulled into the parking spot and tried to quiet the roaring in his head that swelled louder and louder with every passing second.

Fiona had begun to fuss, and the sound sent him spiraling over the ledge. Silas gripped the wheel, staring vacantly out the car window, unmoving.

Maeve was gone.

He was Fiona's only parent.

Fuck, fuck, fuck.

A knock rapped on his window, startling him. He glanced to the side to see Taran standing there, a hesitant flicker in his deep brown eyes.

Silas shut the car off and opened the door.

"Look, you can tell me to go home, and I won't be offended," Taran started. "But the last thing I wanted to do was leave you hanging when you're dealing with something big. Even if it's just helping feed Fiona while you handle what you need to."

Silas stared at him. Maeve had left just like his father—ditched because life got too hard. Yet here was this amazing man who showed up when life got hard. Even when he didn't have to. Nic and the others might give Taran shit for being weak, for helping people who didn't deserve it, but damn, that took some sort of courage. His eyes burned, and a hot, shameful tear slipped out, trickling down his cheek.

Taran's eyes widened, and he leaned down and brushed the tear away with his thumb. A moment later, Taran's lips pressed against his, not with any demands, but with smooth, comforting strokes. Silas sank into the feel of Taran's hot mouth against his, the way he cupped his cheek, the way he grounded him even when he was spiraling out. The taste of tea lingered with each stroke of Taran's tongue, each press of their lips together. Even though his mind swirled, his fingertips still numb, he existed in this kiss, this connection, which kept his feet on the ground.

When Taran finally pulled away and waited for an answer, Fiona's "I'm hungry" cries beginning in the back, Silas summoned his words.

"Please stay," he murmured.

Taran nodded and headed to the backseat of the car, opening the door and already starting to get Fiona's car seat out. The way the man stepped in without needing direction, how he came to his aid with no questions, needing no answers—the wall around Silas's heart had cracked open a while ago for Taran Shah.

Together, they headed to Silas's front door in silence interrupted only by the sounds of Fiona's fussing as she made her demands for food. When they got in, Silas didn't even need to direct him—Taran headed for the kitchen and started getting her a bottle prepped. Silas took Fiona to the bedroom and began to change her diaper, focusing on the process rather than indulging in the way his mind was spinning.

Within minutes, Fiona was changed, and Silas settled onto his couch while Taran brought the bottle over. His throat squeezed tight with his swallow as the tiniest hint of relief threaded through him. Even if all Taran did was sit in the room, his presence here helped. In a moment where Silas should feel utterly alone, this man filled up his empty spaces.

Fiona chowed away at the bottle, and Silas sank into the couch a little deeper, his mind whirling. Taran settled in beside him, but he wasn't pushing or even shooting questioning glances his way. He just offered silent support while he sat next to Silas. As Fiona continued to pound down the formula, Silas found the words coming from his mouth unbidden.

"Maeve left her parents a note," he said, staring at a crack in the hardwood floor. "She doesn't want to be a mom, so she ditched."

"Oh, fuck," Taran breathed out.

"No idea where she went, so it looks like I've got Fiona full-time now," Silas muttered, trying to stave off the persistent burn in his eyes, the threat of more tears impending. Just a month ago, he'd barely been able to wrap his mind around the idea of having a daughter. Now he had to face the reality that he was the only parent here.

Unless he ran off too.

The thought smacked him in the face with guilt, and bile rose in his throat as he stared at Fiona. She clutched the bottle, her chubby cheeks a bright pink as she stared up at him with those earnest blue eyes.

Fuck, she deserved so much better than the cards she'd been dealt.

Silas glanced Taran's way, and the realization slammed into him full force. She wasn't the only one who deserved better. "Look," he started. "I know you didn't sign on for this…."

Taran's brows lifted, and he gave him a sharp look. "You'd better not be trying the martyr route with me, Silas King. I'm the ultimate martyr, and I won't tolerate being dethroned."

Silas sucked in a deep breath. The fierceness in Taran's tone surprised him, but he needed to get this out. "Yeah, but you started dating someone who was co-parenting, not taking on a kid full-time. Everything's going to be different."

"Are you saying that for me, or for you?" Taran asked, those words slicing like a razor. "Because I knew what I signed up for the moment I started dating someone with a kid, whether you had her full-time or not."

Silas's argument dried on his tongue. He wanted to lash out, to push him away on instinct, but the firmness in Taran's tone made it clear he'd see through all of his attempts. The confusing jumble of emotions threatened to overwhelm him, and his eyes stung again for about the thousandth time since he left Maeve's parents' place. He gazed down at Fiona, who hadn't looked away from him once, those big eyes fixated on him.

Silas tilted his head back, relaxed into the couch, and stared at the ceiling. Taran didn't say anything else, but he reached over and rested his palm on Silas's thigh. Silas swallowed at the wash of relief the comforting touch brought. Fuck, he wanted to be better than this. Taran deserved someone who wasn't going to use him, who put him first. Silas couldn't do that when he had to prioritize his daughter's needs. For one brief moment, he'd believed he might be able to balance it all.

And then Maeve left.

The thought still made rage burn in his chest, but it was soon chased by the hollow tang of bone-deep grief that his little girl would grow up never knowing her mother. His stomach clenched hard at the memory of his father's cigarettes, how their smell had lingered in the house long after he'd ditched. Until they didn't anymore, and no matter how much Silas tried to recapture the phantom scent, it was as gone as his father.

"The last thing my father said to me was that I was nothing but trouble," Silas said, not even recognizing his own voice. All he could hear were those rough words, the low tone, the disgust there.

Taran's stance shifted, but he didn't look at Silas, as if he knew some fraction of what this admission cost him. How his skin itched like he was covered in hives, and his heart ached like someone had taken a hammer to it.

"When did he leave?" Taran asked, his voice soft.

The lump in Silas's throat grew, and it was a miracle he managed to speak. "When I was six. Came home from the park and saw he'd ditched, no warning. Apparently, he jotted down a note, but my mother still hasn't told me what it said."

"And now Maeve is doing the same thing," Taran murmured. Silas managed a nod, but he didn't trust his voice. Silas clutched Fiona a little tighter to his chest.

Taran leaned in and pressed a kiss on Silas's cheek—soft, gentle, and so pure, his heart ached. His lips brushed over the shell of Silas's ear as he whispered. "You're so much more than trouble, Si. If he couldn't see the protective, loyal, and passionate person you've always been, then he didn't deserve you in the first place."

Silas's eyes burned, and another tear trickled down his cheek. Fuck. He hated feeling this weak. Yet, those simple words from Taran wrapped around his heart and squeezed it tight.

No one had ever viewed him that way.

This man hadn't just seared himself into Silas's bones but branded himself on his very soul. He'd never met another like Taran Shah, and he knew deep down, he never would. As much as he'd tried to keep his distance, he'd fallen head over heels for him.

Taran pulled back, but instead of going to his side

of the couch again, he leaned against Silas's shoulder. Silas cradled Fiona in his arms, feeding her the bottle, and the warmth in his lap, the heat of his boyfriend by his side—for the first time since he got the news, he managed one long, deep breath.

Here in this bubble, maybe he could dare to believe that he could conquer this, one day at a time.

CHAPTER 21

Taran stretched as he sat in the stiff wooden seat at Chesapeake Brew. It had been comfortable at first, but after spending hours in the chair, his entire body was aching. Either that, or the sleeplessness had caused it. A week had passed since Maeve had left, and while her parents stepped in to help watch Fiona when Silas worked his shifts at Port of Call, his boyfriend was still adjusting to taking care of this little girl every night. Taran had made the call to take a week off work. He stockpiled more vacation days than anyone else and never got the chance to use them, so when he'd asked, they'd been quick to grant his request.

However, today Si was home with Fiona, and Taran decided to work through some of the bugs and comments coming up from Barter's beta launch. He'd already helped Silas set up a profile on it because if his boyfriend could find an exchange for some steady childcare, that would make a huge stride in starting to feel stable.

The screen glared at him, and when he stared out the big glass windows, the sun barely registered. Taran lifted his cup of tea to his lips and took a sip, this one still warm since he'd just ordered his third. Or fourth? No wonder parents always looked like zombies. The kiddo wasn't the worst sleeper on the planet, but the wake-ups that happened a couple times a night threw him for a loop. Si kept telling him to go home and get some real sleep, but Taran couldn't pull himself away.

Silas had never asked for his help, but he'd be getting it anyway. The fact that Silas never asked him left a deep imprint. Out of all the guys he'd dated, Silas was the one without an agenda. He wasn't trying to use Taran like a responsible-boyfriend prop, and he wasn't trying to score some free babysitting. If anything, he'd tried to push him away, to do this on his own.

Silas's care, his fierce protectiveness, and the tender way he looked at him—all of it was real.

For the first time, Taran wasn't some caricature or playing some part.

Silas *saw* him.

"Tar, how's the beta going?" Nate asked as he strolled over.

Taran glanced up, blinking a few times to clear

the spots from his eyes. Damn, he needed to take a walk or stretch or something. He forgot what a hunched over recluse he became when he got sucked into a project like this. At least he'd forced himself to work out in public instead of holed up in his room.

"I'm getting a fair amount of participation," he said, rubbing his eyes with his palms before looking over at Nate again. "There are already some bugs I've been trying to fix, and a few design flaws pointed out that I need to tweak too. Like with the bartering aspect. If the offered service wasn't a clearly stated category, people were using the 'other' classification to send dick pics. And if someone wants to barter sex for things, that's their own prerogative, but this isn't the site for that."

Nate peered over his shoulder and let out a low whistle. "I always knew you were smart, but this is next-level stuff. You should be super proud."

Taran flushed and gripped the back of his neck. "It's just a project I was tooling around with for fun. Not like I'm rescuing puppies out of trees or curing MS."

"Yeah, but you have no idea how helpful that'll be for people who do trades or hobbies and need services. I mean, Linc could trade some quick jobs for things we need, and that's really unique." Nate rested his hands on his hips. "Plus, it's a great way for the community to get to know each other a bit better."

Taran's smile warmed. "I'm glad you get it. While this town does talk and most folks know one another, people aren't always comfortable with bartering like they used to be. I was hoping this could change that. It's why I put in the radius aspect to keep jobs local."

Nate glanced at the door, but there were only a few folks scattered around the coffee shop in seats. None of them were approaching the register. "How is Silas doing? We heard about Maeve running out of town."

Taran worked his jaw. Silas hadn't reached out to talk to anyone about the situation, but in this town, news spread like wildfire. While Silas had opened up on that initial night and the raw anguish had cracked Taran's heart in two, he'd gotten quieter ever since—more subdued. The man's world had been upheaved, almost as much as it had when he'd found out he had a daughter in the first place. Taran could be patient.

Yet sometimes he couldn't help the trickle of fear that Silas would shut him out entirely.

That he'd decide having a relationship on top of all this was too hard, so he'd cut the cord.

"If you don't want to talk about it, that's okay," Nate rushed to say.

Taran shook his head, a wry smile on his lips. If anyone's anxiety could give his a run for its money, Nate's could. "He's surviving. I mean, that's all you can do in that sort of situation, right?"

"If he needs anything, though, you'll let us know,

right?" Nate said. "Both Linc and I tend to be home on weeknights if he wants help with Fiona. I'm sure Beck would be thrilled to have a little munchkin around for a while."

Taran's heart squeezed tight. Nico and Hudson had offered Silas days of leave if he needed them, a flexible schedule, and whatever they could do to assist him with this transition. Taran loved his friends, big-time. He shouldn't have been surprised they'd rally like this. Mama had cooked Silas enough food for weeks, which Taran brought over at once.

"I'll make sure to tell him," Taran murmured, meeting Nate's eyes. "Thank you."

The front door jingled, and both their gazes swept in that direction.

Silas stepped inside with the baby carrier on and Fiona solidly in the center. Even though Silas still rocked the leather jacket, his hair windswept and stunning, and the snug fit of his jeans placed that stunning ass on display, the sight of him with the baby carrier enhanced the protective vibe he had going on, and that alone made Taran's heart soar. Fiona wore a sunshine-yellow hat to shield her from the sun and waved her tiny arms around. The little girl had already won Taran over from the first moment he held her.

"Is he summoned like Beetlejuice if you say his name three times?" Nate asked, his eyes dancing.

"Only on Tuesdays," Silas said, his smooth-as-sin

voice sending a pulse of warmth through Taran. Even though Taran knew what strain the man was under, in public Silas was all casual smiles and jokes, same as always. Only Taran saw the toll this had taken on him.

Silas swept up next to him, the rich scent of his cologne an immediate comfort. Taran glanced at him, not quite sure how to handle public situations still.

Silas solved it for him when he leaned down and gave him a sweet kiss on the cheek. "Hey, babe."

Taran's heart fluttered at the casual affection, which was enough to make him swoon. He was so gone for this man it terrified him. He reached up and offered a finger to baby Fiona. "Taking her on a walk?"

Silas nodded. "Thought we'd get out of the house and pay you a visit. How's work going on the app?"

Taran pushed his laptop a few inches away. "It's all troubleshooting at this point. I'll probably be able to launch Barter in a couple of weeks."

Fiona let out a happy burble, her eyes crinkling with the newfound smiles she'd discovered. Taran's heart thudded harder at the sight. Nate leaned forward, cooing at the baby and playing with her chubby fists.

"I think I've got a bite from the profile you set me up on there," Silas said. "A stay-at-home mom was interested in trading weekly meal prep for taking Fiona during some of the weekday hours."

"You know I can help on any weekends," Taran jumped in. The last thing he wanted was for Silas to feel like he needed to shoulder all of this on his own.

"Yeah, but they're your weekends," he said, his eyes darkening a shade. "You're already giving up some of your vacation time to help me get adjusted."

Nate looked back and forth between the two of them, as if sensing the slight strain in the air. "I've got to go man the register." A quick glance told Taran no one was there.

"Yeah, but we're a team," Taran murmured, his voice soft.

"I'm not going to be another asshole out of the long line of them to take advantage of you," he snapped. Taran flinched, and Silas's expression softened as he continued. "Look, this isn't me pushing you out. But you deserve the best. Definitely better than this mess."

Taran crooked a brow as he leaned on the surface of the table. "I'm pretty sure I'm the one who decides what I deserve. And picking the guy who cares about me, the one who's willing to fight for me when I might not be able to—yeah, that's no hardship at all. And I adore both you and Fiona."

Silas leaned down, and this time, his lips brushed over Taran's. Taran melted into the kiss, even with Fiona finding and clutching the neckline of his T-shirt. As Silas tried to pull away, Taran let out a laugh and untangled her little fingers from the fabric.

"How are things going with Maeve's parents?" Taran asked. Their plans and intentions had been a massive question mark ever since Maeve vanished last week. Not only were they reeling from their daughter's disappearance, but they'd made it clear they didn't want that to mean Fiona left their lives as well.

Silas's brows drew together, and a little divot appeared between them. "They're... enthusiastic about helping out with her. I think we're still trying to figure out where the lines are. My mom's been excited to come help too. She already volunteered to pitch in and watch Fiona whenever she can."

Taran tilted his head in Nate's direction. "Same with Nate and Linc."

Silas ducked his head, a brief flush rising to his cheeks. "I don't get why so many folks are jumping in right now."

Taran's throat squeezed tight. In getting to understand Silas, one core fact had emerged every time—the man had seemed to take his father's final words to heart.

"Because they care about you, Si," Taran said, reaching between them to weave his fingers with Silas's. "Because more people see the real you than you think."

"They're clearly all insane," Silas muttered, even though he squeezed Taran's hand tightly. The charged air hung heavy between them for a moment, and quiet descended.

"Well, that is a requirement for living in this town," Taran responded eventually, the dry sarcasm cutting through the silence. "Check your sanity card at the bridge."

Silas flashed him a crooked smile. "You're something else, beautiful."

Those damned butterflies returned every time Silas called him beautiful, every time he looked at him with that genuine expression. Taran was so far gone for this man that his brain had begun imagining scenarios he normally didn't permit—lazy mornings together, walks in the park with Fiona, nights of horror movie marathons after they put Fiona to bed, or fucking each other into oblivion before they fell asleep. The coziness of the picture overwhelmed him, the ache persistent because it was every damn thing he'd been looking for. And if this app took off down the line, he might even be able to quit his job, giving him a more flexible schedule.

Silas kissed the top of Fiona's head, and Taran fell in love all over again.

The longing in his chest threatened to drown him, and fears were tugged in the wake—that this was Silas's first relationship. That they were too new.

But the worst fear was the lesson he'd learned years ago in his own family.

That anything this perfect was destined to break.

CHAPTER 22

A few weeks had passed since Maeve had left, and by some miracle, Silas kept pulling through each day.

The exhaustion was enough to drag him to his knees sometimes, but he still got to work and made sure his daughter was fed and had slept. Taran stayed by his side through it all. He honestly wasn't sure how he would've managed any of this without the man. He hated how much he'd come to rely on him—he didn't want to be another asshole taking advantage. However, the more time that Taran spent with them and he, Taran, and Fiona all coexisted in each other's lives, the more a steady warmth blossomed in his chest.

A stability existed in the routine they'd begun to develop, one he'd have bolted from a year ago. Even though he couldn't look too far ahead without wanting to internally scream, he'd come to appreciate the quiet moments with Taran. The quick kiss before heading off to work, or the way they both sagged into bed together after a long day and curled up together. And whenever they got the opportunity, their hands were on each other's bodies, whether it was a quick suck or jerk, or he had the chance to pin Taran down and fuck him into oblivion.

Silas sat on his bed, rocking Fiona back and forth to get her to sleep for the night. The little girl had conked out, snoozing steadily enough that he was about ready to transfer her to her bassinet. The slightest sounds snagged his attention because Taran would be coming over any minute now. He'd spent his Sunday morning with them, but then headed over to his mom's for dinner, an invitation he'd extended to Silas and Fiona as well.

Silas had declined. As much as he wanted to meet Mrs. Shah as Taran's boyfriend, he didn't want her to see him as this hot mess who'd just become a single parent. Guilt still weighed him down too. Maybe if he'd sucked it up and tried to fake a relationship with Maeve, his daughter would still have her mom around. The thought caused his stomach to clench, but he couldn't shed the insidious tendrils of guilt, like he could've done something more to make her stay.

Fiona's eyes were firmly clamped shut and light snores were coming from her small mouth, so he lifted her up and settled her into the bassinet. She barely moved as she lay there on the mattress, fast asleep. Silas switched on the monitor, grabbed the other one, and headed out of the bedroom, closing the door behind him.

A creak sounded as the front door opened, and Taran stepped inside.

Silas swallowed hard at the sight of him. He'd dressed down tonight in jeans and a maroon tee with "Have you tried turning it off and on again?" across the front. His ink-stain hair was swept to the side, and those dark brown eyes filled with a warm affection the moment they landed on him. Silas was a hundred-and-one percent sure he'd never been in love before because he'd never felt anything close to this for another human being.

Being with Taran was like sitting under a sky full of stars in the middle of summer—a slice of the infinite within his grasp.

Silas had been circling around telling him these past couple of weeks, not wanting to be selfish and burden him with these feelings. Yet for some reason, the sight of him tonight had those words leaping onto Silas's tongue.

He'd always believed falling in love would be difficult, that dating someone would be the ultimate burden. He'd learned from the best when dear old dad ditched.

However, being with Taran? The support, the effortless affection, and the way the man lightened his heavy moods with humor—none of it was the nightmare he'd once perceived a relationship to be. This man made everything in his life easier, even when there were uncertainties or they butted heads.

"Hey," Taran said in a low voice, heading over to Silas.

Silas met him midway, crossing the room until they were a step away from each other. Silas grabbed him by the fabric of his shirt to pull him in close and planted a kiss on his lips, tasting the strong spice of tea as he sank into the heat of his mouth. A shiver ran through him at how right this felt, how perfect. When everything else in his life was falling apart, this was the one thing going well. The truth terrified him, yet he couldn't deny those feelings anymore.

When he pulled back, Silas didn't relinquish the grip on Taran's shirt. "I love you," he said, his voice surprisingly steady.

Taran's eyes widened with surprise. "Are you sure?"

A laugh escaped Silas as all the nerves evacuated his system. Of course that's how Taran would respond. Before Taran could work himself up into an anxiety spiral, Silas stepped in. "Yeah, I'm damn sure."

Taran's jaw worked for a second, a flicker of disbelief in those pretty eyes. Silas reached between them to cup Taran's cheek, brushing his thumb across his cheekbone.

"I... love you too," Taran murmured, his cheeks warm with a blush. "Though I'm guessing that isn't a shock, considering both my best friend and brother spilled the beans that I've had a thing for you next to forever."

Silas shook his head. "Crushes are different than reality though. This between us? It's all real." His heart thudded hard at putting those words out there in the open. That he'd admitted them to anyone, and that someone had genuinely returned the sentiment. He wasn't a lovable guy. Rough around the edges, known for lashing out and making bad decisions. Never in a thousand years would he have believed someone so good, so pure as Taran Shah would take an interest in him and they'd actually work well together.

"Are you sure you weren't body snatched or something?" Taran asked, his gaze searching. "The Silas King I knew was not only anti relationship but would never dare say those three little words out loud."

Silas shrugged. He'd spent so long fighting the idea of letting anyone in, yet Taran had slipped in with no effort, like he'd always belonged by Silas's side. "A lot has changed in a short amount of time. Makes you reevaluate your priorities."

Taran nodded, even though a flicker of doubt flashed in those chocolate eyes. Before Silas could reassure him, Taran lifted the bag he still carried in one hand. "Mom told me to bring you more food. In case you had a hankering for samosas or goat stew."

Silas crooked a brow. "I won't turn food down, but I've got a hankering for something different." He didn't bother to hide the heat in his voice.

After his confession, he felt like he'd stripped down and stood on display, skin taut and ready to get sliced into. He needed to feel Taran's body against his, to lose himself in the man's warmth, to solidify the connection between them in the best way he knew how.

"Oh, yeah?" Taran asked, his voice coy as he placed the bags of food on the kitchen counter. He glanced over his shoulder at Silas, those lust-drenched eyes his undoing. Silas prowled toward him, placing the baby monitor on the kitchen counter alongside the food. He sauntered behind Taran and gripped his hips tightly, closing the space between them as he sank his teeth into Taran's shoulder. His cock stiffened at the sweet moan coming from Taran's lips, and he leaned in to nudge his erection against that sexy-as-sin ass.

"You look fucking edible," Silas murmured, the tip of his tongue darting out to trace a line along Taran's neck. With the way they were pressed against each other, he could feel the man's shiver, the motion fueling the furnace within him. "I want your cock in me tonight."

Taran froze.

Silas's heart pounded hard. "That's only if you want. If it's not your thing, that's completely okay," he murmured in Taran's ear, trying to soothe the man.

Taran turned to face him, but Silas kept his hands around Taran's hips. Any distance between them felt like too much right now. Had he overstepped tonight? Was Taran not feeling this as much as he was?

"I'm into it," Taran responded, his voice hoarse. "I just didn't think that's what you did. With anyone."

Silas swallowed hard, the truth causing his skin to prickle. "I don't."

Taran looked at him, his gorgeous chocolate eyes so lost, a little helpless. "Why me?"

The realization crashed over him. Taran wasn't pushing him away—he was just dealing with the damage all those assholes he'd dated had inflicted. "I want to murder every last bastard who told you that you were boring, or weird, or not fucking enough," Silas growled. He tipped his forehead against Taran's. "You are *everything* to me, Taran Shah. I didn't date anyone because everyone just wanted the image of me. You managed to see the real thing. And I've never bottomed for anyone because I've never trusted anyone enough to let them in. I've never told anyone about my dad's last words to me—not even my mom."

Taran's eyes widened, and they grew a little

glossy. "I've wanted you for so long that I can't believe this is real. I feel like any moment now, I'm going to wake up in my bed, alone, and this will all just be some fantasy. How was I invisible all those years and now you're suddenly seeing me?"

The fragile tone of his voice broke Silas's heart, and he swallowed hard. He wrapped his arms around Taran and brought him in close until they were chest to chest, and Silas rested his chin on Taran's shoulder. "Because I was so angry back then, not sure if I wanted to prove my father right or wrong. I've had time to reflect since then, I've had time to fuck up plenty, and I've had time to start to see what's important. So, I might not have seen you then, but I see you now."

Silas felt the tremble that rushed through Taran.

"Fuck, I love you more than you'll ever know," Taran murmured. The certainty in those words reassured him like nothing else.

"Back atcha, babe," Silas said, drawing in a deep inhale of the amber-and-sandalwood cologne that would forever remind him of Taran. He nestled deeper into the crook of his neck and pressed his lips to the side of Taran's neck, feeling the flutter of his pulse. Silas continued to explore the expanse of soft, warm skin with his lips, his tongue, his teeth. With each nip and lick, Taran sank against him a little more until a low moan escaped his lips.

"Couch tonight?" Taran asked between heavy breaths.

"Hell yes," Silas breathed. The idea of having Taran thrusting inside him sent a secret thrill up his spine. He hadn't bottomed before. Not because he wasn't curious, because he'd fucked himself with toys plenty—but he hadn't been lying—he'd never trusted another soul like he did Taran. A jittery rush traveled all the way to his fingertips at the prospect of doing this here, with him. Silas sank his teeth in the crook between Taran's neck and shoulder, eliciting another moan before he pulled back. "Let me go grab the lube and condoms from the bedroom."

Taran nodded and stepped away from him, already heading for the couch. Silas walked into the bedroom as silently as possible, trying not to even let the floorboards creak as he navigated around Fiona's bassinet where she lay swaddled and sleeping. One wrong noise could end the night early. The lube and condoms were in the top of his nightstand, and he managed to retrieve them both with minimal sound. He paused on the way through to check on Fiona, whose chest rose and fell in slumber, before heading back out of the room.

When Silas closed the bedroom door behind him and looked up, he stopped.

Taran stood behind the couch, resting his palms flat on its back. His shirt was off, putting those lithe abs on display, the light glinting over his nipple piercings. His jeans were still on, but the top button was undone and the zipper down, making the bulge of his cock very, very clear. His night-dark hair was mussed, and an intensity lit his eyes that drove Silas wild.

Silas couldn't help but lick his lips. Fuck, he was so turned on right now.

"Get over here," Taran said, a command in his voice that surprised Silas just when he thought he couldn't get any hotter. "I'm going to bend you over this couch and fuck you until your legs are shaking."

Every time. Every damn time he thought he knew all there was to know about Taran Shah, the man threw him a curveball. And this was one ridiculously sexy, bossy curveball.

"Fuck yes."

CHAPTER 23

Taran braced himself against the couch.

His cock was beyond hard, his heart still racing, and his mind whirling with the possibility spread before him.

Silas loved him.

Silas *loved* him.

Giddiness threatened to overpower everything, even if the surprise of the admission had scared him half to death. Disbelief still tickled the edges of his mind, yet the sight of Silas approaching him scorched everything else away. All he could see was this gorgeous man heading toward him, tattoos peeking out of his black tank top, ripped jeans clinging to that fuckable ass, and his feet bare. Silas's ocean blues were a little bit wild, a little bit vulnerable, and the sight stole Taran's breath away.

Never in a thousand years did he think Silas

would let him top. Knowing he was the first? He wanted to make this unforgettable.

Silas slunk over to him, each movement oozing seduction as he sidled up to Taran and licked a stripe up the side of his neck. Taran swallowed hard, the sinful sensation coursing through him. As much as he loved being at this man's mercy, he loved to be the one calling the shots even more.

Taran reached between them and unsnapped the button of Silas's jeans, following with undoing the zipper. "You're overdressed for this party," he murmured against the shell of Silas's ear as he dragged the man's briefs and jeans down. His palm skated over that hot skin, brushing along the hair of his thighs, the thatch of pubes surrounding his cock, but never actually touching his erection. Taran's dick was hard as hell in his jeans, but he didn't pull his pants down yet as he thrust against Silas's bare ass.

"This needs to go too," Taran murmured, dragging Silas's tank top up and over his shoulders. It hit the ground as well, and then the man was bare as hell and looking like a work of art. Taran rested his palms on Silas's hips and centered himself behind him, drawing his tongue up Silas's spine in one slow roll before sinking his teeth into his traps. Silas let out a loud moan he tried to swallow when he glanced at the door.

"Fuck," Silas cursed, thrusting his ass back again. "Why is you being bossy that fucking hot?"

"Because," Taran said, continuing to place nips along his shoulders, up his neck, enjoying the way he shivered, "someone's got to bring your wild ass in line."

"Yes, please," Silas moaned, gripping the back of the couch. Taran plastered himself against Silas's back as he reached around to pinch his nipples first, eliciting low curses from Silas. He then trailed his fingernails down along those washboard abs, his cream skin and the dark lines of his tattoos such a mesmerizing sight. He continued to stroke down-ward, close to but never touching his cock. The glisten of precum on the tip might make his mouth water, but Taran was having far more fun unraveling Silas King.

He might've spent half of his high school career eye fucking Silas's ass, but none of that compared to having those muscled glutes backed right up against him. Taran's heart jackhammered as he continued to run teasing strokes along Silas's chest, enjoying the steady stream of curses that came from the man's mouth. This wasn't just a casual fuck for him—he wanted to make this memorable for Silas, to somehow communicate the love that bottomed his stomach out, that sent him reeling every time the man walked into the room.

Taran leaned in until his lips brushed against Silas's ear. "Bend over, ass out."

Silas glanced back, a flash of surprise in those pretty blues.

Taran's mouth quirked as he descended to his knees behind him.

He grabbed Silas's cheeks and spread them open, revealing his pretty pink pucker and putting it on display. The man's earthy musk was delicious, and if Taran wasn't already hard, he'd be bursting through his jeans. As it stood, the layers of fabric were driving him nuts, but he was nothing if not patient. He leaned in and drew his tongue along the perineum, taking his time as he licked a stripe all the way up until he skated across the tight bundle of muscle.

"Holy hell," Silas breathed as his grip tightened on the back of the couch.

Taran reached up to clutch Silas's hips hard and then dove in. He attacked Silas's hole with his tongue, alternating between lapping at the ring and thrusting his tongue inside. Garbled noises poured out of Silas's mouth to the point where he needed to bite on his fist to keep quiet. He loved watching how responsive Silas was, how he didn't try to hide himself away here in this space between them. Taran used tongue and light nips with his teeth as Silas's entire body quaked.

When Taran started to drive his tongue in more, Silas thrust his hips back in time. Taran soaked in the sight of his man coming undone before him, his one hand white knuckling the back of the couch. Based on the muffled sounds Silas made, he was sinking his teeth into his fist so hard it would leave marks. Taran's heart squeezed tight at the possessive thought, and suddenly he needed to sink deep into Silas right now. He wanted to bury himself inside the man until they were so connected they'd never be able to be severed.

Taran pulled back and flattened his tongue against Silas's hole, giving it long, slow strokes that had him panting.

"I need you inside me, babe," Silas gasped as his legs trembled. "Fucking hell, that feels… ungh."

Taran dragged his tongue down, bringing its tip across the perineum again in precise licks that brought a fresh new string of hushed expletives from Silas's mouth. He shifted back and dragged his palm across his aching cock still covered in denim. Taran squeezed Silas's hips as he rose from his knees. He pulled his zipper down and leaned past him to snag a condom and lube from the couch.

"Oh, thank fuck," Silas cursed. Even though he was attempting to keep quiet, he was the most vocal lover Taran had ever been with, and he adored it. Everything about this man made him fall a little harder in love. Taran swallowed the lump in his throat at the realization as he pulled his jeans and boxer briefs down to his thighs before rolling a condom over his cock. After a few long strokes, lube coated his length.

Silas stood before him, ass thrust out in invitation as he clutched the back of the couch with a desperation Taran loved.

"Need something, Si?" Taran purred.

Silas looked back and arched his brow. "Where the hell is my pure, sweet boyfriend, and who's this filthy-talking, bossy sex god?"

Taran smirked. "Don't know what you're talking about. I'm simply asking a question."

"You know what I goddamn want," Silas shot back.

Taran closed the space between them to press his length against the crevice between Silas's cheeks, but then he reached around to pinch his nipple. He stroked his fingers down Silas's side again, enjoying the shuddering response. His cock protested, but he was having far too much fun to rush in.

"Fucking tease," Silas muttered. He softened and stared back over his shoulder at Taran, those intense blue eyes locking in on him. "I need you inside me."

Taran swallowed hard. The flash of vulnerability there did him in—by far the sexiest thing he'd ever seen. "Let me prep you first."

"My fucking god, Taran Shah, if you try to prep me, this is all going to be over before it starts. I'm ready for you." Silas thrust his ass against Taran's cock in a clear demand.

Taran reached between them and ran his fingertips in a few teasing circles around Silas's rim, which was enough to cause the man to jerk forward.

"I'm two seconds from just coming all over the couch," Silas said, bracing himself to the point his knuckles turned white. Taran didn't miss the sheen of sweat on Silas's forehead whenever he glanced back.

Taran lined the head of his erection with Silas's hole and slowly pushed in. Silas sucked in a sharp breath, and Taran waited until his breathing returned to normal before nudging in a little farther, making it past the initial tight ring of muscle. Silas reached back, grabbed Taran by the hips, and slammed himself the rest of the way onto Taran's cock in one, smooth stroke. The squeezing heat surrounding his cock had Taran's eyes rolling back in his head.

"You feel so damn good," Taran said, his voice coming out low. He sucked in a sharp breath and began to move, pulling away before sinking back in with a little more force, testing out the stroke and rhythm. The man's tight heat was perfection. Taran was likely to blow faster than anticipated from sinking into this pure, scorching heaven. Silas's breaths came out quicker as Taran picked up speed.

"Hell yes," Silas moaned, the husky tone of his voice sending a shiver down Taran's spine.

Silas thrust his hips back in time with Taran's movements, taking him as deep as possible. Sweat pricked on Taran's brow, a drop tickling him as it trickled down his cheek and slid down his neck. He snapped his hips forward as he buried himself in Silas's sweet ass again and again and again. The way they joined together shattered him, a completeness that filtered through his entire body. He'd never experienced anything this powerful before in his life.

Fucking Silas King was a goddamn awakening.

He'd had good sex before, but the connection between them enhanced each thrust, each moan, each brush of his hips against that lush ass. His mind spun with the headiness of the sensations as he drank in the scent of sweat and cloves surrounding him and sinking into his very pores. Taran wove his fingers through Silas's hair and tugged the silken strands as he fucked him harder. Silas gripped the couch, his fingers digging into the fabric as it shook each time Taran thrust into him. Smacks and grunts filled the air, a melody Taran lost himself in as pleasure coursed through his veins.

Taran's cock was ready to blow, and based on the quickened breaths from Silas, he was just as close. His balls drew up, and he let out a shaky breath. Taran reached around to wrap his hand around Silas's cock, feeling the wetness of precum at his tip.

"Come with me." The command was effortless as he stroked Silas in time with his thrusts, the smack of their skin, the snap of his hips, and the heady moans taking him to unparalleled heights.

All too fast, Silas was coming, clenching around his cock as he spilled on Taran's knuckles. The way

Silas's channel squeezed him tight took Taran over the edge. His orgasm swept over him like a spring storm, bliss saturating him from head to toe. His release flooded out of him, and he floated on the waves of ecstasy as he gripped Silas's hair in one hand, the other on his hip, curling over him as he came.

Their sharp breaths sounded through the room, only interrupted by the crackle and pop of the baby monitor. Taran came back to earth, the carpet soft on his bare feet and Silas's cum cooling on his knuckles. He leaned down and pressed a kiss to Silas's back, his heart squeezing tight. He didn't want to pull out. If he could, he'd stay buried here forever, even if that might make life awkward as hell.

"Goddamn," Silas breathed out. "That was…."

"Yeah…," Taran agreed as he slowly drew his cock out. He took the few steps over to grab a washcloth from the kitchen cabinet and ran it under warm water. He tied off his condom and tossed it in the trash before returning to Silas's side. With the warm washcloth, he took his time cleaning them both up, his strokes careful. When Silas finally pushed up off the couch, his legs were quaking.

Taran's lips curled. "I keep my promises."

Silas scanned him, his gaze a lazy, heated caress. "Damn right you do." He plunked onto the couch and crooked his finger. "C'mere."

Taran couldn't help but obey. He kicked off his

boxer briefs and jeans the rest of the way and sank next to Silas on the couch. The man's arms wound around him, and he was tugged in to cuddle with his back pressed against Silas's chest. He sank into the cocoon of warmth, their sweaty legs tangled together on the couch. They reeked of sex, and Taran drank in the musky scent.

"I definitely wouldn't mind doing that again," Silas murmured, his lips brushing against Taran's neck. "You've made me a bottoming convert."

"I'm glad it was good for you," Taran said, his voice wavering with the realization that he'd been Silas's first.

"Everything's good with you," Silas mumbled against his shoulder, his voice growing slow and tired. The words caused Taran's heart to throb. He reached for Silas's forearm and clasped it tight, his eyes welling up from the intense emotions rolling through him.

Silas had always been the unattainable one, the daydream he'd never thought would be fulfilled.

Yet here he stayed, pressed against him, loving him in a way none of his boyfriends had done before. The sheer care and tenderness Silas showed, his passion, his loyalty—all of it was everything Taran had ever hoped for. He sucked in a shaky breath.

All of this—Silas sweaty and pressed up against him, their takeout abandoned on the counter, and

Fiona asleep in the bedroom—this was the future he'd always dreamed of.

This, here.

Taran gripped Silas's arm a little tighter.

And now that he'd seen it, what terrified him the most was the idea of it getting ripped away.

CHAPTER 24

Silas raked his fingers through his hair as he stepped up onto the walkway to Maeve's parents' house. Exhaustion weighed on him big-time today. Fiona had slept like shit last night, so both he and Taran had suffered. And then the early shift at Port of Call had been one mess after another—broken plates, burned dishes, and enough irritated customers to put everyone in the back of house in one hell of a pissass mood.

He was just grateful Maeve's parents were still willing to watch Fiona. But for how long? That was another headache he'd been trying to coordinate—childcare, or how half of his paycheck would now be going to pay for that, unless the Barter deal he'd started figuring out pulled through.

His little girl was worth it, though, and the thought of bringing her home and Taran joining them at his apartment later—fuck, that had his heart racing.

Silas didn't bother knocking. He turned the knob and stepped inside of the Pier 1 chic place that he still didn't feel comfortable inside. How they managed to deal with an infant in their house which looked more like an art gallery half of the time was beyond him, but he appreciated the help while he had it. There hadn't been any discussion of when this arrangement would end, but given the fact that Maeve's parents liked to vacation, he wouldn't put stock in them sticking around to help permanently.

Which meant he needed to have a plan in place.

First the "You're a father" news, then the Maeve-leaving bomb, and…. Yeah, he wasn't going to get the rug pulled out from under him a third time.

When he headed into the hallway, the sound of happy baby gurgles echoed from the living room.

Silas's chest warmed as he rounded the corner to see Mrs. Johnson holding Fiona, who was making a valiant effort to try and grab her hair.

"Hey," Silas said, and Fiona perked up at the sound of his voice. Fuck, that never got old.

Mrs. Johnson looked up at him. "Hi, Silas." Her tone felt a little more formal, and based on the intent look in her ice-blue eyes, Silas's warning bells started to ping. A creak sounded from the other room followed by footsteps, and a moment later, Mr. Johnson walked into the room. Silas closed the distance and scooped up Fiona on instinct, needing the cuddly warmth of his daughter as he braced himself against whatever problem would be knocking him off at the knees next.

Probably just wanted to tell him they couldn't watch her anymore.

"Ah, Silas, I'm glad you're here," Mr. Johnson said, not meeting his eyes. Goddamn, this was about to get awkward. Maeve's father let out a low cough and gestured toward the couch. "Why don't you take a seat?"

Discussions that started out that way were never good ones. *Here, take a seat so when we slice your Achilles you don't collapse on the floor.* Silas settled into the proffered couch, clutching Fiona tightly as he barely rested against the cushion.

"What's going on?" Silas asked, unable to stave off the wariness in his voice. This year had been one curveball after another.

"We wanted to discuss something with you," Mrs. Johnson said with a prim smile. 'We understand the position you're in. You had a fling with my daughter that happened to result in a child."

The phrasing there had him bristling. It might be true, but he was the one who sang Fiona Iron Maiden songs at three in the morning when she woke up, and he was the one she looked for in a room the moment she heard his voice. They even had a dumb game they played that involved saying "Ahhh" over and over again until she gave him a huge gummy smile. That felt like a whole lot more than her grandparents had insinuated there.

"What my wife is trying to say is that we've grown attached to the little girl," Mr. Johnson interjected. "Even though Maeve doesn't want to be a mother, we'd like to have Fiona around… on a more permanent basis."

Silas's stomach sank. This was going in a different direction than he'd anticipated.

"Well, I'm not making any plans to move," Silas offered, even though his intuition was currently screaming. "So, you're always welcome to see her as much as you'd like. I only live a few minutes away."

"Ah, see, we were thinking of offering the same," Mr. Johnson said. He had the audacity to clasp the back of his neck in an "aw shucks" move. The reality of what the man was suggesting slammed into Silas's chest full force, and rage bloomed within him.

"We know you didn't plan for this," Mrs. Johnson jumped in, clearly trying to smooth over her husband's words. "And we understand if you intend to keep her. But if you wanted the chance to go back to your former life, we would happily take on this little girl. She's an absolute joy."

Silas's chest stuttered. At the mention of his former life, a brief flare of selfishness rose to the surface, the memories of lazy mornings sleeping in, not having to worry about childcare or bottle times or nap times. Of being free to move to whatever city he chose at the drop of a hat.

Guilt smothered him a moment later, the feeling so staggering he could barely breathe. He looked down at Fiona and clutched her closer to his chest, hating that he'd even contemplated it for a second. Her big blue eyes stared up at him, those thick lashes fluttering as she got tired of cooing at him and let out a big yawn. The tug in his chest was the fiercest thing he'd ever felt, a protectiveness he'd never anticipated.

"Look, son," Mr. Johnson said, the exact phrase that set Silas off again. He braced his shoulders and prepared himself for a fight. "A single parent working as a sous chef…. Not the sort of situation to give a kid a solid future. It's not like there's a college degree to fall back on, and Maeve told us you have a history of getting into fights. We heard about you decking someone at the festival."

Cold leeched into Silas's bones.

Their slimy condemnation echoed the same things he'd been telling himself from the moment this began.

Those words echoed his father's.

He was nothing but trouble, which was exactly what he'd bring to this little girl.

A lump formed in Silas's throat. But she was *his*. Her mother had already abandoned her, and he couldn't put her through that too. "I'm sorry, Mr. and

Mrs. Johnson, but she's my daughter, and I'll do my best to make sure she's got a better future than I had. My mother can attest that a single parent gets the job done just fine."

Even as he said the words, shame filtered through him. He'd never been the shining example of a good kid, and he'd caused his mom so much heartache over the years.

"If you'll excuse me," he said stiffly. "I've got to get my daughter home."

"Just think about it," Mrs. Johnson said, her cajoling tone like a vegetable peeler to his skin.

Silas didn't justify her words with a response. Sure, they might care about Fiona, but if they really did, they wouldn't be trying to pry her from the only immediate family she had left. He clutched her tightly, plucked her diaper bag up off the floor, and headed for the door. Neither of the Johnsons followed him, and he was grateful for that because the temptation to rip their heads off grew with every step.

However, the bitter tang of Mr. Johnson's words left in his mouth hit worse because it was the truth he'd been trying to ignore for far too long now.

Silas was a shit excuse for a human. How had he gotten it in his head that he could be a decent partner? A decent father?

Maybe his little girl deserved better, but he

wanted to fucking try. He wanted to be good enough for Taran, for Fiona.

He swallowed the bile that rose in his throat as he exited their suffocating home. He needed to find other childcare for her. Yet Mr. Johnson's words sent an alarm prickling in the back of his head. Would they try to fight him on Fiona's custody? There had been a hint of warning in Maeve's father's tone when he brought up the news of Silas decking Kevin. That had been right in front of Fiona too. A-plus parenting on his part.

He jammed his fingers through his hair, letting out an explosive breath. Fiona looked up at him with wondering eyes as he carried her over to the car and strapped her into her seat. His throat tightened as she reached out to clutch his fingers, offering him one of those pure, gummy little grins that had stolen his heart. This girl deserved the world, and if he were honest, all he could offer was what Mr. Johnson had detailed so explicitly. He wasn't loaded, and she'd never have the best on his income as a sous chef.

He'd love her more than anything on the planet, but was that enough?

His eyes stung as he squeezed her fist before prying his finger free and heading to the driver's side. Silas settled into the seat and drove down the road. "Okay, Fi. We're going to get you changed up, and then there's another bottle in your near future."

The drive flew by too fast, his mind a jumble of regrets and fears. He should talk to Taran about the Johnsons' proposal. Guaranteed, the man would have some sensible view on the situation or at least be able to joke about it enough to take some of the heaviness away. How Silas had survived without Taran in his life was a mystery. Even in his relationship though, some guilt chipped away at his happiness.

Taran had helped him from the beginning—with figuring out how to take care of Fiona, watching her when he couldn't, and making sure the laundry was started or the trash got to the curb when Silas was ready to lose his mind from all the pressure. And Taran grounded him, supported him, understood him when no one else did. The man gave him so much, but what the hell did Silas have to offer back?

A lot of stress and extra work.

Who would want that long-term?

Fuck, he needed to derail this pity train before it started heading toward Run Away Station.

Silas hated the Johnsons for dangling the option over him—not just because Fiona was his daughter, but because hell, he was fucking tempted. And that only made him hate himself even more.

Silas pulled up in front of his place and wrangled both Fiona and the diaper bag. She'd fallen asleep during the short car ride, and even as he headed into his apartment, she still didn't wake up. She'd soon be in for a rude awakening because changing time had arrived.

He flung the door open and dropped the diaper bag by the entrance as he made his way over to the bedroom. The sooner he got her situated, the sooner he could kick back with a beer, because fuck, did he need one after the way this day had panned out. Fiona began to stir in his arms the moment he stepped into the darkened room. He flicked the lights on and headed for the changing table.

His head felt like he'd welcomed a nest of bees into it, and it was buzzing with thoughts that made him feel loathsome, desperate, or downright terrified. His stomach churned as he set Fiona on the changing table. She was nice and sleepy, which meant this should be an easy diaper change.

He glanced at the place where he normally kept a stack. Fuck, he was out of diapers.

A fresh pack lay on the floor. Silas bent down to grab them and tear them open.

He straightened up in time to see Fiona roll.

Right off the changing table.

Silas darted down, but he'd barely gotten his hands underneath her when her head gave a loud *thunk* on the floor.

The sound sent a sickening jolt through him as his mind blanked out. Fiona looked up at him in shock for a moment before her ear-splitting scream echoed through the room.

Fuck, fuck, fuck, fuck.

A bump was already beginning to form on her head. Fuck, he needed to get her to the hospital. Now.

Ice filled his veins as he lifted her up and strode toward the door. Shit. He probably needed her diaper bag. Her desperate wails sent dread rushing through him with every single one. His eyes heated. Had he paralyzed her? Done brain damage?

He should've fucking kept his hands on her.

He rushed down the steps with her, strapping her into her car seat at a lightning pace. Her face had turned purple at this point with how hard she was screaming, and the panic just rang, rang, rang through him. Each and every one of her ear-piercing screams sent shards through his heart.

Silas raced to the hospital, his fingers numbed and his whole body cold.

He wasn't meant to be a father.

He should've known he'd just fuck this up too.

Those loud, heartbreaking wails had his stomach churning like he'd drunk a vat of coffee as he soared to the hospital.

Fiona would be better off in a real home, not with a disaster like him.

CHAPTER 25

Taran had a bad feeling from the moment Silas stopped responding to his texts after work.

The sinking in his chest hadn't abated even when he pulled in front of Silas's apartment and spotted his Kia.

Not that Silas couldn't take his time answering texts, but it wasn't like him. Or, hey, maybe Taran was catastrophizing again and just looking for reasons for this relationship to fail. Healthy habit he had. Great way to take something perfect and ruin it.

Taran squeezed his steering wheel before he got out of the car and headed up the walkway to Silas's apartment. By the time he had used the key Silas had given him to open the door and step inside, he knew something was wrong.

Silas sat on the couch, slumped forward, Fiona

asleep in his lap. He wasn't moving, his head hung forward and his eyes vacant.

"What's going on, Si?" Taran asked, closing the door behind him after he entered. He approached with careful steps, not wanting to disturb the little girl's sleep.

Silas didn't respond. He just leaned forward like a husk of himself, staring at the blank wall as if it held answers. Taran lowered himself onto the couch next to Silas, not sure if he should reach out to touch him or not. Everything about the man screamed unapproachable, a desperate energy radiating off him that made Taran pause.

His gaze traveled down to Fiona who slept soundly, curled up in a blanket. He didn't miss the little white bracelet around her wrist. Taran's stomach dropped.

"What happened to Fiona?" he asked, worry swarming him in a guerilla attack. The little girl's breaths seemed even, but as he scanned her for signs, he saw the massive lump on the back of her head.

"Fell." The word came out rusty from Silas's mouth, as if he hadn't spoken in hours.

Taran's heart constricted. "She's okay though? Of course she is," he mumbled, anxieties running away with his tongue. "They wouldn't have let her go home if she wasn't."

Silas still hadn't glanced up at him, still frozen on the couch. The haggard look in his eyes conveyed the horror of watching his daughter fall and smack her head. "Just need to keep an eye on her for concussion symptoms," Silas said hoarsely.

"It happens to a lot of parents," Taran tried to reassure him, the heaviness in the room smothering. "Did she roll? They start that around this age."

"Fiona deserves a better parent," Silas muttered, a withering deadness in his tone that dried up Taran's veins. "She deserves a better home."

Taran opened his mouth to argue, but Silas swung his head to look at him. Those blue eyes were shattered, his mouth a thin line, and all the cockiness, the sarcasm, the intensity leeched from his expression.

"Maeve's parents want to take her," Silas continued. "Permanently."

Taran's stomach bottomed out.

The buzzing in his ears started out slow, increasing in crescendo with every passing second that Silas didn't step in with righteous indignation, didn't claim Fiona's place was here, with him. With them.

"Her mother's gone, and all she has is me," Silas said, his voice heavy in the pristine silence that had descended between them. "And I can't do this. I don't know what the hell I was thinking when I came back to town to be a parent to this kid."

"That's the fear talking," Taran said, stepping in, his voice gentle even though the terror slicing his insides to shreds was anything but. The resoluteness in Silas's gaze devastated him. While he'd been in love with Silas for far longer than he'd had a kid, Taran had fallen for Fiona too. If she wasn't in the picture, if he could just give his kid up because it got tough….

Taran didn't know how he could reconcile with that.

He'd lost his father in the middle of high school, and he'd do anything to get another second with the man. Mama and Nico shouldered different wounds after the car crash, but Taran had been left with an unfillable sense of longing for the family they'd been, the togetherness that had never quite been the same after his loss.

Dad's death had broken them all differently, but Taran had been fighting to fill this emptiness ever since. The closest he'd come had been this—his time with Silas and Fiona.

Knowing Fiona would be growing up nearby, her father not having anything to do with her life? That would break Taran's heart. It would be Dad's death all over again, cracking apart the family they'd formed—but she wasn't gone. She'd be right there.

Except he couldn't force Silas to step up.

Bile rose in his throat.

Silas shook his head. "Not fear. Just fucking reality," he spat. "The Johnsons are well off. They'd make sure she was taken care of, had the best of everything."

"Except she wouldn't have her father," Taran responded, the answer coming out with a bite. "Si, you can't just give her up because it's convenient."

Silas's blue eyes flashed with anger. "That's not your damn choice, Tar. She's not your fucking daughter."

Those words hit him like a slap, and Taran sat back. Coldness filtered through him from head to toe, dissolving the brief flare of anger.

Silas didn't seem to register the words pouring out of him. "If she went to the Johnsons, she'd have a real chance for a good life. And hell, I could even go back to Philly, find a better career for myself. Maybe I wouldn't be such a damn disappointment then." He clutched Fiona tightly, the little girl's chest rising and falling in slumber.

To Philly.

Without him.

Taran's hopes shattered like the windshield of his father's car.

This was where he'd usually just nod and go along with it. Time after time, boyfriend after boyfriend, he followed along as they broke his heart to pieces. As they dragged him through the dirt. And he let them. He didn't fight back. He didn't walk away. He was always the one who got dumped in the end.

And Silas was the one he'd always wanted, the guy he'd been dreaming of forever.

If there was anyone he should just bend to, it should be him. He could follow him to Philly, and they could still be together.

His gaze drifted down to Fiona in Silas's lap. Except every time he saw Silas, he'd be thinking of the little girl in Chesapeake City wondering where her mommy and daddy were. Taran swallowed hard.

He couldn't.

"I can't do this, Si," Taran said, his voice thick as his eyes burned. Agony throbbed in his chest, a living, writhing thing. "She's not my daughter, but I love her. And I love you too much to follow you in this and watch this decision tear you apart over the years." Silas's head swung in his direction, shock painting his features. Taran continued, desperate for some sort of response. "Please, tell me I'm wrong. Tell me you need time to adjust, that you're just scared."

Taran waited for him to jump in, to take back his plan, to refute everything, but Silas just stared in silence.

The silence told the story his words never would.

Silas was choosing fear, and Taran couldn't follow him there.

Silas's mouth formed a thin line, and he refused to look at Taran. His heart cracked open at the closed-off expression, so different from the man he'd come to know.

Taran rose from the couch even though his limbs

begged him to stay. Every fiber of his being wanted to remain here in this place with them. Except all he could see was the empty spot at the table after his father died, the damned yearning in his chest for what they had. The same yearning that pushed him into relationship after relationship, searching for more. Searching for what he'd found with Silas and Fiona, here in this bubble.

One that would be ruined the moment Silas handed her over to Maeve's parents.

Taran was going to be sick. He leaned forward, brushing a kiss first to Fiona's tiny forehead. The little girl's skin was so soft, and she barely stirred. And then he pressed his lips to Silas's, stealing one last selfish kiss for himself. He drank in the leather scent, the crisp taste of beer on his lips, the molten heat of his mouth that captivated Taran every damn time. Taran lost himself in those sensations for a single moment, everything he'd ever hoped for wrapped around this man.

Taran's eyes stung and glazed over as he pulled away. "Please don't give her up," Taran whispered. Any louder, and his voice would crack, those tears would spill.

He turned on his heel and headed for the door, each step echoing as he waited for Silas to speak, to beg him to come back, to change his damn mind.

But silence followed instead.

Taran stepped out the door, but he only walked a

couple of paces before he crumpled to the ground. The promise between him and Silas might have once had starry sky potential, but as he walked away, those precious, glittering stars winked out of existence, one after the other.

The sobs wrenched from his throat, his entire body quaking as he fell apart in the middle of the corridor, knees digging into the sallow carpeting. All that was left of their promise was the stale flickering light of the hallway sconces, hollow and destined to die.

CHAPTER 26

Silas thought he had been miserable when Maeve ran off.

That misery paled in comparison to what he felt when Taran walked out the door a week ago.

Silas couldn't blame him. He should've said something, anything. Except he couldn't bring himself to lie, and he still wasn't sure what he should do. The Johnsons had been pushing him for an answer, especially after they'd found out about Fiona's hospital visit. And Mrs. Johnson had left him with a reprimand that had dug in with claws—that he was a danger to his child.

Yeah, lady. Didn't take a genius to figure that out.

He pulled up to his house on his Triumph, his heart in the gutter. He'd been a complete zombie through his week at work. The thought of Fiona not being there at the end of the day had his chest aching almost as much as the void of texts from Taran and his empty bed. His eyes burned with a phantom ache. When Taran had left that night, Silas had broken down, snapped like a matchstick.

What made it all worse was that he understood why Taran left. In a twisted way, he was proud of him for finally standing up for himself. It had taken bravery to walk away, and he deserved better than Silas and his never-ending shitfuck of a life.

Silas speared his fingers through his hair. His throat tightened. His mother had been over during the three days he needed childcare coverage, but he said they'd need to talk tonight about his current situation. No way would Silas drop off Fiona at the Johnson household while he was trying to make this decision. He wouldn't be surprised if they disappeared to their Florida house with Fiona in tow, just like their daughter had vanished into the night.

He knew the bubble he operated in would burst soon. The Johnsons wanted an answer, his mother was curious, and Nico was definitely biting his tongue because guaranteed he'd noticed something different with Taran. The urge to just hit the road on his Triumph reared in his mind stronger than ever.

Silas stepped into his apartment, and the sight of Fiona curled up in his mom's arms slammed him in the chest with grief. His little girl looked so pristinely happy, those long lashes shut in slumber, innocent to how fucking terrible this world could be.

Her bump had gone down, and she seemed to be in the clear as far as concussion symptoms, but Silas was still out of his mind at the idea of her getting hurt again. The crunch of her head hitting the floor had imprinted in his brain as the most terrifying moment of his life.

"She's been sleeping like a champ all evening," Mom said, glancing up toward him. "How was your shift?"

"Work was work," Silas managed, a lump in his throat. Gratitude warred with shame. Mom had no idea about what the Johnsons had said and what he was considering. If she did, she'd be so disappointed in him. Just like Taran had been.

Fuck, he missed Taran like his next breath.

"Where's your boyfriend been?" Mom asked, a knowing look in her gaze that pierced right through Silas. He turned toward the fridge, ready to go get a beer, when he realized he'd run out. Probably better off so he didn't continue trying to numb out the pain with alcohol. Great way to follow in dear old dad's footsteps.

Silas plunked onto the couch beside her, attempting to ignore all the memories embedded in this ratty thing—from curling up with Taran after a long day to holding Fiona while she took a nap so often that he'd left an imprint in the cushion, and when Taran had fucked him braced against it. He missed those moments with a desperation that ached, yet he only had himself to blame. He was the reason Taran walked away.

Mom didn't push, but her gentle stare peeled back his layers the way it always had—whether he admitted he'd gotten into a fight at school after one of the "bros" found out he was bi, or telling her how he couldn't summon the energy to care at school when everyone already thought he'd turn out just like his dad. Taran had operated like his mother did —it was no wonder Silas opened up to him in a way he hadn't to anyone else.

"We broke up," Silas muttered, staring out the window rather than at her.

"That's a shame," Mom responded. "I really liked him."

"Me too," Silas said, forcing the words out. He reached over and stroked Fiona's hair, feeling how low the bump had gotten.

"You made a mistake," Mom said. "We've all done that as parents. She's okay, sweetheart."

Silas tried to ignore how his eyes burned. He'd gone years without crying, yet Fiona and Taran had unlocked that part of him effortlessly. "She'd be better off with someone else. I'm not meant to be a father. You should know that better than anyone." He hadn't meant to admit the last part, but it slipped out nonetheless.

"Silas James King, look at me," Mom said, her voice firm.

He shifted on the couch so that he faced her, and she handed Fiona over. In transition, Fiona shimmied a little and let out an adorable yawn with a squeak. Silas buried his face in the crook of her impossibly soft neck, just breathing in her scent for a moment.

"You aren't your father," Mom said, her brows drawn together in seriousness. "And don't dismiss me the way you always have. I should've told you this before, but to be honest, it didn't seem appropriate at the time."

Silas nuzzled against Fiona, and his little girl cuddled back, the warmth and proximity the closest thing to soothing the aching void Taran had left when he walked out the door.

"Your father and I were the classic case of high school sweethearts who ended up getting knocked up too early. He was about to go to college, but when I found out I was pregnant, I begged him to stay. The idea of raising you on my own terrified me, and he eventually agreed. But he was never happy about it. Those regrets were clear on his face each and every day—of the life he felt he'd missed out on. By the time you turned six, he snapped, but the signs had been there for a long, long time."

Silas swallowed hard. While the immediate thought that bubbled up in his mind was of how that only proved his father never wanted him, he didn't miss the point of his mother's story. In fact, he'd just been having those same notions of running.

Just like his father—the man he'd never wanted to become.

"What if I can't do this?" Silas asked, his voice barely above a whisper. "She's only been with me for a month, and already she got hurt."

Mom toyed with the malachite bead on her pendant. "If you can't do it, then you can't," she said. "Your father tried. And I didn't miss the comments he made to you, the digs you *never* deserved. I hate that I allowed it to go on as long as I did."

Silas shook his head. "You did everything you could for me."

"Just like you're doing for your little girl," Mom said. "Your father's fear might've left a mark on you, but I see the way you look at her, how you're both clutching onto each other for dear life. There is no doubt in my mind you love that little girl with all your heart. Kids don't need buckets of money or fancy houses, sweetheart. They need love and a community, and that's something you have in abundance."

Her words stripped away every argument he'd been making the past week.

Fiona didn't just have him. She'd had Taran, Nico and Hudson, Linc, Nate, and Beckett, Sarah, his mom, and even Jamie, the woman he'd planned on sending Fiona to who was raising three munchkins of her own.

Taran had tried to get him to see the truth, but he'd been too scared to face it then.

God, he'd fucked up so badly with Taran.

His chest ached something fierce. The Johnsons' words had sunk in deep when he was vulnerable, and he hated the way he'd let them get to him, how he'd even considered what they'd pushed. In the face of the truth, their manipulations shone clear as day.

"I've always been proud of you, sweetheart," Mom said as she reached over to squeeze his shoulder. "Even when you make mistakes. Lord knows, I've made plenty."

Silas sucked in a sharp breath to try and keep from bawling all over his daughter. If he could be a fraction of the parent his mother had been, he'd be happy. "I fucked up with Taran," he admitted, running his thumb over Fiona's cheek. "I... wasn't ready to hear what he was saying."

Mom's lips quirked. "My son? Stubborn? I never would have suspected it." She let out a sigh. "I wish I could say there's a miraculous way to fix things, but I've never been great at relationships. What I do know is, that man loves you. He looks at you like you lit each star in the sky just for him. I'd start by doing the thing you hate the most."

"Talking," Silas muttered.

"You're doing a decent job so far," Mom replied as she pushed up off the couch. "I'm going to get myself some more tea. If you want to chat more about Taran, we can, or you can tell me about work."

Silas nodded, gratitude welling in his chest. He'd never needed two parents—not when his mom had loved enough for both of them. As she bustled to the kitchen, Silas pulled out his phone and stared at the text chain between him and Taran that had been silent since the day Taran walked out the door.

He owed Taran so much more than an apology though.

An idea took root as a shaky resolve settled through him.

He knew what he needed to do.

He only hoped Taran was willing to listen.

CHAPTER 27

Swedish Fish did not go well with vodka straight from the bottle.

Duly noted.

His stomach still felt a little sour from heaving most of it up last night. Sarah had loitered outside of the bathroom and offered to hold his hair while Taran flipped her off. Taran had barely left his place, to the point that Sarah, Nico, and Mama had all threatened to drag him out. Cole had already dropped by earlier in the week and they'd talked Barter. Taran wasn't ready to speak about Silas with anyone yet—and besides that, he wasn't about to put pressure on him at work if he spilled the situation to Nico. The screen glowed back at him, his steadfast companion in the pre- and post-work hours.

He'd been living and breathing Barter.

The soft launch had happened a few days ago,

and that kept him busy. Busy was good. Busy kept him from thinking about every damn thing he'd lost. Busy kept him from sniffing the shirt Silas had left at his place because the leather-and-clove scent made him want to sob. Oh wait, no it didn't, because he'd cried enough into the shirt to wash the scent away.

Still, Barter was the one thing going right in his life now. It had taken off, and troubleshooting the app issues that cropped up and beginning to work on the marketing launch of the thing occupied him even as he made too many screw ups at his day job. The couple of times he'd ducked out of his house, he couldn't help but strain to look along the sidewalks on the off chance he spotted Fiona and Silas. If Silas hadn't already handed her over to the Johnsons.

His stomach soured, and not just from the torment he'd subjected his insides to last night.

Sarah stalked into his office and plunked into the reading chair they'd stationed right next to the book-cases. "You should bottle up this scent and sell it as Eau de Misery," she said, picking up one of the Clive Barker novels from the shelf and flipping through as if she planned on reading the book.

Highly unlikely.

He hadn't missed the glint in Sarah's eye. This was an interrogation. Cole had left him alone because he knew Taran needed the space, but Nic and Sarah weren't that sort. They smacked you with their care like it was a cudgel until you felt it the next day. If he were being honest though, sometimes he needed the push.

"What happened between you and Silas?" Sarah asked, glancing at her nails as if she couldn't be bothered. Taran knew better. Despite the space he and his roommate gave each other, their friendship was like a glacier: plenty beneath the surface. "We gave you a week," she said. "Nico's going crazy trying to not dive into your business, and everyone's worried about both of you."

Taran sucked in a sharp breath. He didn't even know what Silas had ended up doing because he hadn't heard a damn word from him. In his defense, Taran was the one who'd left. However, he wasn't going to blast Silas's business all over the place. "We split up," he said, shocked the words came out as steadily as they did. The admission rocked him off-kilter again, like he'd slid from one side of the room to the other. "He made a decision I couldn't back, so I walked away."

Sarah stopped pretending to read the book. "Wait, you left him?"

Taran's throat felt parched at the thought, and he couldn't summon a response. He swung his gaze back to the computer screen, even though the code he had up glared at him petulantly. Well, it could go screw itself too.

"Tar, I've lived with you for a decent amount of

time, and I've known you even longer. You've never broken up with someone."

The shock in Sarah's tone irritated him. Yeah, she was right, but he didn't need that pointed out right now when ninety-five percent of him wanted to go running to Silas and beg him to take him back.

"Yeah, we all know I've got no spine," he shot back. If that sounded bitchy, then so be it. He wasn't in the mood to placate, and he was pretty sure he'd forgotten to eat dinner—if his stomach would even let him. Thinking he'd been bummed out over losing Kevin was laughable. This pain that carved him to pieces over losing Silas and Fiona? He hadn't experienced this intensity of grief in years, the sort that numbed his fingertips and strangled his heart.

The sort that would linger for years, leaving him with flashes of what might have been, of the future they could have had. Waking up next to Silas in bed, taking Fiona to the playground when she got old enough, heading down to Cozy Café for a family breakfast on the weekend. Everything he'd silently hoped for from the moment Silas let him in, when the locked door finally swung open.

And then Taran had been the one to shut it in the end.

Because if Fiona wasn't a part of the picture, he couldn't stand by and let Silas live with those regrets. If he was the man Taran had believed him to be, giving up Fiona would ruin him.

Sarah slapped the book down onto his desk. "You're missing the point entirely," she said, drawing his attention. "You broke up with him. You chose to walk away because you cared that damn much. If that's not growth, I don't know what is."

"Look at what all my growth's left me with—nothing," Taran responded, unable to keep the bitterness out of his tone. He couldn't help but wallow. The thought of Silas in his apartment just minutes away was driving him out of his mind.

"You're not hearing me," Sarah said, leaning forward. Her dark eyes settled on him, and he had to look away under the scrutiny. "You've been searching for a relationship almost as much as your brother had been searching for a stiff cock." Taran mouthed, "Ew," but she continued. "But you were compromising yourself for the sake of your goal, dating these guys who took advantage of you over and over again. Even if things between you and Silas don't pan out, something amazing came from your time with him because you cared about the reality more than the future you wanted from him."

Taran's heart squeezed tight. His time with Silas had been everything he'd been looking for. Who needed future dreams when he'd been living one?

"The situation between you guys," Sarah said, "is it not something you can talk out?"

The night he'd left, he'd been so sure there was no way to discuss through this problem. Silas was gearing up to run away, and nothing could get through to him.

Not your fucking daughter.

Those words still stung. Somewhere along the way, Fiona had begun to feel like his too, and the reminder had devastated him. Except over the past week, he'd been wondering if he hadn't closed the door too soon. If he should've waited until Silas was calmer to talk with him, to try and get him to see reason. He'd been freaking out just as badly when he bolted, even if it hadn't been external.

Taran let out a sigh. "It might be."

Sarah raised her hands. "Look, I'm first on the ditch brigade when things get rough. But you spent a long-ass time giving second chances to guys who weren't worth it when it sounds like this one is."

Taran glanced at his screen, the glow less than comforting. Would Silas even be willing to talk? If he was still prepared to hand over his daughter, Taran would just close the door again, but if he'd changed his mind... fuck.

Being with Silas had been every dream fulfilled in that brief time, and the potential there... the starry skies couldn't compare.

A *bing* came from his phone, the sound he'd attached to the Barter app. Taran's brows drew together. He'd gotten a few bites already and there were some interesting offers, including an inspection at the mechanic's up the road for some coding work on their business, as well as free meals from Cozy Corner for the same offer.

He couldn't help but check. The app was so new that every barter offer to come his way had his pulse jumping.

None like this one though.

His gaze zeroed in on the user and the barter on offer.

Barter: 1 hour of coding.

Offer: A lifetime.

Meet me at Elk River Park.

He recognized the user profile immediately because he'd helped set that one up.

Silas King.

Taran pushed up from his desk, his pulse racing a thousand miles a minute.

"I've got to go."

CHAPTER 28

Silas's heartbeat hadn't slowed from the moment he sent the Barter request.

He sat at the pier where he'd taken Taran over a month ago, which wasn't long, even though it felt like a lifetime had passed.

When he'd explained his plan to his mother, she'd agreed to stay and watch Fiona. A thousand and one things could go wrong—Taran could ignore the message, or he might not check it tonight. Or worse, he might check it and decide he was done with Silas regardless. Not like Silas could blame him. He'd acted like a complete fucking asshole.

But he wouldn't run. Not anymore.

The breezes had turned warmer than they'd been the last time he was here with Taran. The summer was creeping in. Already, the trill of cicadas wove through the trees, and the bright moon overhead coated the trees and the lake with a silvery glint. This had been his refuge so many times throughout the years that it was only fitting he waited here now. Whether Taran showed or not, he was in the one place he wanted to be.

Out here, his head began to clear for the first time in weeks. With full-time care of Fiona on his plate, he hadn't been able to just escape like this. He'd forgotten how much the gentle wind off the lake filled with that crisp scent filled his lungs, clearing the excess baggage, how the moonlight filtered into the jagged cracks of his soul, lighting him up in a way the sun never did.

Out here, he could see where he'd gone wrong with Taran, how he'd let his issues and the Johnsons muddle what should've been a clear choice. He'd come back to Chesapeake City for Fiona, and she was his little girl. End of story.

He picked at a hole in his jeans, tugging at one of the errant threads. He wasn't sure if minutes or hours had passed, but he'd left his phone back at the car. Either Taran showed or he didn't, but Silas didn't want to be checking it every five seconds out here.

He could handle being alone—after all, he'd done the loner thing through most of his life. Hell, he kept even his closest friendships at a distance. Yet with Taran that had never been an option. The man made him realize that hard truth, and in the short time they were together, he'd found himself forging deeper friendships with old friends like Nico and Linc as well as the newer ones he'd begun to make here.

No matter what Taran chose, Silas would always be indebted to him for that.

Even though his heart ached at the idea that it might never be more.

A crunch sounded from behind him.

Every ounce of his being begged him to turn around, but he couldn't bear the disappointment if it wasn't Taran. Instead, he hunched forward a little more, staring out at the lake.

"You know, sitting out here like that makes you prime serial-killer bait." Taran's voice sounded from behind him. The dry comment had Silas's heart squeezing hard.

"I was hoping Jason would show up, but apparently I'm not slutty enough to attract bad eighties horror icons," Silas responded. He still hadn't budged, even though his heart nearly leapt out of his chest.

Taran had arrived.

The creak of the weathered planks sounded beside him and a second later, Taran's shadow appeared first before the man himself stepped into view.

"I got your message," Taran said as he lowered himself onto the pier next to him.

Silas sucked in a breath. "I owe you an apology. The things I said…. I was wrong. You mean a ton to that little girl, and I hated those words the second they came from my lips. Fiona's not going anywhere. I called the Johnsons and told them what I should've from the start. I'm Fiona's father, not them. They can be in her life as long as they understand the bottom line. My only regret is that it took losing you to realize the truth." He stole a glance then and there.

Taran leaned forward, dressed down in black jeans and a simple white tee. His dark hair was brushed to the side, glossy under the moonlight, and those molten eyes stared at him with a gravity he'd missed so damn much. His mouth dried at the sight of this man. Taran was all fine features and a pouty lower lip Silas wanted to sink his teeth into. He'd memorized every detail about him, from his elegant fingers to the way a single brow arched when he made a wry comment, and he'd missed all of it this past week.

"Did you mean it?" Taran asked, a resonant hush to his voice that reflected their surroundings, from the gentle, shimmering lake to the broad expanse of stars above them.

Silas knew what he was asking. However, the words he summoned failed to capture everything he'd meant when he sent the request to Taran. From the moment they'd gotten together, he'd seen forever in this man. That should've terrified him.

It didn't.

Silas leaned in closer, until their faces were inches

apart. "'Our truest life is when we are in dreams awake,'" he murmured.

Then he brushed his lips against Taran's.

There had only been a few times Silas felt this way—when he'd first returned to his mother's home after moving away, seeing all the charming disarray around the house, her plant collection in full bloom. When he came to this spot at Lums Pond at night, a sanctuary against the chaos of the world and the chaos of his mind. And when he first saw Fiona after a long day at work and a smile lit her face.

It had taken him a long while to realize the preciousness of those moments, those places, those people after a lifetime spent running away.

However, Taran made him want to come home.

He sank into the sweetness of his mouth, the heat blooming between them as Taran melted into the kiss. The week apart had shredded him to pieces, but as their lips met again and again, he could feel himself becoming whole once more. Silas dipped his tongue into Taran's mouth and could've drowned in the bliss shuddering down his spine. This was where he belonged.

Here. With him.

When Silas eventually pulled back, Taran's lips quirked to the side. "Quoting Thoreau again? I'm starting to think you've got a hard-on for that guy."

Silas tipped his forehead against Taran's. "Better than having a hard-on for horror movie monsters."

"True," Taran murmured. "It's incredibly inconvenient."

A laugh slipped out of Silas, the first genuine one all week. "Fuck, I missed you."

They slowly pulled away, but Silas was glued onto Taran, as if at any moment the man would disappear and he'd realize this was all some dream.

"I missed you too," Taran murmured, resting his hand on top of Silas's. "I… I'm sorry too. Not for standing up for myself, because I should've started doing that a long time ago, but for shutting the door when I could've left it open. You were freaking out from one bad situation after another, and I should've tried to contact you after the dust settled."

Silas shook his head. "You're here now. That's all that matters." He glanced at Taran and winked. "And anyway, if someone would accept my Barter request, we'd have a hell of a lot of time to figure things out."

"A lifetime?" Taran asked, the hopeful note in his voice too much. Silas's heart was too full, too complete right now, all the joy mere seconds from spilling over.

Silas wove his fingers through Taran's. For once, he didn't need to look to the sky to see all the promise he'd been yearning for—he'd found it right here.

"Sounds perfect to me."

EPILOGUE

TARAN STEPPED INSIDE HIS PLACE, HEADING STRAIGHT for the case of beer they'd stacked in here. The party was in full swing, and people had been tearing through Chesapeake Brewery's wheat beer that he and Sarah had picked up in abundance. The summer day was an effortless one, filled with solid blue skies, pastel clouds, and the scent of grilled meat wafting through the air.

Sarah poked her head inside. "There you are. I wasn't sure if you were refilling the cooler or if I was."

Taran's heart twisted at the sight of his roommate decked out in summer goth attire—a short black lace dress and a choker.

"I've got it," he said. They'd worked seamlessly at hosting shindigs for ages, and this one was to celebrate Barter's success. If the figures kept up this way, he'd be quitting his job in six months to work at this full-time, which still felt unreal. All the better, because then he could help cut down on Fiona's childcare expenses, since his schedule would be way more flexible.

As much as the Johnsons had offered to help pitch in with her care, Silas was leery to accept after the way they'd tried to push him, and Taran couldn't blame him. For the time being, Silas maintained strict boundaries with Maeve's parents—and of course, they'd heard no word from Fiona's mother since her disappearance. They made do on their own and with the help of friends, family, and both Silas's and Taran's moms who were fast becoming friends.

Sarah stepped up to him and tugged the case from his hands, her black sparkly nails on display. "End of an era here, isn't it?"

"I'm sure you'll find another awkward, sarcastic roommate to fill my room," Taran said, even though his heart twisted. Five years of living together, and now he was leaving. As much as he couldn't wait to move into the new place he and Silas picked out—a two bedroom so Fiona had her own space—he'd built a lot of good memories here.

Sarah arched a brow at him. "You know that's bullshit. You're irreplaceable, Tar."

Taran ducked his head, trying to hide the way his cheeks heated at the compliment. "Or you could catch the relationship disease that's spreading and find yourself with a hot girlfriend."

Sarah snorted and headed for the door, which Taran propped open for her. "The rest of you might have abandoned me for grossly happy relationships, but I am living for playing the field. Get those match-making paws away from me." She tossed him a grin before she headed for the coolers.

Linc had declared himself grill master at their party, mostly because someone needed to keep Taran from his normal designated role since they were supposed to be celebrating his business launch. He skimmed across the back lawn of his and Sarah's place to soak in the last barbecue they'd be co-hosting.

Beckett and Rae rolled around in the grass together, the kids exploding into fits of giggles, and Nate, Rae's mother Everly, and Hudson kept a close eye on the pair. Mama was sitting down by the table next to heaps of food—half of which she'd prepared—chatting away with Silas's mom, Beth. The women got along better than he could've ever hoped. Mama's outspokenness seemed to mesh well with Silas's mother's gentleness, and they'd bonded immediately over the struggles of raising boys by themselves.

Mama had also accepted Silas with open arms,

and she was beyond thrilled about getting to dote on Fiona.

Silas and Fi gathered by the fence alongside Nico and Cole, all of them deep in conversation. Taran's heart thudded hard at the sight before him, so overly full it ached. Forget the launch of the app, leaving his job, whatever—this was the real success here, everything he had dreamed of.

His gaze zeroed in on Silas as he approached. Today he was wearing a tank top that put all those delicious tattoos on display, and his black jeans highlighted what a gorgeous ass he had. However, what stole Taran's breath away was the smile on his face and the rough laugh that lit the air—genuine. After years of watching the guy's fake smiles, seeing the raw, real happiness on his face struck Taran square in the chest.

Silas King might've been his high school crush, but the man he'd become was far, far better than anything Taran could've imagined.

And the way Fiona's full-body baby giggle followed her father's joy sparked Taran's own. He stepped up to them and extended his hands out to take the little girl. Silas looked up at him, those deep blue eyes filled with a tenderness Taran still couldn't believe some days. Fiona snuggled up against his body, and a second later, her little claws were searching for the edge of his shirt to grab.

Silas leaned in to press his lips to Taran's in a

sweet kiss filled with the promise of a sunrise. "Please don't tell me you're still fussing over everyone at your own party."

"Okay, I'll tell you I'm not," Taran responded, unable to keep the wryness from his tone.

"Sit back, have a beer," Cole jumped in, thrusting an open one in his direction. "You deserve it, man."

Nico glanced between Silas and Taran, and then shook his head. "Still weird."

Silas leaned in, and a second later, he was licking up along Taran's neck. Taran couldn't help the shiver rolling up and down his spine. He shot a heated look at Silas and mouthed, "Later."

"How about that," Silas shot back at Nico, looping an arm around Taran's shoulders and squeezing tight.

"Yeah, gross," Nico said, arching a brow. "I know way too much about your past to imagine you being with my little brother."

"Quit imagining it then," Taran said, taking a sip from his beer. The crisp liquid rolled down his throat, relaxing him almost as much as the heady summer sun.

"Besides, your brother makes me look positively vanilla in comparison," Silas responded with an amused smirk.

Nico blanched right as Hudson clapped hands on his shoulders.

"What's wrong, gorgeous?" Hudson asked, amusement dancing in his light eyes.

"Your boyfriend's distraught that his brother has a sex life," Cole responded as he leaned back on the fence. "I'm just watching the show."

Hudson nodded. "The Brothers Shah tend to put on a good one."

Nico rolled his eyes. "That's not a thing, babe."

"Mr. Taran," a small voice called out behind him. Taran turned in time to see Beckett racing his way. He skidded to a halt right in front of him, some dirt clods flying with his enthusiasm.

"What's up, Beck?"

Nate jogged after him, running fingers through his sweat-soaked strands. "Jesus, how are you so fast?"

"Can I hold baby Fiona?" Beckett asked, those big, dark eyes pleading. The kid looked like a miniature version of his father.

Taran glanced at Silas who nodded, fighting with a smile.

"Sure thing," he said, starting to lower down. "Extend your hands out and make sure you've got her head supported." He placed Fiona in Beckett's arms, and she began wiggling at once in excitement, making gurgling noises and trying to grab Beckett's nose.

"Ahhh, she's moving," he exclaimed, his eyes growing impossibly huge.

Nate chewed on his lower lip, biting back a laugh. The love he had for Beck shone clear in his eyes, though, giving Taran hope for his own future as a part of Silas and Fiona's family.

"You're doing a great job, kiddo," Linc said, his voice a low rumble as he approached. "Burgers are ready."

"Oh, I'm hungry," Beckett said as he looked up at Taran. "Can you take her back?"

"Give her here," Taran said, scooping up Fiona with ease. She curled into his arms like she belonged there, a warm little bundle still even as she'd started to become grabbier and more mobile. Beck raced past his father in the direction of the food table now filled with fresh burgers to accompany Mama's butter chicken, chole, and naan dominating the table.

"Want me to get you a plate, babe?" Silas asked, following the others who were heading to load their plates.

Taran nodded. He watched his friends and family gather around the table, their laughter filtering up to the achingly blue sky. The scents of grilled burgers and hot dogs competed with the coconut of sunscreen, and the tang of his beer remained on his tongue. This was one of those perfect days he'd catalogue away in his memories.

Life might be messy, rife with losses, curveballs, and days when going forward seemed impossible. But then there were moments like these—serene in their simplicity, just filled with the laughter of his friends and family, the warmth of a beautiful summer day bursting at the seams with color, and a calm that quieted the buzz in his mind.

He could weather all of those ups and downs with this fierce, loving community by his side. Whether it was stopping by Cozy Café for breakfast on the weekend with Nate, Linc, and Beck, or ducking into the bank to see Sarah, the familiar faces of the people in this town brought him such immense joy, he could never imagine living anywhere else. Even Cole was only an hour away, and he'd always shown up when Taran needed him the most.

His loved ones had left their imprints all over Chesapeake City, from Hudson and Nico's co-owned restaurants to Nate's coffee shop and the countless businesses Linc had revitalized himself. They'd made the town this beautiful, welcoming place to live, a place he now offered his own contribution to as Barter took off, especially in this area.

However, it was the little girl in his arms and the man approaching him with a plate full of food that brought him home, every time.

Taran had spent a long time dreaming of his future, but he'd found it at last.

Yet to read the rest of the series? **Stronger Than Hope** Is now available. Plus check out Katherine's delicious MM romantic suspense **Midnight Heist**.

ACKNOWLEDGMENTS

There are so many people who helped make this book possible. A huge thanks to Zoe Allison and Lynn Burke for offering insightful critiques, and to Landra and Cate for letting me brainstorm plot and character issues. I'm so, so grateful to the amazing team at Hot Tree Publishing for giving this series a chance and making it thrive.

A huge thanks to my husband and daughter—they were massive sources of inspiration from the beginning to the end of this series, especially since I was writing this book while raising an infant. And a big thank-you to my readers whose enthusiasm keeps me going, and my author friends who brighten my day.

If you're not ready to let the Chesapeake Days universe go, stay tuned. I've got a spinoff series planned called Chesapeake Nights...

ABOUT THE AUTHOR

Katherine McIntyre is a feisty chick with a big attitude despite her short stature. She writes stories featuring snarky women, ragtag crews, and men with bad attitudes—and there's an equally high chance for a passionate speech thrown into the mix. As an eternal geek and tomboy who's always stepped to her own beat, she's made it her mission to write stories that represent the broad spectrum of people out there, from different cultures and races to all varieties of men and women.

Website: http://www.katherine-mcintyre.com

Newsletter sign-up: http://eepurl.com/duIScb

facebook.com/kmcintyreauthor

twitter.com/pixierants

instagram.com/authorkmcintyre

bookbub.com/profile/katherine-mcintyre

ABOUT THE PUBLISHER

Hot Tree Publishing loves love. Publishing adult romantic fiction, HTPubs are all about diverse reads featuring heroes and heroines to swoon over. Since opening in 2015, HTPubs have published more than 300 titles across the wide and diverse range of romantic genres. If you're chasing a happily ever after in your favourite subgenre, HTPubs have you covered.

Interested in discovering more amazing reads brought to you by Hot Tree Publishing? Head over to the website for information:

www.hottreepublishing.com

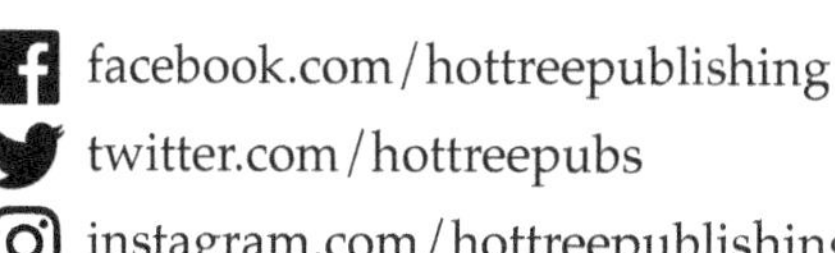

www.ingramcontent.com/pod-product-compliance
Lightning Source LLC
Chambersburg PA
CBHW060736190726
48285CB00001B/237